Praise for *The Mar*

8-8-8-8-8-8-8-8-8-8

‘Put down whatever you are reading and pick up this book.

What an absolute gem of a read from a place of sheer brilliance... Conceptual, yet simple and one of the most un-put-downable reads I have come across in a very, very long time. Bravo’

Lee A Jackson – ‘Dreaming Falling Down’

‘A well-conceived sci-fi exploration of the human mind and its capacity for empathy’.

Kirkus reviews

‘An amazing read from an amazing mind; brilliant, highly original... it should be made into a movie’

Renee Paule –
‘On the Other Hand: The little anthology of big questions’

'The Many Lives of Adam Capello' is a deeply captivating, thought-provoking and philosophical read

Katja Leslie – ‘The spirituality of incarceration’

The Many Lives of Adam Capello

By M.W.Taylor

Published by Savant Press

www.savantpress.net

Facebook "The Many Lives of Adam Capello"

Please support by leaving a review on www.Amazon.co.uk

www.savantpress.net

First edition October 2016

Published by Savant Press

ISBN: **978-0-9954762-1-9**

How does anyone deal with the knowledge of a thousand lifetimes? What does it do to you? Our minds are better used, our universe expanded to the point that we feel we can touch the stars, but through all of that do we lose ourselves?

Our core identity is our personality, the identity that we grow up with, the perfect mix of nature and nurture that we rely on to take us through this amazing adventure called life.

And yet we still want more...

Prologue

My great grandfather is the greatest link to the past I know. I have experienced so many events in history in my mind, but talking to him gives it all some sense of place. It is as if hearing his stories of things from as far back as the 20th century is the correct and natural way to pass on history. I on the other hand am in the process of completing my Awakening foundation and it has changed my world completely. It is also leaving me very confused and thus I found myself airing my dilemma to one of the few people I know who has chosen to stay the way he is. I looked at him, not knowing where to start.

“You know gramps, it’s weird knowing everything without experiencing it in my new body. It takes the fun out of life. I’ve been there, done that, but not as a whole, only as a part. A part of me that was alive, but long ago in a different time, with different ideals, different objectives, and to all sense and purpose, I was a different person. It feels like I have watched all my lives on T.V; remote, detached. I miss people that yesterday I didn’t even know existed, and my heart aches for faces that I don’t recognise yet.

Not surprisingly with that statement, my great grandfather looked at me as if I'd been speaking Greek. Like so many of his generation who felt that they were already too long in the tooth to change their lives so drastically, he had chosen to opt out of any Awakening process.

"Well Adam," he began, thinking so carefully that I could hear the steam driven cogs revolving slowly in his head, "I have seen you grow up from a little baby learning to talk, to a happy child always wanting to play games, but now I feel like I'm speaking to a university professor. I don't understand everything you say, and I can only begin to imagine the things you have told me, but I do know this, if you open up Pandora's Box, you might not like what you see but you can never close it up again. Some things are better left in the past, that's why I never got caught up in all this nonsense." Then he gave out a long sigh that spoke a thousand words.

Even with the past memories of a man close to my great grandfather's age, I find it sad that we have this obstacle in our communication, a generation gap of unparalleled proportions. My experiences hold no reality within his consciousness.

And so great grandfather, I have written this book for you, and others like you, to try and explain what Awakening is and how it has affected me. I want you to know though, at the heart of it all, I am still the Adam you know, it's just a little bit harder to see me under the coat of identities I find myself wearing.

The reason a person goes through Awakening is to reutilise all that we have learned in the past. It's a way of reclaiming our experience, knowledge and wisdom that comes with it.

It is also seen as a way of achieving immortality by being able to keep our personality and memories intact from body to body. To be born again gives us all a new bite of the cherry, knowing that you get more than one chance and making you feel that it is never too late to try something new.

In effect, it makes us look forward as much as we look back.

Chapter 1 – Questions

March 30th 2061

I'd been nervous of course, who isn't? And had considered joining that small club of people who prefer not to know, but the peer pressure was so great, so high, so expected. Why is it that people have to interfere in my life, expect me to want to delve so deeply into my past?

And so I found myself with my "guide" at my side going to my first Awakening. My guide is very pretty, nineteen, auburn hair, a great figure that she shows off in tight sweaters and even tighter jeans and she's a real chatterbox. So of course I fancy her, I'm fifteen years old, I fancy most girls.

Millie held my hand (unfortunately in a motherly way) looked at me with those big brown eyes of hers and soothed me into submission. She has been through this process already of course, and even though she'd had doubts when it had been her turn, her parents were even more worried about being seen with a daughter who only has a limited set of life memories. It's amazing with all this accumulated enlightenment how people are still trapped by their wish to fit in.

My parents are next door, they'd opted not to watch and that suited me fine. Looking into my past lives was going to be weird enough without having my parents watch me absorb some of my past characteristics. Millie talked me through it.

"Don't forget Adam, during Awakening, you relive the past life in real time, which makes it feel very real. As such, all the old habits of voice control or language and personality traits come back as if they'd never left. You might not be a teenage boy anymore; you could be any age, sex or creed."

Mum and dad might see their fifteen year old son suddenly become a seventy year old judge or a thirty year old hooker, anything can happen. When you come out of your session, the years fade away and your current present day identity re-asserts itself. It takes control but leaves you with the benefit of that past knowledge / experience, not all of it of course, but enough to make a real difference.

New languages are a common plus, although ironically, this has had the effect of transforming modern English, French and Spanish into a new tri-universal language. People are so comfortable with it, a new amalgamation is forming. "Frenglish" seems to be the cool language of the day. That, mixed with text speak and gadge keeps everyone on their toes. I could of course try to learn it all just as me, but what's the point, all that effort, all that studying, just so I can keep my current core identity intact? Don't forget the extras such as science, literature, history; everything! You just can't catch up with thousands of years worth of experience in one lifetime of study.

Okay, so you don't necessarily need all that experience, but some employers have started requesting at least your last three Generations (3G's) listed on your CV. The world has gone crazy trying to unlock the secrets of the past in an attempt to deal with the problems of today. The total collapse of the world's economic system in 2027 had left everything in tatters. Savings had gone, society had broken down and it all had to be rebuilt from the bottom up. Thank goodness for Martin Kale.

Martin Kale

Martin Kale had come to most people's attention through his T.V show. He was an expert in human psychology, hypnotism and theology, and that's just for starters. He understood the human mind in a way that set him so far apart from anyone else that it worried people. His specialism, if you could call it that, was in how other people like himself could use or abuse their insight, mostly in the form of con artists, showmen, shaman, witch doctors, faith healers, psychics and of course, politicians. These people had used their "powers" of observation and control to manipulate others around them.

Martin Kale was a savant; an individual with amazing cognitive skills and a didactic memory, usually seen in people with autism. Unlike most people with autism though, savants are able to communicate in a near normal way, thereby having all the benefits, with few of the side effects. In fact he was a savant amongst savants if you know what I mean. He never agreed to an IQ test, saying it was too rough an instrument, too clumsy to truly illustrate an individual's intelligence and even though I think it was just a cover, I'd say I have to agree with him.

His understanding of the human mind wasn't just the application of hard study, it was the ability to see signs that no one else could. It was the ability to remember every subtle clue, and process all that data in that incredible mind of his. In essence, he could see into your soul. He even mixed in a little sleight of hand, anything to distract whilst he could study you further. No wonder he became an entertainer, he'd have been hated otherwise. People always fear what they don't understand.

His TV shows would give it all an air of mysticism, but on a level that made it look like trickery. The real trick was that he could all but read our minds but no one believed it, even though he would dangle that information in front of our faces. The ultimate con; real magic disguised as entertainment. Until of course he developed his "Awakening process". How ironic that the Awakening process had to be developed by one of the few people who didn't need it. He had enough going on in his head without the distraction of countless lives whispering in the back of his mind.

Now I'm no expert, so maybe you better Wiki if you want to know more about Awakening, but here is a quick summary. Using a psychological profile as a base point which is built up using methods developed by Kale, it is mixed with personal details extracted using a cognitive polygraph and a light hypnotic trance. With this process, Kale was able to unlock certain areas of the subconscious that had previously only been stumbled upon by hypnotists.

Augmented with memory tricks and bolstered by acute visualisation, past lives were revealed. Apart from the volunteers "seeing" images and hearing voices from the past, CAT scans were showing regions in the brain lighting up like a Christmas tree. Those so called clumsy IQ tests were now being used as a measure of improvement. Kale was changing people's lives, empowering them with greater knowledge and self awareness. Some rumours even started circulating that he was the messiah. This was the second coming in the second Millennium in our hour of need, and with that followed his assassination.

He was shot dead at a mass conference in London at Wembley stadium. Robert Bains entered infamy as his assassin and is still paying the price today. Without Kale at the helm, his Awakening process lost steam, relying on the few elite volunteers who had been Awakened to try and carry on with his methods.

I am not a religious person, few are these days, but twelve years later, a ten year old boy announced that he was Martin Kale. He was the first and so far the only person to ever "Self Awaken." His depth of knowledge about everyone mirrored Kale's abilities, but it was the fact that he knew a secret password that Kale had left in his will that removed most people's doubts. The messiah had resurrected.

Kale never made any claims to be a messiah, in fact he would play them down at every opportunity, but this only made people believe in it more. His return gave his process a momentum that could never have been attained without his death and resurrection. Now his process was offering everlasting life; immortality through new bodies, and it was to change the world.

Now it was my turn to experience the Awakening process. I'd had my psychological profiling, been briefed on any possible risks and been matched up with Millie to help me through my initial Awakening process. I'd had the history explained, as I have already related to you, but also some of the rumours of personality quakes dispelled. Stories of talking in multiple tongues or getting trapped in time, never being able to wake up. These are stories usually told in whispers by people airing their greatest fears. Of course, some fears are greater than others, and some fears become reality.

Adolf Hitler

A few years ago, a Jewish girl in New York suddenly discovered she had been Adolf Hitler. Imagine the horror, the irony and the shame. She was counselled, as were her parents. Her great great grandfather had been in a prisoner of war camp in 1944, so the story could not have been any bigger. How do you deal with that though? After extensive tests, it was unfortunately confirmed to be true. Sometimes people "see" past lives that didn't actually happen, so strong is our subconscious imagination.

Once confirmed, the girl was given a lethal injection. Most people guessed this would happen, the situation had already been hypothesised and it had been decided that Hitler's punishment should be to lose ten G's. It was argued that ten lives were nothing compared to the millions he had killed but that an example needed to be made to help avoid any such despot or serial killer thinking they could get away with murder in this life or the next. Murder rates have already come down a long way as it is now very difficult not to be found out. Murder victims are beginning to come back and point out their killers. As a result, murder by subterfuge is the new way forward: poison, sniper fire, masked killings, anything that will keep the murderer's face hidden.

There was a big outcry, thousands of people protested at this young girl's death, but already people were seeing that we are not limited to just the person you see in front of you. That is just the façade, the face of today. What lies beneath is the darkened tainted soul of an evil person(ality). Personally, I saw a young girl losing her life, a girl, who for fifteen years had led a good life and in keeping with society had submitted herself to this Awakening process and was now having the murderer within killed. She was just an innocent bystander. Or was she?

You have to ask yourself this. What is stronger: the soul, spirit, personality, memory, life force, or whatever you would like to call it, or the body with its current memories? Don't you think it is a bit of a coincidence that Hitler would become a poor defenceless Jewish girl? It's as if his malevolent spirit had chosen the best place to hide. If we talk about being born again giving immortality through interchangeable bodies, then surely that leads to the point that the body is just a shell. Yes it develops its own personality, and up until a few years ago we figured we were just that, a person with one chance in this life, but now we are so much more.

Thus logic dictates that this girl, though young

and pretty and apparently a nice person, is just the current shell. You must not be able to escape your crimes just because you change your mask. Don't get me wrong, I'm just playing devil's advocate here but you can't argue with the logic.

This same logic has completely re-written many of our old laws. Murder now can be investigated back at least three G's, more in extreme cases. Suicide bombers are now being tried; a twist that no one could ever have foreseen. Of course, those same bombers also thought that they would be going to heaven for their personal sacrifice. What a shock they must have had!

Suicide has risen to new highs anyway. Life is less precious, the usual fear of death, the great unknown, is not so unknown. If you have a body that doesn't work properly, get a new one. If you suffer from depression, get a new life. Tragically some people commit suicide because they think they are ugly.

Old age is another dilemma. What do you do, get older and more infirm, or swap it for a new one? If it were not for the fact that you have to wait to be reborn, and then at least another fifteen years to have your old identity Awakened, even more people would be contemplating suicide. You also don't want to leave your loved ones, so there are still more ties than you could ever imagine, but it completely changes the way in which you view the world. Peter

Pan gleefully declared, “To die would be an awfully big adventure.” Well sorry Peter, it turns out that it’s just more of the same old crap.

Millie is a shining example of how it can all go so right though. She’d not been particularly bright, scoring just average grades at school and she lacked confidence, but as she went through her Awakening, her mind just opened up. The world was unravelled, giving her an insight she could never have dreamed of. She didn’t have any murderers in her psyche (although she had robbed a bank and enslaved a few Phoenicians, but that’s just cool) and her confidence, along with her intelligence, soared.

She finished the Academy of Advanced Generations with flying colours, rounded off all those skills and experience, and is now specialising in land regeneration for third world countries. I only hope she’s able to stay in the country long enough for me to finish my Awakening programme, which could be anything between two to four years depending on how far back in time I go or how tricky it might turn out to be.

My father thinks he can remember flying a war type aircraft on another planet. Whether this was just his imagination or an amazing far reaching latent memory has not been verified. One thing that is certain though, Awakening has answered a lot of questions in this world, but it has posed just as many.

An oddity remains. Nobody remembers being an animal, but animals seem just as alive as us and they obviously have some form of intelligence. Where are their spirits or memories? Why are we not interchangeable with them? That is an area of generational research that is very popular. Can you imagine being the person who finds the missing link and discovering what, or how an animal actually thinks? It would be a form of communication, but oddly only through animals that have died.

What a strange way to listen to animals; through the living human shell of their reborn bodies. And what lessons we have been learning. History has gone from being a dusty old subject where facts were dragged out from years of research, going through old texts or digging in a field, to interviewing people alive today. Tours of Old London are given by people who died in the plague or helped put out the Great fire in Pudding Lane.

So many questions...

As with my father's perceived memory… was there once life on other planets? How far back can we go once Awakening processes are tweaked and improved? Most importantly, how do we remember all of this without anything physically transferring from body to body? Do memories need a physical host? What happens to us between bodies and why don't we remember those in between times? How long are those gaps, how conscious are we in that spirit state? Do we have any choice of our new bodies as was posed with the Hitler scenario?

Nobody really knows but it's a fascinating field of study, and one I'd like to take up. As you can imagine though, it's a very competitive occupation and is populated by the best minds of the day, all headed up by Kale. Yes, Kale has resumed his name from his last G and is leading us even further into the light, a brave new world, borne from the scared old world. Where will it all end?

Millie suddenly looked a little more serious than she had been, caught my eye, and said "Come on Adam, it's time to meet your former self."

Chapter 2 - Old Man Kirk

If you think I'm going to describe in great detail the process of my first Awakening session, you are going to be sorely disappointed. I can't. Well not in a way that makes any sense. Apart from the usual technical stuff that Awakening entails, my consciousness of my surroundings seemed to narrow and fade.

Millie had told me about several of her sessions, but I'd still expected more. More lights, more darkness, more memories, more feelings, smells, senses overloaded. To be lifted to a higher plane.

In all honesty I missed the point at which I stopped being me. Well, now me, not past me. Past me just took over. I became… someone I didn't know but do know: Intimately. It was like peering through a keyhole to spy on someone, only to discover that you're spying on yourself. Then you get closer. You forget about hiding, so much of your attention is drawn to this person that you approach quietly, closer and closer until I found myself looking through his eyes. The shock was short lived because I think I started forgetting who I am (*me* me, not *him* me) and became... him. I warn you, it can get confusing, so I'll try to avoid such viewpoints in future.

I am an old man, Victorian era, setting up an old camera. I've never seen a camera like it before; huge, wooden, beautifully crafted in mahogany with brass rails and leather bellows. I just know this of course, remembering that it had cost me a small fortune, my present self standing aside to watch and experience this setting.

I'm in what appears to be a photographic studio. Prints framed on the wall of very stiff, formal couples. In contrast to these stiff lifeless portraits on another wall are beautiful graceful yachts, exquisitely caught in action, their sails catching the wind. This is my first love, the portraits just pay the bills.

I'm inhabiting this body and I'm obviously new to this. I'm not in control because all that I see has already happened and therefore unchangeable. It's weird beyond weird. Knowing you are this person, not only in an intellectual, thought out way, but just knowing… as you do when you wake up in the morning and see your arms and legs.

So knowing you are this person, thinking their, sorry, *my* thoughts, but I can't change the thinking. You are a voyeur, but of your own past through your own eyes with no control and only a limited ability to remember further back, just like remembering what you did last week. But when you remember last week, you have a point of reference, it is still there, buzzing around in your head on the surface of your subconscious waiting to be re-ignited. Trying to remember what I was up to almost two hundred years ago without any reference points is like racing through toffee. I was catching glimpses of his memory, but as he chose to remember them, not me.

Millie had warned me about this apparent lack of control and said that once a memory is glimpsed, you then have the reference point and you can, with a little practice, open it up and explore your past. I had no such luck, but then I was too enthralled with what was going on in the present of my past. One memory point was enough for this Awakening rookie.

Due to the old age of my body and its brain, my memories were pretty clouded. I had some very clear images brought up from when he was much younger, but had trouble remembering current events. Booking times, prices, customer's names. The camera settings I knew instinctively though.

I watched through my eyes as this old body took full control of a young couple for a portrait. He was posing them, setting the timer, then aperture, and softly getting them to relax in this ultra formal setting. Most amazing though was my voice. I could hear myself in a pitch and timbre that was so far removed from my own that I thought something must have gone wrong and that I had mistakenly inhabited someone else's body instead of mine. Of course, that's silly, that's impossible.

"That's right Mrs Hampton, just relax on the chair whilst the good captain stands by your side." His voice had a slight tremble, but was still strong and had an air of confident authority.

The captain looks a little puzzled. "So we will not need the neck braces then?" He asked.

I chuckle, just to show good humour without being rude or patronising. "No no, captain, this is my instantaneous method, no long cramped sittings here. Your photograph will be taken in less than a second."

He seems pretty pleased about that and then I get a few flashbacks; memories of him developing his "Instantaneous" method. I see experiments in the dark room; mixing of chemicals, underexposing glass plate negatives, overexposing, over developing. Playing with silver nitrate, alkaline levels, bromide, and albumen prints, anything I can do to refine and improve on this fledgling art. I don't know about any of these things but I understand the instant I see them; it's "look and learn" to the extreme.

Then I witness his real breakthrough, with him tinkering away in his workshop. His instantaneous method isn't a faster photographic emulsion as I'd thought; it's a rudimentary mechanical shutter that has been the real source of his success. His ability to photograph the beautiful yachts in action has brought him great acclaim and secured a lot of work.

Then I find myself back in the studio with the good captain and his wife. The captain is wearing dress uniform; very smart, laundered and pressed, giving it a crisp, first time worn look. The word impeccable comes to mind. He has a perfectly trimmed beard with matching moustache that makes him look older than his years but gives him a regal touch. My present mind jumps back in momentarily so I can make a mental note to myself; I'd quite like to try and grow one of those beards for myself when I can, Millie would love it.

Marching through the Victorian studio, I'm pulling the blinds away to let the glorious sunshine come through the glass eaves. The painted background lights up, as does the skin of the pretty and prim Mrs. Hampton. Again, her outfit is immaculate, but flowing, soft and alive in stark contrast to her husband's stiff, sharp suit that has been tamed by a firm hand.

Tiny particles of dust appear like miniature fairies, suddenly caught out by the midday sun, fluttering and drifting towards the dark corners, looking for somewhere to settle and rest their wings. The level of detail astonishes me and makes me realise how little I look at the world around me during a normal day in my present life.

Within minutes I have moved reflectors to ease the harsh shadows and it is time to expose the film. I do this by grabbing a mahogany dark slide from the writing desk and running a finger over the polished wood. A small ivory disc with the number ① is inlaid on one side, with a matching disc showing the number ② on the other. Placing it on the camera top, I then put my head under the black cloth at the back of the camera and am suddenly a little disorientated as I am now looking at the Captain and his wife through the camera, but they are upside down and back to front. My older self is unperturbed though, thank goodness he knows what he is doing and I feel for a ridged brass knob on the side of the camera and twist. The image pulls in and out of focus until I'm satisfied.

I set the aperture a little higher than needed for the depth of field required, instantly remembering that depth of field is the degree of focus needed to get the foreground and background in focus at the same time. I am doing this for insurance against my old failing eyes and I'm happy that my new faster film gives me such luxuries. Promptly I press the trigger, releasing a spring mechanism to click the 'Instantaneous' shutter (my 4th version thus far). Subtle tiny hydraulics ensure a smooth exposure, such is the skill of the old man's craftsmanship.

"One more photograph please." I say it as a command rather than a request but delivered with polished professionalism. Then I push the dark slide back into the camera, pull out the whole film plate holder, twist it round, inserting it back into the camera and pull the second dark slide out in a blink of an eye. We don't want the young couple getting restless.

It's at this point that I regain a little more of my current core identity and start trying to delve into some more of his memories. I see lots of faces and I realise that I am able to remember them better than he can. How strange is that? How can my memory be better now? I then remember that I've had the advantage of Kale's memory techniques and I'm under some form of hypnosis.

My mind flits again, leaving the Captain and his wife, searching through Kirk's memory until I see an old man sitting in front of me. His clothes are clean, but nowhere near as pressed as the captain's. He has grey, itchy looking trousers on, a black waistcoat and a dark green coat. It is then that I realise that I'm seeing all this in colour! The only other images I have seen from this era have all been in black and white, colour had not been invented yet, but now I'm seeing it with my own eyes and with that the reality sets in. I look closer at the man sitting before me, slowing time so that I can study him without my host looking at something else.

He has a receding hair line, slicked back and all white, supported by a matching Quaker style beard that hangs from his chin like a mane, his chin and cheeks free from any facial hair and I definitely do not like this style. It's also hard to place an age on him, apart from saying he looks old, especially with the white hair and pallid skin, but his eyes have fire in them, showing an iron will and a fortitude that will no doubt keep him alive to a ripe old age.

The sail boats displayed on the wall are also there in his memory, right by moments of walking along the promenade with children in sailor outfits skipping up and down. I see him photograph these graceful vessels from the corner of a marine promenade, then flash forward to him printing them with a sepia tint. Written on the glass plate negatives are the names of all the yachts so that they will come out in the photograph when printed.

Veshelda, Candida, Shamrock, Astra, Brittania, and there, right on the end, was the name of my business. Kirk of Cowes - Copyrt.

With that I started seeing the name emblazoned on the back of countless other photographs. W.U.Kirk & Sons in beautiful flowing script, Portrait, Landscape and Yachting photographers.

Another listed my patrons: Royal patrons no less.

His Majesty the King
His Imperial Majesty the German Emperor
His Imperial Majesty the Czar Nicholas of Russia
H.R.H The Prince of Wales
H.R.H Princess Victoria
H.R.H Princess Louise (Duchess of Argyle)

H.R.H Princess Henry of Battenburg
H.I & R.H Princess Stephanie (Countess Lonyay)
H.R.H Princess Victoria of Schuamberg-Lippe
H.R.H Princess Henry of Prussia
T.H.R Prince Nicholas and Princess Marie of Greece
H.H Princess Victoria of Schleswig Holstein
H.H Princess Aribert of Hainhault
H.H. Prince Batthayny-Strattmann
T.H. Prince and Princess Henry of Pless

An incredibly impressive list, but all of them names I'd never heard of in any of my history books.

I pushed for my full name, my curiosity driving my consciousness into my control but all I kept getting was the name Captain Hampton, mixed with his head thinking of exposures, further bookings, the pain in his left knee, a chill on his neck.

I'd taken my attention off what was happening and as a result, I was disappearing from the here and now. Flashes of different events, weeks or years seem to be passing by, but who can tell? Only to be broken by a vision that suddenly jumps out at me in a crowded market place. I'm confronted by an odd looking poster on the wall showing a skull. It's advertising a magic show for the supposedly world famous "Sandris," a Native American mystic from Lake Timran in New Mexico. The skull looks Aztec or Mayan in design and has that special illusion of eyes that follow you wherever you walk.

It grabs my attention from past and present, my heart beating wildly, not understanding why I am seeing it or what it means as it sends a shiver down my spine. Somehow I knew that this must be relevant to me in a very big way, but I didn't know as Kirk or me as Adam Capello. It felt timeless, as if it could be from any point in my life or lives. Thankfully it was short lived, my grip lost on any temporal point, and I started shuffling again, trying to find Kirk in the confusion.

Eventually time settled and I found myself in an office, books and ledgers everywhere, and a rather grand writing bureau. It was a relief to be in one temporal time point again and gave me a chance to look around. Next to me was someone rather important to him, I knew this because I could feel lots of mixed emotions.

He was a man in his mid to late thirties, with a slicked parting, deep set eyes and a hook nose. He looked a little more "modern" though, with smart but still stiff clothing. He was sitting writing a letter, with meticulously small handwriting. I concentrated on the emotions trying to amplify them, feeling love, regret and worry.

At this point I then realised that this was Kirk's son. As I looked at him through the photographer's grey old eyes, I could feel his sadness too. He was worried about his son but I couldn't tell why. He had pride in him because he had also become a successful photographer, carrying on the family business in an art, and trade that was still very new and fashionable, but why was he so sad?

William. William. I kept getting this name in my head. Was it the father or the son? As my old self looked around, he had some quarter plate photos printed with another selection of crests on their backs, but this time they had his name in full. William Umpleby Kirk.

Umpleby? Surely not? How Dickensian…

Somehow I knew it was time to go back and find myself.

Chapter 3 – Research

And that was that, my first Awakening; my enlightenment. I didn't know what to make of it really, so much information to take in. So much experience, and yet so little seen. Somehow I'd expected to see my whole life flash before me, gain every insight and morsel of information but instead it was just a glimpse into a strange new world.

I could remember my aching limbs as I worked Kirk's large heavy camera and I could still feel the pride in my chest at the photographic studio business I had built up. I'd been a pioneer! Not of another country, but of a new science and art form. I was at the cutting edge of my day, improving the science myself in a way that was virtually impossible to do in today's world without a super computer and a degree in I.T or biomechanical engineering.

It was a simpler time, but one where Britain was near the height of its empire, an empire that spread throughout the world holding its head high with other royalty. All those kings, queens, prince and princesses of places I'd never heard of but now remembered as if whispered in my ear.

"Come on lazybones, some of us have work to do." Millie was the one whispering in my ear now and a welcome sight if ever there was one.

"How long was I in the session for?" I asked, my voice sounding strange after the older, deeper voice of the photographer.

"About an hour."

"Wow, only an hour, it felt so much longer" I squeaked, a lot higher than I meant to, excited and elated that I'd finished my first session.

I then looked a little closer at Millie, something was different. "You look younger somehow, have you been at the Botox?" I said with a mischievous grin.

She looked at me indignantly. "No, but thanks for the compliment... I think. Actually it's quite normal after your experience to look at people a different way, according to the age of the last body you visited. I'm guessing you were someone a little older than yourself?"

"You could say that, possibly fifty or sixty years older, I can't remember. It was amazing though, he was a photographer in this old studio and he wa…" I was interrupted by Mike, my Awakening facilitator (Observer) from the Kale institute who'd taken me through my first regression. He'd just re-entered the room.

"How was it Adam?"

"Good thanks."

"Any residual memories making it hard for you to concentrate?"

I had to think about that one, went over my 12

times table and recited the current date just to test my memory. Mike looked into my eyes with a light, tested my pulse and breathing. “Yep, you’ll live, glad to have you back in the 21st century” he quipped.

And with that I went on to tell them both about my experience and how it made me feel.

“For the first few minutes it made me feel strange, as if I was in two places at the same time. I then started to forget me as myself, as you do in a dream.”

Millie nodded her head whilst Mike acknowledged verbally, showing that he was listening and found nothing out of the ordinary.

“Looks like you will have to Google this Kirk photographer when you get a chance” he said, smiling. “I’m really into the Victorian era, took me over four years before I realised that I‘d been living in China during most of that period, so I‘ve missed out completely. If only I could tap into other people‘s heads and see what they see. That’s why I love being involved in the Awakening process, I can see your memories through your experiences which can be fascinating. You should hear some of the situations some people get themselves into.” He gave a little laugh, a few stories evidently running through his head as he spoke.

“Now that you have 'Seen' Kirk, you should be able to tap into that part of your past easier than the others. You have set up reference points that you can use to pry yourself back in. Looks like I might have to ask to be assigned to you for a little while." He chuckled, as if this was meant to be a mild threat. Mike is cool, easy going, thirty-five or so and makes me feel at ease, a must for any observer really.

"Any skeletons in the cupboard then?" Millie asked, half teasing, half concerned.

"No, thank goodness, but I can still feel the sadness he was feeling when he looked at his son and I don't know why," I said, looking to her for some kind of answer.

"Ha, don't worry about those, every lifetime has its emotions and that's part of the whole experience. Just remember to leave them at the door though," she softly warned. "Don't transfer them into this life, they can take over if you're not careful."

I'd been told about this a few times before, and again had heard some of the horror stories. No wonder Awakening comes with counselling. Just one hour in a session and that sadness had me wondering why. It then dawned on me why Awakening could take several years to just complete basic memory restoration. If you can afford to, most people carry on delving into their past for the rest of their current lives. It made me wonder, in the following life would you get all the memories packaged into one? Surely that must be the case. To remember your last lives and then just delve one G away rather than have those memories scattered through countless G's over thousands of years again; a tidying up process, similar to defragging your hard drive, putting your memories into an easily readable logical order.

As part of Martin Kale's Awakening process, Kale had always stipulated the importance of exercising your memory. My school included his fundamental processes in their syllabus but I'd never pushed for the more advanced classes. With my recent exploration melting away like ice cream on a hot summer's day, I was having regrets. The better my memory control, the better my Awakening visualisation and retention. Kale's principle cognitive steps are known the world over and I'd learnt them by the time I was ten like most kids. They are debated every now and then on television and it is more than likely that the more advanced classes will become standard teaching within the next few years.

As Mike had mentioned, now that I have a handle on my Kirk identity I can now use the memories to delve back in. The better my memory technique, the easier it would become. My curiosity about this old Victorian photographer was sky high and I was looking forward to my next session so I could meet the old fellow again and ask him some questions. The time in-between would give me the chance to think of those questions and my mind to fix a point on where that memory was retained.

Mike left to start his next session, leaving me with Millie so that I could tell her the whole story. As I was describing the Victorian photographic studio, it amazed me that I still knew all the correct names for the equipment and chemicals. It wasn't like being told once in a classroom and then having to practice those new skills to learn them, it was as if I'd already done all the theory and practice in one go, and of course that's exactly what was happening. I'd had a lifetime to learn these skills and they were fixed in some form of ethereal long term memory. I knew everything I'd seen rather than remembered everything I'd learnt. Could this extend into memories that I'd not witnessed through my last Awakening? Could I tap into deeper memories now that I had created / re-established a link to my former life?

Millie said she'd test me.

"Vous verrez que beaucoup de Victoriens de la class emoyenne s'exprimaient raisonnablement bien en Français. Vous m'avez bien compris?"

I stared at her, my mind clicking and whirring. I heard what Millie was saying but wasn't sure if I'd understood her or not.

"Pardon" I uttered with school boy brevity.

Millie laughed and patiently repeated.

"Vous verrez que beaucoup de Victoriens de la class emoyenne s'exprimaient raisonnablement bien en Français. Vous m'avez bien compris ?"

This time my mind echoed it as… "You will find that a lot of middle class Victorians spoke passable French. Do you understand me?"

"Yes, yes, I do" I screamed – "Oui, oui je comprends."

"But, I feel like I'm tripping over my words a little and… - Je me sens comme si je cherche parfois mes mots et…"

As if to prove my point, I couldn't think of the word for strangely, so I broke back into English; defeated.

"How do you say strangely?"

"Curieusement," she answered without even blinking.

"Ah, biensûr. Curieusement je me sens comme si je parle l'Anglais mais en se faisant l'écho du Français - Ah of course. Strangely I feel like I'm speaking English, but echoing French."

We then dropped out of French for my sake. For her it was effortless, every intonation and pronunciation was, to my untrained ear, spot on. She sounded so… French. It was fantastic, and a part of the Awakening process that I'd been so looking forward too. This was definitely one part I didn't expect to come so quickly.

Millie gave me a teasing, disapproving look. "Yes, and your French is very formal and rusty, definitely an Englishman speaking French than a native. One day, if and when you remember a French life, your French will be a lot more informal and come to you without the echo. That's just your mind translating from English to French. This honeymoon period of linking into past skills will fade after a while, but you will retain some skills, so keep looking back and practising, otherwise you will lose it."

I went to speak to my parents while Millie looked at the digital recording of my session. They were relieved that I was ok and curious to know all the details from me first hand. On talking to them both, it occurred to me that we had opened up a new chapter in our lives. Everything that I have become so far in this world I owe to them. They have nurtured and guided me as well as any loving parents can, and for that I will always be grateful.

This one short session had given me a small inkling into what it is like to be a parent, with Kirk's love and concern for his son still strong in my memory. The details of what happen in life fade fast, but the feelings, they linger much longer. After all their care and attention, they had to watch me take my first steps into my past and therefore begin to shape my future, which in turn will make their role smaller; their influence eroded, but not broken. I only hope that when I come to the same point in my life, I can give my children the love, support and independence that they will ultimately require.

I told them that I loved them, something long overdue, and I could see in their faces how much it meant to them. I'd never stopped loving them of course, it's just that it became more and more difficult to tell them. I had lots of things going on in my life, what with friends, clubs and school, but I guess, in truth, I thought I was too cool to tell them, it felt too awkward. Now, with a slightly more mature outlook on life, I guess that cool doesn't matter. In fact, it's cool to be able to tell anyone that you love them. Unless it's your teacher of course, that would just be wrong.

I suppose it means that Awakening isn't just about finding out what happened in your past lives, it's also about how you are going to use that information to shape your new life ahead. We are all of a relatively new generation and the first to have our minds opened up by this amazing process. It is still so new that there are millions of questions posed by these experiences, and most of them unanswered.

My brother Ben is only eleven, so was still at school that day, safely wrapped up in his childhood, his innocence preserved for a few more years until it will be his turn to tentatively take his first steps into his past. I might finally be able to have a sensible conversation with him when he starts his Awakening.

My parents walked me over to the centre's internet café before they set off. I'd arranged to meet up with Millie again for a drink and to look at Google Generations. Google Generations is part of Google's search engine specifically optimised for searching for details found during the Awakening process. I'd messed around with it before, but this was the first time I'd be using it as a fully fledged 'Lifer'.

Cola and pizza by our side, we keyed in "William Umpleby Kirk". I was so excited that it took me by surprise. This morning I'd been a little reticent to start the whole process, but it had been inevitable. Even though I'd been scared and my parents had been willing to let me back out at any moment, I'd known that I was going to have to go through this process sooner or later. Now I was on a high and couldn't wait for my next Awakening. What a difference a day makes.

Several links inevitably popped up, but so did a couple of images. These photographs showed beautiful old yachts sailing across the water, their sails full, the waves breaking across their bows, all displayed in glorious sepia, just as I'd seen in my Awakening. Google the images if you want to see them.

Dates of birth and death were also supplied, it was all so easy, or so it seemed at first. As usual with any web search, it takes a lot more digging to get underneath the surface information.

I will not bore you with all the details, this was

my life after all not yours. Suffice to say I'll break it down to the bare facts. I found that due to the hard work of keen photographers and yachting societies on the Isle of Wight, a lot of my work had already been done so I would like to thank them for their efforts.

William Umpleby Kirk 1843-1928
Sons: Photographers – Edgar and Arthur

William Umpleby Kirk was born in 1843 at Hull, the son of an auctioneer William Kirk and his wife Mary Ann, both from Leeds. At the time of the 1851 census, 8 year old William Umpleby was living with his parents and two older sisters at Market Weighton, about 15 miles northwest of Hull. In the 1861 census, William Umpleby was found lodging in Birmingham.

In 1865 at Scarborough, William married Ada Elizabeth Parkin from Seacroft, Yorkshire, the daughter of butcher & farmer William Parkin. The couple set up home in Market Weighton where their first son Arthur Henry was born in 1866. The 1871 census records William working as a glass and china dealer living on the High Street. Another son, Edgar William, was born there later that year.

It was at Market Weighton in the early 1870's that William Umpleby Kirk set up a photographic studio, possibly as an adjunct to his glass & china business. A photograph of the period has been found with the imprint on the reverse "Wm Umpleby Kirk, Photographer, Market Weighton". However, by 1874 the family had moved to Walthamstow, East London, where two more children were born; Ernest Oliver in late 1874 and Minnie Blanche in early 1877.

By the time of the 1881 census, the family was living at High Street, Northwood, IOW, with William being described as a photographer employing two boys and a girl. Also living with the family was a 20 year old nephew William Raintill from York described as a photographer's assistant, a servant and lodger. Although not identified as such, it is probable that other of William's children made up the complement of assistants. Indeed, the two eldest sons, Arthur and Edgar, later became photographers.

Minnie's birth in early 1877 at Walthamstow effectively establishes the earliest date of the family's arrival on the Island.

At the time of the 1891 census, the family was living at Clarence Cottage, Bath Road, Cowes, with William being described as a photographer and Edgar a photographer's son. Older son Arthur was not present and was to be found living in Ashford, Kent, employed as a photographic operator. Arthur, then 24, was boarding with widow Mary Barns from Ashford who was also a photographer and had a 24 year old daughter, Nelly, working for her as a photographic retoucher. Arthur married Nelly Barns early the following year in West Ashford.

By the time of the 1901 census, Arthur Kirk had returned to the Island and was living at Palmerstone, Freshwater Bay, Isle of Wight. The census records him as being a photographer on his own account and a widower. Research shows that his wife, Nelly, had died in early 1900 at Lewisham, London, so it is possible that Arthur was operating as a photographer in that area in the 1890's.

Also in the 1901 census, William was described as a photographer employer at home, and living with him were his two sons Edgar and Ernest, both described as photographers.

William Umpleby Kirk died on 20 Jan 1928 and was buried at Northwood Cemetery.

And I also found this:

In researching the Race (Cowes yacht) history a long lost photo archive has also been unearthed. A photograph from the 1932 race was found framed on the wall of another Cowes-based photographer leading to the re-discovery of the Kirk of Cowes archive and the unfolding of a fascinating story. William Umpleby Kirk lived in Cowes, Isle of Wight from 1870-1928. It was here that he captured the first perfect image of Queen Victoria's yacht, earning him a Royal Patronage. After his death, his son Edgar carried on the family name and captured images of the Race in the 1930s

And so, with a little time and lots of pizza, my lifetime was exposed, catalogued for me to put the pieces back together. Google Maps brought up the relevant sites, giving me the eerie experience of looking at my own grave in Northwood cemetery and showing me the approximate area of where my studios had been on the Isle of Wight. Everything seemed different though; new developments obliterating what was left of the past. Millie then pointed out the links to the "Past maps" section where I could view fantastic World War II aerial photography, and there, in surprisingly high resolution, were roads and shapes that were more familiar to me. God this was exciting.

It's just as well that it started off as exciting, because the research became slower and slower as the facts dried up, taking it from fast, almost too much detail, to repetitive blind alleys.

I wanted to know more about the man himself; his wife, his family and how he ended up being a photographer at such an interesting time. How did he gain royal patronage from so many different royal families?

Of course, I was also curious to know what was causing this sadness in my former self; my heart went out to him, supplying yet another odd experience of feeling sorry for myself, but in the 3rd person.

Mike was right; this was a fascinating period in Britain. A time of innovation, character and national achievement, a time of great pride, something that seems to be missing nowadays. All these feelings, all these questions posed by just one Awakening session. I had so much to learn.

There was only one way to deal with this, and that was to go back and pay old man Kirk another visit.

Chapter 4 - Young Man Kirk

"This time concentrate on William Kirk, remember his every characteristic. How he moved, was he a nice man or arrogant, what memories did you pick up from him? You have already done the hard part and located him in your past, now all you need to do is focus on him. He is you and you are him, you are one and the same, separated only by time."

Mike was leading me into my regressive state but part of me was resisting. I couldn't get comfortable, my nose itched, I began to get pins and needles in my hand and my fingers felt cold.

"Don't worry Adam, just relax. Remember your breathing exercises. Breathe in deep… now hold in for two seconds… and release. Calm your mind and stop thinking about Kirk as someone else. Take possession of this identity that was yours and will be again." Mike then looked down at his notes from my last session, and I could feel myself letting go.

"That's it William, relax and tell me what you can see."

I didn't notice him changing my name at the time, but Mike was addressing my former self to bring Kirk back. My mind had cleared and was now remembering the time in the studio. The pain in my knee came back, but so did his professional confidence as he was dealing with his clients. I remembered the feel of the ivory number on the dark slide and could smell the soft leather bellows, and with that I relaxed even further, knowing I had found him.

I began to see through his old eyes again and saw my son Edgar, complete with the sadness I'd felt before. I couldn't believe I'd managed to get back to the point at which I'd last left him. With my new found confidence, I tried picking up William's / my past thoughts to see if I could see what problem he'd had with Edgar, or at least stick around and try to get something from their conversation together.

They spoke a little about business matters, their manner together a little formal, but with an underlying softness. Again I tried prodding Kirk's memory, but all of it seemed recent and irrelevant and to be honest I was getting a little bored through my lack of control. Being a passenger in a car gives the greater view, but it's not as much fun as taking over the wheel when you are on a good road.

I could feel myself mentally yawn as my old hand dipped into my pocket to check the time on my silver Hunter pocket watch. Now, with my attention down, everything lost its colour, weirdly giving the impression of looking at the world as if it was through an old black and white photograph, just as it would have been at the time. The photograph loses contrast and begins to fade as the watch face grows bigger. A loud clanging sound rings through my ears as the watch face somehow becomes a clock face at the top of the town hall, striking ten o'clock in the morning.

This magical transition leaves me elated as I suddenly find myself surrounded by colour so vibrant, it feels like the Wizard of Oz in glorious Technicolor, enriched by the busy sounds of a town market. The smell of fruit and vegetables fill my nostrils, all adding to the verisimilitude of the scene; it could not feel any more real. Maybe that's how I let go, my senses assaulted from every angle to make me truly believe I was where I was. Mike's couch was not there anymore. I, as Adam, did not exist. I was now William Umpleby Kirk, and I was young again.

Gone is the pain in my knee, gone is the sorrow I'd been feeling and instead, making a welcome return, is my sharp eyesight and a spring in my step. Why my mind has taken me here I have no idea but I feel great. The sun is shining brightly in the sky, which gives the market an amazing brilliance that naturally lifts the soul, but it seems more than that. What can it be? Why am I on top of the world?

Love. I am in love. I can feel butterflies in my stomach when I think back to last seeing Ada, but the memory feels like it was only yesterday. I'd seen her at the Sunday service of St. Mary's church a couple of times since my return to my home town of Market Weighton last month. This is my first experience of love, both as William and now as Adam, and it feels amazing. At least I think its love, how do you know you really are in love when it is the first time? I'd felt attraction and lust before, Millie is testament to that, and whilst this feels similar, it is also strangely different. I want to spend my life with her, even though I have no idea what she is really like.

Like a bolt out of the blue, Ada caught my eye during the vicar's sermon and I'd had to wait an age before I could subtly persuade my father to introduce me to her family. During that wait, she glanced over a few times as if surveying the architecture of the church, carefully making sure that her eyes never rested on me for more than a second. For a lady to openly look at a man, especially during a church service, would be heavily frowned upon, such is the restrictive etiquette of Victorian society.

"William, I'd like to introduce you to Mr. and Mrs. Parkin. Mr. Parkin owns Parkin Farm in Seacroft." Father's rather formal introduction allowed me to approach closer. "And this is their daughter Ada."

With every ounce of restraint that I could muster, I spent the next five minutes making small talk with her parents, occasionally asking her polite questions on current fashion, of which I honestly knew nothing. Happily, I knew more about fan etiquette though as she quickly fluttered her fan at me whilst her father was talking to mine; my former self grew quite excited. In those days, fans could be used as a form of semaphore to coyly signal a lady's interest in you. Is she really telling me she is single? Wow, if only fans were popular in 2061, things might be a little simpler on the dating front.

Of course, I was to find out later that the complications of Victorian courtship mixed with the convoluted mechanisations of marriage were to be anything but simple.

My mind returned to the market place and its cacophony of sound, for I was on a mission. Ada's father had just opened up a butcher's shop on the corner of Finkle Street and I'd made my mind up to pay him a visit to ask if I could take Ada to the Summer Ball at Hitching Court the following week. My mind was racing away with me, reviewing and editing the conversations I had planned in my head a thousand times already.

Should I buy something first? No that would be too obvious; it could make me look naïve and stupid. But what if there are customers in there? I'd definitely have to buy something then without asking my question.

My nerves were getting the better of me so I started rehearsing our conversation in my mind.

"Ahem, good day Mr. Parkin, I thought I'd take a look at your new shop." Hmm, should I say shop or establishment? Establishment sounds a lot grander, less common.

"Good day Mr. Parkin, I thought I'd just pop in to see your new establishment and wish you luck." Mr. Parkin would reply and I would listen patiently, waiting for the appropriate moment and then ask how Ada was. Oh for the love of God, why is this so difficult?

My heart is beating rapidly now, to the point that I'm sure other people can hear it too, like a drum setting the pace of life. On the way out of the market I suddenly see the skull poster from my first Awakening, like an overlapping memory, only this time it doesn't affect me at all, its eyes are dead; impotent and completely without power, so curiously I am able to carry on unheeded. How strange that I should "see" the same point in time, but from two different viewpoints, but then I guess memories are always affected by time and can become bigger or smaller events in their recollection. On this occasion, all I'm left with is the drumming of my heartbeat eerily chasing me past the poster.

I march on, turning the corner into Finkle Street. Mr. Parkin's new establishment is not big enough to be an establishment… so shop it is then. My mind made up, I approach the window with more than a little trepidation, and berate myself for it. I'm a grown man, twenty years old for goodness sake. I have even lived in the city of Birmingham for two years making it on my own, so why is this so difficult? It was time to have 'The talk'.

On looking back at this moment, I, as Adam, am in the very strange position of knowing the fate of my former self. I am here as young Kirk seeking permission to take a beautiful stranger to a dance and nervous as hell, but I have already spent time as Kirk as an old man, possibly forty years later. I vaguely knew the outcome of this conversation and the very complicated but exciting two years that was to follow, for Ada was to become my wife.

So how can I explain to you how out of time I suddenly feel. I am a fifteen year old boy in 2061, looking back through the eyes of someone who was me over two hundred years earlier. I don't really know him, but I begin to recognise certain traits within my own personality.

In addition to being a passenger within Kirk's body, I have no powers apart from that as an observer and the ability to see into the future of this portion of me. Even if I was to know that I was going to meet some terrible death I would be helpless to do anything about it, for I have already played my part, and thus everything is written in time.

It makes me realise now how lucky we are to be

living in the present, with the freedom to do what we want and the power to make things happen. The impotent role of observer has always been an uncomfortable one for me. In this case though, I knew it to be filled mostly with happiness, although you would not have guessed it at the time.

My talk must have gone well with Mr. Parkin though, as my memory suddenly took me to the Summer Ball with Ada. My own father had not been so happy. He had other plans for me in terms of marriage and business, which had started with him bringing me back from Birmingham to sell his glass and china in an outlet for some of his auction goods. As head auctioneer, he had built up a lot of professional respect in our market town, putting us in a much better position within society. He wanted me to marry a girl of equal or higher standing in order to elevate us to even higher social status.

Mr. Parkin was doing well financially, but he was still a farmer and butcher and that was on the lower end of middle class. Ada, in my father's words, was not quite good enough for me. He could not argue with her beauty though, even if he thought she was a little too clever for her own good.

"Women should be looking after the home and their husbands rather than taking up hobbies such as this new fangled photography." He added gruffly.

And there it was. That little nugget of information that makes everything come into place.

It had been Ada who had introduced me to photography and it had been the large dowry from her father that had changed my father's mind and had enabled us to open up a photographic studio in Market Weighton a few years later. Ada had the creative flair, whilst I had inherited my father's business acumen, which was just as well, as it would not have seemed right to have a woman owning her own photographic business in those days.

She blessed me with three boys, saving a bonny girl for last in the form of Arthur, Edgar, Ernest and Minnie. The last two had been born in Walthamstow, London, where we had moved our studio to take advantage of the extra trade.

London had turned out to be too noisy and dirty for us though and we longed for the sea air. We had contemplated Brighton or Bognor, but luckily I had seen an article describing the Cowes yacht race on the Isle of Wight. Property prices were more affordable due to the slight inconvenience of living on an island and so we were easily able to move everything to our new studio on the parade. My love of yachts grew, as did the children, until Arthur and Edgar were photographers in their own right.

If only it had ended like that; a happy marriage and a moderately successful business allowing us to live our golden years in paradise, but life is never that simple, as with every up, there seems to be a down, **the universe breathing in and out.**

In 1898, Ada caught a chill which led to a fever. Three weeks later she died in bed surrounded by her loving family. I can still feel the grief at losing my soul mate. She had been with me for thirty-six wonderful years and we both knew we had been lucky enough to find each other when so many others were stuck in unworkable arranged marriages. From that point on I knew I would feel alone for the rest of my life.

As if to prove that point, I took refuge in my own company, often hiding away in my workshop and leaving the running of the business to my sons. It wasn't fair to them, after all they had just lost their mother, but they were able to plough their grief into their work. I didn't seem to be able to cope at the shop front.

So with that sorrow I could be found tinkering away in the workshop with several different projects to keep my head occupied, until I found I had devised a simple prototype film shutter using just cigar boxes and some rubber bands. Simple, but very effective and I continued to make many mechanical improvements over the following years, using tiny hydraulic parts from France. Now I could take photographs in a fraction of a second rather than in the usual one to five seconds at that time. Not only did this enable me to take more natural portraits, it also made it possible to photograph a yacht as if it had been frozen in time.

My "Instantaneous Method" had been born, and with it I had caught the eye of Queen Victoria and Prince Edward after photographing the royal yacht in action. When my royal patronage became public, we were inundated with work, and thus I was forced out of my workshop and back into the business again. Even after her death, Ada had played a part in keeping the studio going. I would never have been focused enough to have spent all that time alone otherwise.

Although I have described this to you in a few paragraphs, in reality of course, it was quite a few years, and some of the worst of William's life. Thankfully I became so busy that it gave little time for any more reflection. Arthur left to set up his own studio back on the mainland, leaving just Edgar and me to run the family business. I was sad to see Arthur go, but we had never really seen eye to eye, whereas with Edgar… he was so much like his mother; creative, kind of heart and full of ideas. He had inherited her eyes, but sadly also her lack of business sense, but I was glad to have him at my side.

As the years passed, I caught up to the point in which I had first 'met' Kirk. William was now known locally as Old Man Kirk and a pillar of Cowes society, and this is where the memory came full circle, for as I looked at the silver Hunter pocket watch, I remembered that it had been a silver anniversary gift from Ada to me to mark our time together. So when I had looked at the watch, it had reminded me of that beautiful day when I had passed the market square so nervously, trying to gather the courage to ask her father for permission to take her to the summer ball all those years ago.

This is probably why I felt so sad looking at Edgar as there is so much of his mother in him and I never stopped missing her. She would have been so proud to see the business grow with my invention and she would have loved the photographs of all the graceful yachts sailing majestically across the Solent.

As Adam, I often wonder where Ada is now and have fought the temptation to try and find her through a multi-generation dating agency. I'm too early into my life for that, but maybe one day we will meet again.

Chapter 5 - Reclaimed skills

You might be thinking that my vocab is a little advanced for a fifteen year old boy. Well, this is for two reasons.

1: By the time I finished this journal, I was eighteen and thus able to go back and edit some of the finer points of my experiences through my Awakening foundation.

2: Due to the many experiences that I have now been through, I have of course acquired an extended range to my vocabulary, but you probably would have guessed that.

My life in this period has changed dramatically in terms of my awareness of the world around me. I find myself jealous of my younger brother Ben in his pre-Awakened mindset as his world is very personal, extending only to his family, friends and favourite TV shows.

I know I am lucky. I live in Tunbridge Wells, a large, attractive, affluent middle class town nestled in the South East of England and yet less than an hour away from London, where we go quite often for days out to the theatre, galleries or shopping.

I do miss the innocence though, and the freedom of having little, or no personal responsibility, but that's all part of growing up I suppose. Ben is okay as a brother really, but the four year age gap seems huge sometimes, even though he is always trying to "fit in" with my friends and me.

I guess my parents are pretty cool for their age. Dad designs bridges all over the world and Mum now runs her own clothes upcycling store where people either bring in their faded or out of fashion but sentimental clothes and have them "remodeled" or buy clothes already redesigned by her.

Toby and Max are my best friends from school and have also started their Awakening foundation. Our conversations have shifted from Superheroes and computer games to girls and music but the strangest conversations now are shared histories or similar experiences. Toby's first experience was in Paris around the turn of the new millennium, about twenty years before I had a lifetime there. After we both had that experience, we were able to talk about the same places and even a couple of the same cafés we used to love. We often wonder if we ever saw each other in the overlapping years, maybe just passing each other on the metro, or indeed, in one of the cafés. Mind you, my French identity was already playing tricks on my mind in regards to Toby, but that's another story.

Max had quite a scare, reliving his time in the trenches in the First World War. Apart from having to shoot a few soldiers as they came over the different battlements, Max remembered being trapped into a corner, leaving him no other option but to charge towards his opponents armed only with a bayonet. All went blank as he made his charge, leaving him to think that maybe he had been shot before he reached his quarry. I don't know if he was more disturbed by that, or finding out that he had been German!

Many people argue that fifteen is too young to go through the Awakening process due to the graphic experiences endured, not to mention the loss of innocence, but society as a whole is keen to regain its past lives as soon as possible, thus keeping the idea of immortality alive. Kale has also argued that it is the perfect age to introduce new ideas to the mind as it is mature enough to cope with the experience but still malleable enough to be open and question what it sees.

I have also picked up quite a few new languages from my identities, but most of them are quite dated, with Ancient Greek and 15th Century Spanish not being that useful on my holidays. I think Middle English is quite cool, but when someone hears you using it in conversation they think you are quite geeky, as if speaking Elvish or Klingon.

The Greek and Latin are useful as far as most

things academic, I'll give them that. A whole new world has been opened up to me in which I can see the roots of names for anything from medicine to dinosaurs (terrible lizards) to Philosophy (love of wisdom). It reminds me of when I first learnt to read; I would scan anything and everything to test my new skills. Ah, my parents' joy at watching me grabbing words from shop fronts, posters and food tin labels until even they began to tire of it. With these skills comes confidence, and a realisation that there is nothing that you cannot learn. Yes, we are still limited by our IQ; God's hand still playing a part in this new age of knowledge, but everything is within reach, graspable like those tins in the supermarket.

With these new powers of understanding comes a new breed of intellectual. For those lucky few blessed with an intellect that matches their experiences, it is as if Einstein or Sir Isaac Newton had lived long enough to acquire enough knowledge and experience from those lives to think on a completely new level, like the Gods themselves looking down upon the mere mortals that inhabit this earth.

Can you imagine a room filled with Newton, Einstein, Hawking, Da Vinci, Plato, Confucius, Galileo, Mozart etc? It could be fantastic. Unfortunately it could also just be a room full of super egos, such is the nature of man.

Quite often we are reborn with minds not able to cope with the inner abilities of the soul. When Shakespeare came back the whole world was excited to see his first new play in over 400 years but it was bitterly disappointing. It would appear he has lost that special touch, that intangible "it" that separates the genius from the mundane. Unable to cope with his celebrity status and failure, he became an alcoholic, and is currently trying to "clean up" at the Betty Ford clinic. So much talent locked up within his tortured soul.

Maybe that just makes room for a new wave of intellect, armed with the combined experience of millions of years and free of any language barrier, the tower of Babel a distant memory. Could it be possible that one day we will put Eve's apple back on the tree? Would that appease our gods?

If this is so, maybe we would not need our bodies any longer. Whilst they provide a useful purpose on this earth and can be fun, they are also difficult to maintain and very distracting. Is this where Awakening will lead? To the end of our physical vessels, to a point in which we can still retain our identity and the essence that makes us sentient?

The bible says that we are all made in God's image, if that is so, is this the point in which we realise our full potential? Is this the point in which we all become gods? And by doing so, we merge and become "The almighty God." That image holds a lot of poetic license, but how else can we even begin to fathom the complexities of divine power? How can you describe something that has never been seen before? It would be like describing a computer to a caveman.

It is at this point that I have to ask myself this question. As free spirits in an "energy", that for the sake of convenience we might call God, and where we all realise our full unified potential, would we be happy? Kind of screws with your mind doesn't it? The whole purpose of doing everything that leads to this point should be to create happiness, both for you and everyone around you, and yet of course we spend so much time trying to create a safe and secure and fulfilling world around us that we forget to just enjoy being us, and to derive the simple pleasures that this can provide. Hopefully, and I really mean hopefully, we can realise this point one day. Then the world, or universe or whatever we may find it to be, will be a better place.

I better get off my soap box now and try to highlight some of the good and bad things that Awakening has brought to the human race. They are ideas I think about a lot these days, and help serve as my personal justifications for following this yellow brick road to Awakening.

Good points:

- Immortality through re-birth into new bodies with recoverable memories.
- A greater attitude to looking after our planet, as now we will be there to reap the benefits.
- A greater knowledge of our past.
- An end to the barriers of language.
- A new wave in spiritualism with a more universal concept of God.
- Greater conversation, rather than the old topics of football and sex (although it still happens; obviously).
- A reduced fear of death, thus giving consolation to those affected by illness or tragedy.
- A hope of everlasting peace through greater understanding of each other.
- A new breed of intellect to steer our future onto the right path.

- An improved sense of global community.
- Timelessness.

Bad points:

- It can bring back very painful memories.
- Less value placed on the life of the bodies we have.
- Difficulty in balancing our current identity with our generational, or principle core identity, i.e. nature vs nurture.
- Being in love with someone from another life and trying to reconnect in your current life, as there can be a huge age gap - an uncomfortable side effect from G-dating (chapter 13).
- Having to cope with a famous / infamous past.
- Knowing you have had an amazing intellect in the past, but not having a suitable brain to deal with it in this life and thereby unable to fulfill your potential.

My experiences have changed my world, and if I'm honest, have probably made me a much better person. My understanding of the world is at a level that I could never have reached at this point in my life, as I have lived amongst different cultures under different circumstances as both man and woman, black and white, rich and poor. I have an insight that would have been impossible without Awakening. This insight gives me the patience needed to deal with matters calmly, and it gives me the wider tolerance to accept the imperfections of life.

It arms me with such a heightened understanding of what it is like to be in the mind of so many different lives that I now realise how easy it is has been to make mistakes without even knowing I'd been making mistakes. With that realisation I understand how others make the same mistakes and I can therefore accept and understand the reasons behind the thinking. I react less to what seems to be stupidity and respond better to respect when given. In essence, it makes me a better, more patient, more tolerant person.

It is still early days in the era of Awakening, and not everybody is lucky enough to be given the opportunity. Many third world countries just cannot afford the facilities or the time to undertake such a huge period of learning, but we are changing that.

A lot of countries are also at war, stupidly fighting for religious reasons or over land. The irony is clear and has been put forward to them. If they went through Awakening they would realise that we do not own a country. Our time within a certain land is fleeting in the context of countless lives and those countries have also migrated or changed over the millennia to a point in which they are unrecognisable now.

In relation to religion, many faiths have been challenged in terms of their vision of life and death, and this has broken many of them down. However, the breakdown of most religions has seen the unification of them with similar religions. For example, the many forms of Christianity such as the Catholic Church and Judaism, The Church of England, Anglicans, Lutherans and so on, are now able to look back and see that their differences were borne of time and circumstance, not from right and wrong. Those that believe in a certain faith have now realised that they have previously been involved in many different religious beliefs in the past, so now they have a real understanding of the viewpoints of them all.

As a result, faiths are coming together and convincing the rest of the world that a unified faith holds part of the key to world harmony. Earlier I spoke of mankind giving up having bodies in the future, and that their souls, or energy, would mix and become God. This mix of science and religion seems to have a similar goal, as it seems we are all following a similar path that leads to salvation. The science of modern religion is very real now, and could even be called the religion of modern science.

Maybe I'm saying all these things too early in this book, creating a few spoilers, letting the proverbial cat out of the bag, but at this point I am still as unsure of our future as you might be. All we can know for certain is that the better we know our past, the better we are prepared for the future. At long last we have the chance to learn from our mistakes.

It is here that I am trying to connect with you in the most effective way possible. The word **connect** is very important in this context, because it signifies the connection of minds, the greater my ability to convey my thoughts and vision to you, the greater your understanding and agreement. If we can connect in a way that you can see strong elements in your life from my experiences, then we can agree on many elements of what we think our future might be. Hence, from greater universal knowledge of our past, comes greater understanding of our universal future.

Of course, what I have just said makes a mockery of me saying keep it simple, as now I am spouting theories of science and religion, and my personal philosophy, but some subjects demand taking the conversation up a level or two. I guess that is why in the bible, Jesus chose to teach in parables rather than lecture his disciples. Through his stories came greater visualisation, and that lead to greater understanding. Hopefully the chapters dealing with my Awakening sessions will provide extra illumination in the process I am undergoing. Of course, if you were to go through the process yourself, then your understanding would naturally be much greater.

Ah, there I go preaching again.

Chapter 6 – Slave

Mike counted me down this time, my eyes getting heavier as my heart rate slowed and my mind opened up.

"5, 4, 3, 2…" I heard no more; everything just went dark for a second, leaving me hanging in nothingness, wondering whether this is going to work? Am I remembering a time I was sleeping?

All these questions evaporate with blinding light in the midday sun as I'm suddenly surrounded by sugar cane, towering above me until I harvest it with my machete. I'm tall and strong, covered in wiry muscle. I'm also black. Well there's another thing to add to the list, but I don't have time to look around this time, as my mind quickly flits to different parts of my life.

My mind can't settle but it's giving me a good overview of this life. I seem to be living in a small bare hut with chickens running around, the hot sun baking the planks of wood that form a ceiling, making it hot and stuffy. There must be at least eight people in this small room, all sweating, laughing, singing and talking with an accent I can't place. An indistinct mixture of words, with mainly French, some African and a little Spanish thrown in; some form of patois?

And again I'm on the move through another jump in personal time. Now it is late at night and a feeling of extreme tiredness and relief overwhelms me. Is it really possible to feel this tired? Every muscle feels strained as I realise another day is finally over in the unbearable harvest season that leaves me wrecked, but, for a short while anyway, I can rest and see my mother. I'm one of the lucky ones, I was sold with my mother a long time ago when I was still very young: I am about twenty now, so we both wonder how long before she is of no more use to our owner.

This Awakening is so much clearer, all the details coming to me every time I have a question. I feel like I've cracked it except I can't stick to one solid time frame. My name is Cabel, a black slave in Louisiana in the Parish of St. Charles near New Orleans, but my whole life has been spent on this plantation, so I know little else except it is the year 1810 and my owner is called Manuel Andry, who I fear and loath in equal measure.

Now I'm with my… mate? Her name is Charity, and apart from my mother she is the only woman in this cruel world that I love. Where my world is full of pain, she just gives me affection and I don't know where I'd be without her. It's late and we are getting ready for bed, our sexual urges fighting against a sea of fatigue, never knowing what will win until our heads hit the straw pillow. Mating was of course encouraged by our owners as offspring always added extra value to their books, sometimes with their own personal contribution made against defenseless slave girls. As long as the children could be reared as cheaply as possible and it didn't interfere with the Mother's duties, it was cheaper than buying new stock.

I feel like a caged animal, oppressed by my masters and again a huge swell of emotions consume me. Anger, fear, sadness, despair, hate and… hidden, deep within… hope. Now that I have found it, the hope clarifies and brightens. It is in such stark contrast that it stands out like a beacon, focusing my minds onto this fixed point. Escape!

Suddenly my heart is beating in my chest. I can hardly breathe as a sense of utter dread fills me; it is time. After weeks of whispers that could have cost us our lives, we are at last fighting back and somehow I know that it's just after the new year, so it must be 1811 and Charles Deslondes has given the signal for rebellion. Deslondes, a free black refugee from St. Domingue had been working as a slave driver on the plantation. He'd organized the slaves on the plantation and, with the support of runaway slaves who live in the nearby swamps, Deslondes' band has gained our support; this is our only hope.

Now, like caged animals when the trap opens, we are running, grabbing pitch forks, axes, clubs, anything that can be used as weapons to vent our anger. Louis and Caesar are with me, both runaway slaves, and we are heading for the Andry plantation. Caesar is singing and running, completely jubilant in his new found freedom. He then looks me in the eyes, sending a shiver through my spine as I connect through his lost soul.

"Why are you not happy Cabel?" He is asking, genuinely perplexed at my lack of celebration.

I mutter something back, embarrassed by my lack of conviction that this is a good idea, even though it's something I have wanted for so long. Caesar shrugs his huge shoulders, not hearing me and leads us on to the plantation house. It's a beautiful house whose opulence is borne of our sweat and blood, I can't believe the spacious luxury compared to my cramped humid hut.

Now screaming and shouting erupts as we run into the house, some of the other slaves have made it there before us, all with only one target in mind; of killing Andry. So much is happening that my mind can't seem to process all the information quickly enough, and so, like an old computer, everything slows down.

I jump time again; Andry now stands before me and I am blocking his exit, there is no alternative, we will have to fight. My senses go into hyper-drive, giving me the ability to smell the sweat of fear emanating from the frenzied pack behind me. Andry is holding a chair leg, a look of fear and loathing in his eyes, but I hold a small axe, a hand tool from the fields. I try to slash at his face, glancing his shoulder instead, the pain taking the wind out of him. I'm now aware that I am watching this, but unable to stop anything, realising once again I am an observer who has no control. Everything has already been played out so nothing can be stopped and I am terrified.

I'm tempted to will myself out of this experience but held to the spot through a mixture of fear and curiosity. My mind is so caught up in the "now" that I cannot even concentrate hard enough to make my escape.

Again I go in for the attack, this time digging my axe into his thigh as an easy target. He goes down and I can go in for the kill. His screaming fills my ears, but he is not looking at me, he is looking behind with utter horror and it is enough to make me turn round.

"No, no, no, please God no!" Andry's voice chills my heart

I will never forget what I was about to witness and it almost stopped me from taking any further Awakening sessions. There is a reason why we sometimes forget things. Sometimes it is to forget someone you love and sometimes it is to forget something so horrific, that you actively try to block it from your mind. With death I had been granted that luxury, but now Awakening has unlocked that part of my mind. Instead of being hidden, it is highlighted, and I will have to live with it all over again.

Andry's screaming forces me to turn round, just in time to witness Caesar burying an axe into the head of Andry's son. The head just splits apart, blood pumping out, as his lifeless eyes roll back into his head. He crumples onto the floor, his legs twitching and mouth opening and closing like a fish from the lack of signals coming from his brain. Caesar continues to attack and I lose my appetite for more blood.

As I watch in abject horror, his son's skull is glistening white through the blood and hair. I mentally overlay an image of the whole skull for a millisecond, just as I had seen it before as Kirk on that poster in the market place. Was this the reason for my memory playing tricks on me when I saw that image? Will it happen to me now every time I see a skull? Is this the origin of it all, a mental echo caused through the trauma that will reverberate along my timeline? This graphic horror played out before my eyes becoming unforgettable.

No time to think now though, as Andry takes this moment to push past me, his adrenaline giving him the strength to run away, but not before he takes one last look at what is left of his son as he bolts out the door. Still in shock, I weakly tried to pull Caesar off, his face covered in spattered blood, his eyes wild, his mind buried behind animal instinct. Only with the help of Louis could we pry him away. We are not worried about Andry escaping, his wound is deep and he is losing a lot of blood. He will die before ever reaching the plantation boundary.

It may have been bloody and we may have stamped our ticket into Hell, but we are now in control. We found Deslondes and gave him the news. He quickly sent search parties to bring back the body of Andry, keen to show his rebels that we are in control, but an hour later there was still no sign of him. It would appear that he had managed to escape after all; the adrenaline and hatred keeping him alive so that he could muster help in avenging the death of his son.

"How could you let him go, do you know what this means to us?" Deslondes screamed.

He was understandably furious, somehow he knew the implications of Andry's escape and it bore a heavy weight on his shoulders. His instructions are clear though; we are to walk along the Mississippi river until we reach New Orleans, rescuing slaves along the way and torching the plantation houses to send a message of fear to our captors. "We are slaves no more!"

With freedom in our hands and conviction in our hearts, we were able to march against our fatigue. Matters escalated over the rest of that evening with two more plantations razed to the ground; we are on a high. We just walked into those plantations, the planters and their families having fled with the news of our march and thus no more blood is shed.

The next day was not so easy though, as we met our first resistance. Soldiers were waiting for us by the great river and it was to be our first true test. We are mainly armed with just our hand tools but have the bravery of utter conviction that justice is on our side. News of our revolt had reached a couple of other plantations and thus their slaves had also broken free. Our numbers are increasing, building our strength to three hundred or more.

But on that day we were met with the eerie sound of drums as groups of soldiers from New Orleans blocked our path. Whilst we showed resistance, they showed no mercy, it was a blood bath. They were too well armed; the sound of gun fire broken only by the screams of slaves dying.

I was lucky, several shots just missing me by inches as I ran for cover, but eventually we had to retreat. Over the course of the day we continued to build up our numbers by liberating a few more plantations. This strange experience of seeing events flash before me gives a staggered but comprehensive overview to the whole event, but in extreme detail, as if all the highlights have been edited into some kind of gruesome package. It was very surreal. Never as Adam have I experienced this kind of violence first hand, and so, as a passenger observing events from my past, I saw night fall once more, the flames from our last plantation illuminating the night sky. Things slowed down that evening, giving us the respite of some peace and rest. I think I must have been on some night watch for a few hours so that we could get some sleep before the big day ahead. Images of the night sky with a mass of stars making us feel so small in this big harsh world.

Freedom at last

All these memories bombard me. I'm suddenly back in battle, my respite snatched away from me like so many other things in this short life, and short life it was to be. As a few of us run to cover in some bushes nearby, we are snatched from freedom once more by soldiers waiting for us. The ultimate hunting trick; scare your prey into running to your trap with as much noise as possible.

It's a bit of a blur again, but this time each image is encompassed in pain. My face smashed with the butt of a gun, kicks to my legs and kidneys, and then someone stamps on my head; it all goes dark.

There is very little to add to this sad tale. After waking up to a world of pain, I'm pushed and jeered with my hands tied behind my back and I imagine this must have been how my mother had felt when she had first been taken captive. How cruel man can be with no thought about fairness for anyone else but themselves and their kin. I am but a beast and I will be dealt with accordingly.

They ended my humiliation by showing me a rope hanging from a tree. I'd been captured and tried in a matter of hours and now came my execution. My soul rages, but I, as Cabel, seem calm. I'm just glad it's going to be all over, freed by death from the suffering I have had to endure my whole life.

As for me as Adam Capello, two hundred and fifty years after the event, I'm screaming through fear and anger and disgust. My eyes have been opened to the horror of what man is truly capable of doing and I want to be sick. Maybe it was this reaction that saved me from having to experience all of my death or maybe it was just that people very rarely do. It seems that even though we can see back through countless lives over thousands of years, we still manage to block out this most traumatic part of our existence.

My death, my sleep;

And by a sleep to say we end the heart-ache and the thousand natural shocks
That flesh is heir to.

Chapter 7 - Giving up

I was screaming when I came out of that Awakening session. Mike was calming me down, telling me to take deep breaths.

"It's okay Adam, you're back in 2061, back in your present life. You are safe now" he added reassuringly. "Keep breathing slow, deep breaths."

"I'm okay," I rasped, my throat feeling tight with memories of the noose still fresh in my mind.

"You had a bit of a scare this time round, huh?"

"Yeah, too many of them, couldn't fight back." I obviously wasn't making sense.

"Whoa, start at the beginning my friend. Here, take a drink of water."

I gulped down the water, but the residual physical memory still clung on making it a painful experience. Mike could see me holding my neck, his concern growing.

"Are you gonna tell me something about being strangled or hanged?" he asked.

I nodded. "Hanged, but I got out of the Awakening before the…er, end." I felt too embarrassed to say before I died, it sounded too dramatic.

"I could see you were having problems, your

heart rate was up and down all over the place. By the time I woke you up, your heart was touching 172 BPM. Your body will generally wake up by itself before any death experience though, one of its amazing safety mechanisms."

Again I nodded, but I wasn't listening. My mind racing around my latest experience with memories I just wanted to erase as quickly as I'd found them. That unfortunately is not so easy. It's kind of ironic that it is easier to remember details from your past life than to forget them. Sure, hypnosis can be used to suppress memories, but they can be so easily triggered, and that way they will come back and bite you on the arse. It's much better to confront your past, no matter how long ago it was.

At long last the feeling around my neck dissipated, but this just left me free to notice my hands shaking. I knew I was awake and I knew I was back home, but part of my mind was still in the plantation house watching Caesar bury that axe into the head of Andry's son; tears rolling down my cheeks in unison with the blood flowing out of his head. I was a mess and I just wanted to go home.

No more Awakening sessions for me, all the excitement from my past experiences seemed irrelevant now as I had paid the full price for this stupid curiosity. The Pandora's box had been opened and I had stared straight into it. Fucking Awakening! Fucking stupid idea looking into your past lives!

And for what? Yes we regain our past skills, but does it make life any better, any fuller?

I wished Millie was here, but then glad she wasn't as I didn't want her watching my histrionics like some little kid in kindergarten missing his mummy. So I found myself blubbing on Mike's shoulder instead.

"Okay, okay, let it all out Adam. These things happen in Awakening at least once or twice in a person's foundation period. The only problem is knowing when." He handed me a paper tissue from his drawer. "See, I'm always prepared, the ultimate professional" he joked, trying to make light of the situation.

"Sorry Mike, I don't know what came over me, just didn't see that experience coming." I wanted to add that it was going to be our last session, that I was quitting, but I didn't have the nerve to tell him yet.

"Look Adam, can you wait half an hour? I'm going to get Holly to cover my next session so we can have a proper debriefing." He asked, but he wasn't really giving me a choice, the look on his face said "you need this."

I sat in the cafeteria watching the news on TV, trying to block the images still running around in my head. People I recognised were coming out of their Awakening sessions with big smiles on their faces. Their world hadn't been shattered. I imagined them having a great session where they find out that they were some pop star like Elvis or one of the Beatles; living the big time, reining in the creative talent that they had once possessed in abundance.

Of course I knew this was unlikely, and that finding out that you were once so famous creates a whole new set of pressures in your life. Would I want that kind of responsibility?

Counselling session

"Okay Adam, you might not like this, but we really should go to the most traumatic part of your experience. Is that the death of the boy, or your impending death at the end?"

I started playing with my fingers, suddenly obsessed with getting the imaginary dirt out from under my nails.

"In your own time Adam, try starting by telling me what upsets you the most about the death of Andry's son."

"I don't know," I said, shrugging my shoulders. Mike just sat there, silent, waiting for more input. I stuttered on, like an old engine being forced to turn over.

"Okay, it was so much more than seeing something like that in a film. You know this is for real. You can smell your surroundings and have the thoughts of your previous self thrust into your head.

I could hear every little detail, the boy gave out a muffled, hollow, empty groan as he went down, it was horrific."

"You are doing really well Adam, go on."

"I felt so helpless. I was just standing there and yet I couldn't do anything to save him. I couldn't move any of my limbs the way I wanted to, I couldn't shout at Caesar to stop, I couldn't even close my eyes! It's not right. I shouldn't have to remember all these things. Don't you think that maybe death and rebirth is another way of starting from fresh, with a clean slate?" I could see from Mike's face that at least a small part of him agreed with me.

"There will always be reasons for not looking back Adam, but, generally, there are more reasons for carrying on and releasing our full potential."

"Well I don't see how?"

"I have to agree with your frustration at not being in control. That's bad enough during the most mundane parts of our lives, but when action is really needed… Yep, that's horrible."

I felt I was winning him over, that somehow if I could get Mike to agree, he would be able to write off the rest of the Awakening program and I could get on with the rest of my life without any recriminations. Of course, it wasn't that simple.

"But," he added, "By experiencing these things again, it gives us the knowledge, and power, to try and stop anything like this happening again. Through experiencing pain and suffering, be that either our own, or that of others, we can understand the consequences of any actions that may cause them. This is why Kale believes so much in passing Awakening on to everyone. It's the dawning of a new age of understanding."

I looked at him, a little dubious.

"Well, hopefully," he added sheepishly.

"Okay, but I also saw the skull from my first Kirk Awakening, only this time it was glowing over the boy's axed head, it felt more alive in those circumstances. Why would I see the skull again?"

Mike took a second to gather his thoughts. "There are many things we still don't know about past life regression Adam, and images can easily get thrown from lifetime to lifetime as your mind tries to make sense of its surroundings. I'm guessing your subconscious saw the axe embedded in Andry's son's skull and just grabbed at the last similar image it had seen, like jamming the wrong piece into a jig-saw just to finish it off. Try not to make too much of it as it can cause you to "expect" the same residual image again in other Awakenings. More your mind playing tricks than anything else."

I was still looking at him with a little disbelief, but had to admit it made some kind of sense.

"Oh okay," I stammered, "but what about seeing your own death, is that beneficial?"

"We very rarely see our deaths Adam, thankfully we seem to be spared that for some reason, but again, I'd have to say that if experienced and confronted it can only add to our understanding of the universe".

"Huh?"

"Not physically: Spiritually or dimensionally if you prefer. We need to know our place in this universe, be that as a pawn or a king, we need to know where we are and what actions we can take on this chess board of life."

"I hate chess, it makes my head hurt."

"Ha, that's more like it." He paused for a second to reflect and then leant forward. "Now tell me how you felt about Caleb's death?"

"Hmm, no time for jokes then?" I quit smiling and summoned the strength to remember back, and see the noose. "Actually I'm quite calm about that. Caleb was calm, as if he really didn't care anymore. Life had been such a struggle for him, and now his only hope of ever being free had been taken away, no wonder he didn't care. It's as if he knew that through death he would finally be free."

Mike nodded. "Of course, and he was right, that's the beauty of Awakening, we now know that death is not the end. In fact, it's as you said earlier, a fresh start, a new beginning if you like." He uncrossed his legs, leant forward and looked me right in the eye. "I hope you realise that what you have experienced is pretty much par for the course. It's not great, but it's part of the whole experience. You will come out of this much stronger."

I let out a big sigh, reticent to answer his statement but I had to get it off my chest.

"I know what you are saying Mike, I've heard people telling me this and my mum has told me in the past that she has had some bad Awakenings, but she was older than me when she went through it, probably a little more ready to see those things." I hesitated, waiting for a reaction from Mike but he kept quiet. "In all honesty, I don't think I'm ready, fifteen is just too young." There, I'd said it; got it out into the open.

"You know Adam, fifteen is just the age when you can legally start. When you actually do is up to you and your parents and I'll support your wishes either way. There will always be times in our lives when we just feel like giving up though. It usually seems to be the easiest option and it means we can get on with other things in our lives, but it the end it's just an excuse for running away."

I didn't care at this juncture. "So what's wrong with that? We don't all have to know what past lives we have had. Ignorance is bliss as far as I'm concerned"

Mike couldn't help himself, he let out a huge laugh and to my surprise, instead of annoying me, it released some of the tension.

"Yes, ignorance is bliss", he answered. "I often wish I was a lot more ignorant on a lot of subjects. My wife would say I already am of course."

I responded with a reluctant smirk, realising that advocating ignorance isn't probably the best way to get through life. I still had a point though: why is it necessary to dredge up the past?

"Give me one good reason why I really need to go through all of this?" I challenged.

"Well…", he looked back, thinking carefully, "that is for you to find out Adam, not me, but think about this. We are all in a new, incredible position to regain all that experience that we have amassed throughout all our lifetimes. We can potentially go back thousands of years and for a reasonable part of it, schooling has been accessible to a lot of people in the developed world if they could afford it. After spending so many years in formal education and the rest of that lifetime learning a hell of a lot more through life's experiences, why give that up?"

I shrugged, unconvinced.

Mike decided to change tact, open up and speak from the heart.

"Before I was Awakened Adam, I was going through life as if in some kind of trance, going through the usual stages. At your age I just wanted to rebel against my parents. Not because I disliked them, just that I disliked what they had become. They were the result of two people who had had dreams that were so much bigger than the reality in which they were living. Their hopes and aspirations had been dashed by the realities of life.

We quickly grow up, and the playground disappears. We have to get a job, but hey, we can have relationships! Unfortunately those relationships then get more serious and you start thinking of marriage. You get married and you have kids. You have kids and suddenly everything revolves around them. Now you can't leave your job because you can't afford to. You have to live near a good school and you have to steer your kids in the right direction, often thinking that you don't want them to take the exact same steps as you did because you don't want them with that same feeling of **what if**?"

"I don't get you" I replied.

"What I'm trying to explain, is that we spend so much time learning and getting through life, that by the time we get a lot older and have attained that knowledge and the benefit of experience, we feel too old to do anything with it. We have missed the boat as it were. That's why we all wish we knew then what we know now." He gave a loud sigh. "Through Awakening you can know now.You can have all that experience and still be young and free enough to have some direction in your life. All those dreams and aspirations that had been dashed are now possible, doesn't that excite you?"

I looked at him for a few seconds, letting the

details of his explanation slowly seep through my addled brain before finally relenting to his positive energy.

"Okay, give me two good reasons."

8-8-8-8-8-8-8-8

It wasn't easy but somehow Mike had shown me the way back and given me the courage to start confronting my fears. I had nightmares for weeks afterwards, flashbacks of cutting sugar cane under the searing sun, too exhausted to fight against my slave master. Flashbacks of running through the night into the plantation mansion and seeing that skull open up, like an egg cracking against a pan.

Those memories left me with a tinge of hate cursing through my veins and a fear of my mortality. I saw the academy's counsellor a few times, and time took care of the rest, lulling me back into some sense of normality, letting me forget just a little of the worst moments so that I could continue with my Awakenings once more.

Chapter 8 - The feminine touch

Not all my memories come back spanning my lifetime. Mostly they are just pockets of time, recording some memorable event, something that makes it stick out a lot clearer from the rest. With perseverance, scant memories can be expanded, especially if you catch further memories within the memory you are watching, as in the case of my Kirk memories.

If you think about it, there are little things that trigger old memories all the time. Music is a very obvious one, but sometimes it can be something as subtle as a smell, or someone who looks like someone from your past. When Old man Kirk looked at his Hunter pocket watch, it reminded him of when he first met his wife, and thus I was able to see all the memories that linked to that feeling. His wife was a huge part of his life and so there were many interconnecting memories. We don't remember them all at the same time, but the connections are there and can be read with a little practice.

Sometimes we just seem to dip in though; we get a memory that runs close to real time, covering just a few hours. Goodness knows why these memories stick out more than others, all part of the amazing, but usually quite messy filing system we hold in our brains / spiritual memory.

So the next memory I'm going to describe to you has no importance at all in what happened, but it is amusing and I feel I could do with a little light relief after my last experience. It certainly made me see the world in a different way. A change of perspective can do that to a guy… or girl.

It's funny how you wake up one morning as Adam Capello, have breakfast with your parents, cycle down to the Generations centre for your appointment with your observer, and an hour later you are Sophie. What do you mean this has never happened to you?

Sophie

Mike and I had decided to try for something fresh, almost like my first Awakening, which meant entering my receptive state with an absolutely clear mind. Mike had turned the lights down low to stop any visual distraction and had induced me into a light hypnotic state, purely to help me focus. It is very calming clearing my mind of all the detritus that washes up in my head.

There was no calm approach to this body though. One minute I'm relaxing on Mike's couch, the next I'm straight in, looking at myself in a mirror and I like what I see. Ahem, looking back at me in the mirror is a very pretty dark haired girl aged around 19 and she is only in her skimpy underwear.

It's strange how I have dropped into most of my past identities quite calmly, whether I'm a Carthaginian soldier, or a black slave, but seeing myself as a pretty semi-naked girl really threw me off guard. Especially like this; I didn't know where to look. I really cannot convey to you how odd it is getting all pervy about looking at yourself in the mirror. Obviously I was just straight into that body and I wasn't getting much information from her memories so I still didn't really know her, but to look at yourself and go phwoar! It is beyond strange.

It's also just as well I could not control my limbs as I might well have taken things a lot further, it might have been my only chance. This was one experience I was going to find difficult to chat with Millie about.

Then, as if she had heard my thoughts, I found myself (as Sophie) taking my bra off, watching my firm young breasts defy gravity as my fingertips run up from my stomach until I cup them both and tweak one of my nipples, sending a shiver down my spine, much to my body's delight. A huge smile on my face; I'm hot, and I know it.

I can feel every physical and mental sensation and have the mixture of reacting from both her and my perspective. I can feel her soft skin; smell the perfume freshly sprayed on her neck. The combinations of all these elements are hypnotic, and I feel I run the risk of being put in a trance within a trance.

Grabbing a hairbrush, Sophie starts getting ready for the evening. It would appear she is meeting up with her boyfriend Jean Luc tonight at Place de la Concord in Paris for dinner; it is her nineteenth Birthday. The feelings she has for him permeate into my own feelings and for a short while I become… sexually confused.

I have never had any gay feelings and only have a few gay friends, so to be feeling this way about a guy was strange yet again. Yes, I'm using the S word again because I am running out of different adjectives for the word strange. And the things she has planned for him after dinner, I'm blushing just thinking about it. This is one modern thinking girl.

It is at this point that I catch a glimpse of a tattoo on my left calf. It is quite small, a delicate little creation, but it seems to be pulsing; growing before my eyes. I am startled, but Sophie just carries on adjusting her shoe, completely unperturbed by this little token of rebellion against her "sensible" mother. It is a tattoo of a butterfly, a black outline with blue and red wings, but it is changing. It folds into a cocoon then stretches its sides. Gaps now appear in the shape of hollow eyes and grinning teeth to produce a skull just like the one I'd seen superimposed on Andry's poor son, and I'm guessing I must be right about the echo effect. What other tragic images might emerge this way?

And then, just as before, the tattoo returned to normal as if nothing had happened, once more becoming a fun little thing and I wonder why it has had this effect on me. Is this some kind of message from my core self trying relate to me the points of life and death? I guess I am still just spooked by the whole Awakening process. Some people develop real phobias about it, unable to delve back into their past through fear of what they might see. I was still just getting over Caleb's experience after all and this is exactly what I was trying to avoid. That said, it was short lived and so inconsequential. I was still safe and sound. A little part of me is glad that this has happened so that I can learn to confront my demons in whatever form they choose to take.

The next hour was spent going through my outfits, which look very up to date to me and I'm wondering what time period this is. During this whole time little snippets of information present themselves in the form of flashbacks, general thoughts and… feelings. I begin to feel different, more in tune with my body and with that, I guess my feminine side came out.

Now things that would not normally interest me seem more important, my appearance for one. I felt quite excited about applying my make-up, with the feeling that I am wearing some kind of a disguise.

Not a mask as such, just a subtle transformation into an exciting, sexy, woman-about-town look that will boost my confidence and send Jean Luc wild.

It was certainly driving me wild. Now, let me see, what colour nail polish shall I wear? The red is rich and naughty, but the purple shows a little more fun and independence. Really? I was learning a wider spectrum of skills than I ever thought possible.

She checks her mobile phone for the time, and that's when I catch the date. It's April 16th 2029, which is only seventeen years before I was born and I realise that this must be my last lifetime before I was born again as Adam. It really brought home the reality of life before death. Here I was, looking through the eyes of a nineteen year old girl, reading her thoughts and feeling her emotions, and yet my mother would have been about the same age at that time.

It also meant that Sophie must have died young. How could she? How could this beautiful, vibrant, sassy girl with so much life in her die so young? I knew the answer of course, illness, accident or murder, it can happen to anyone, but again the reality of everything hit me. A reminder of our mortality and the fact that no matter how much you think you are safe and well, we never know how long we truly have.

I am consoled a little by the fact that at least we now have spiritual immortality and can therefore continue with our lives in a much bigger future than we ever dreamed off. We can see loved ones again, even though the gaps can be big and sometimes we will both be in new bodies, but it is better than saying goodbye forever to someone you love. Maybe one day I will see Ada again.

I am driven out of this rhetoric by Sophie. She is standing in front of the mirror again, but this time with a killer black dress on. She looks stunning and I am rather proud of myself. I think I look pretty good as a girl. I then make a mental note to myself not to say that out loud to any of my friends.

She lives in the suburbs of Paris in an area known as Creteil, and is taking the metro into central Paris. I have never been to Paris, so to see the beautifully crafted metro sign is both a treat on the eyes and one of the few iconic images of Paris that I have seen in countless films. Walking down the steps I am met by a sea of commuters all making their way home in my opposing direction. Heads down with earphones plugged into their media devices, they are oblivious to the world around them.

We seem to squander so much of our time away, eager to get somewhere else with our head in the clouds dreaming of escape. That last thought makes me stop in my tracks. How strange to think that whilst I am looking through the eyes of one of my past bodies as a helpless but inquisitive observer, that some of the people I come into contact within my past are also playing host to their future selves.

Take it a step further and imagine that I know someone now who I also knew in this precise point in the past. We could catch up with each other in present time, maybe even sharing an Awakening room whilst mentally waving to each other in the past. It's with ideas like this that my head begins to spin; reconnecting with a past love, hand in hand in two sets of bodies in two different sets of time revisiting those most treasured moments.

Back to Sophie, back to the Metro rumbling along Victorian era tunnels heading for Place de Concord and my boyfriend, who I'm madly in love with. It is very difficult to say at which point I am which personality, especially here speaking retrospectively. As Adam, I have entered the Awakening trance with the right level of consciousness needed to tap into relevant memories with at least a small modicum of control. Thing is, the more I become Sophie, the more natural it is to visualise her surroundings, it's a constant juggle of personalities, both vying for control.

Hmm, I'm getting close to my destination now, so I take the time to apply a fresh dab of lipstick. My heart is pounding and those butterflies that hounded my stomach as young Kirk make a welcome return. It feels so good. As Adam, I have never met Jean Luc, but I'm beginning to fancy him a bit myself. I can see his face etched into Sophie's memory.

Sophie's memory is of course her body's local memory. They are the memories physically experienced by her body and the brain that inhabits it. They are the only memories she knows, much as I only knew my memories as Adam before I started the Awakening process. My consciousness though, in whatever ethereal form it may take, holds the link. Am I really accessing memories through time in these bodies via Awakening, or are all the memories held in one place outside of our bodies?

I can only explain it in computer terms, because they have so many similarities. If you imagine that all memories are held in some kind of ethereal memory bank, it sounds like cloud computing. That is to say, the memories are held on a server somewhere separate and can be downloaded down the spiritual internet when requested. If that is so, I do not actually inhabit my past bodies, only the memories made and stored by those past bodies.

This in turn means I never even reach the past; only that I am tapping into the central server that holds my memories. In the example of inhabiting the same time/space as a current friend and mentally waving to each other, we would only be doing that through our server, almost like an internet chat room using avatars as a visual reference.

I apologise as I always seem to go a bit too deep into the thinking behind all this, but how far can it go? Accepting that we are all tapping into our past memories through some form of organic/spiritual computer networked system, how do we know we exist now? If we can visualise everything with every sensory receptor we have, in the smallest of detail in relation to our past, it only stands to reason that we could be doing the same with our present. Nothing is real in a physical sense, it is only perceived. How do I know my future self isn't tapping into me now? How do I know this is the present? Does time really exist, or is it just a matter of everything being filed properly?

And yet… even if we only perceive we are alive, it must be some evidence of existence. Have you ever seen an old film called "The Matrix?" In it, the main character Neo is asked whether he wants to take the blue pill and stay locked into his world; unaware that he is part of a computer programme. Or take the red pill that will enable him to escape his fake life, thus showing him the reality kept from him. Reality turned out to be hard to deal with, to the point that Cypher, playing the part of the modern day Judas, makes a deal with agent Smith to put him back into the Matrix, but this time with a very comfortable life programmed in and absolutely no memory of being who he is now. It is an interesting concept because in reality he wanted to commit suicide but with some control over his re-birth. If you found out you were in a programme but the true reality was cruel and harsh, what would you want?

Questions like these that deal with our very existence all seem too big for the human brain to deal with. They fall under the same category as "What's on the outside of the universe" or "What happened before time existed?" The funny thing is, children are more likely to ask these questions than adults. Is it because only they have the level of imagination needed to conceive the reality of those questions, or is it because we have given up asking and not understanding the answers, if any?

With all these life changing questions evolving in my head as Adam, Sophie is thinking of sex with Jean Luc. I suppose it is sex and money that keeps the world turning round after all. I was still fifteen when experiencing this though, so you might not be surprised to hear that in this lifetime at least, I was still a virgin. I had had brief flashes of sex from older experiences and of course I do know about the birds and the bees, but her thoughts are full on, it's clearly evident that she is no innocent flower.

I was getting a bit worried that I was going to have to experience sex with Jean Luc. I was even more worried that I might like it. I wonder if I could at least induce a headache. Can you imagine? Something so simple that stops sex, which in turn stops insemination, which in turn means your mother is not born, which in turn means you are not born. Just as well I have no control otherwise I might disappear in a puff of logic.

Place de Concord is packed with people and I resign myself to the whole experience of seeing a city from the viewpoint of a local in an era that is very close to my own. As soon as I push past the "Sortie" gate I am met with the traffic making its way up the Champs Elysee to the chaos that is the Arc de Triomphe. I look up to the familiar landmark of Cleopatra's Needle, an icon as out of place as I am in Sophie's head.

Jean Luc is there, and I think he has been waiting a while. Well, it is a woman's prerogative to be late is it not? Damn these heels hurt, but he is worth it. Just look at him, over 1.8 metres of pure hunk, skinny but strong, with long black shoulder length hair and big brown eyes that have a sense of fun shining through them.

He has been waiting; leaning against the pillar of Cleopatra's Needle, smoking an e-cigarette and watching other young lovers meeting at this rendezvous. I wonder if he has been watching the young girls with any more interest than their patient boyfriends.

We embrace and then we kiss. The softness of his tongue is in stark contrast to the stubble on his chin, making me go all gooey inside.

It's at this point that I think I have had enough, especially as they seem to want to kiss quite a lot before making their way to the restaurant.

So with the only control I have, I wish Sophie "À bientôt" and make my way back home past the white cliffs of Dover.

8-8-8-8-8-8-8-8

As mentioned before, for a period after the Awakening, you have a hangover from your past life. Characteristics lingering on, as well as emotions, languages, fears or abilities and as usual, some are good and bad. At least this experience was a lot lighter than the last and left me more with curiosity than anything else.

It also left me sexually confused though, making me look at my friends in a whole new light, giving me unfamiliar feelings, especially towards my friend Toby. Let's just say it was… awkward, and gave me yet another wake-up call to the effects of opening up my memories.

Sophie was my last lifetime and I had been a girl. An attractive, very feminine one at that and it makes me wonder how we can change these feelings from liking women to then liking men. Of course there is gay attraction, bicurious tendencies and people saying for centuries that they are a woman born in a man's body or vice versa and some going the whole hog and liking both sexes, as if taking out the element of chance, not wishing to miss any sexual adventure this life might have to offer. Why limit yourself to only half the world's population after all?

Even though both my previous experiences have been very different, they both left me feeling uncomfortable for essentially the same reason; my perception of the world around me as Adam has changed and even though it is for the best in some cases, I still don't like it.

Millie had warned me about this 'hangover' from Awakenings, but it felt like it was affecting me more than others. Whether that is because I am already very happy as Adam Capello in a very positive, secure family environment or because I just have a natural fear of letting go I don't know, but it was already beginning to bother me, thus instilling some doubts into whether Awakening was right for me or not.

The skulls were bothering me too, and Millie had to admit she hadn't come across them before.

One plus though. Sophie gave me some insight into Millie, letting me read her body language a lot better, understanding her ideas from a woman's point of view and something clicked,

Call it women's intuition if you like, but I could tell for the very first time that there was some genuine affection there for me, held back by the fact that she is older, Something small, but something definitely worth holding onto.

Chapter 9 – Henry and the Mayans

Sophie was my first experience as a woman and of course my penultimate body before the one I inhabit now. I have never visited her again, never seemed to have the time, but I do wonder what happened to her. Google Generations didn't seem to have much to say. I learnt about the area and that there were several Sophie Pardos in the Parisian environs, but so far I haven't found any definite details and that's just the way it is with some lifetimes, most in fact. We rarely achieve anything spectacular such as inventing a cure for smallpox or become Prime Minister of England, we just lead normal lives. The further I look back, the fewer chances of doing anything outstanding happens I guess. I am not saying it didn't happen, my experience as a rebellious slave or from some strange forgotten civilisation are all testament to the sometimes unique opportunities life gives us, it's just that the world has become smaller, and with that we are more aware of the opportunities around us. Through knowledge comes power, or at least the power to change your own life.

After a year of Awakening I had had several past lives where I found myself just wandering around the scrub or jungle, quite often during a hunt or challenging for leadership, anything that would raise the awareness of my existence during that time. During those flashbacks it is difficult to know where or when I am as I really don't think my body knows itself. If it does, it knows as a localised name or time rather than something we would recognise.

The world is always changing as countries divide, conquer or just change their name. Even as recently as the last century, Russia (then known as the USSR) broke up into Estonia, Latvia, Lithuania, Belarus, Ukraine, Moldova, Georgia etc. Siam became Thailand, Persia became Iran and most recently Peru, when it dramatically became Limalia in the revolt of 2042, and these are only a small percentage of countries that changed for so many different reasons. So is it any wonder that when we look back over thousands of years, we do not always know where we are.

Most of the languages are redundant with only Greek and Latin surviving with academic support, Egyptian and Mayan have been discovered, recovered and now largely ignored as we now have G-historians (experts who have a very complete memory of a past life in a high profile time/space era) who specialise in those times and can tell us everything that our traditional archaeologist had to scramble around the ground for.

At last we have the key to our past, so we can see what we have come from and how man has evolved physically and culturally to where we are now. In the process though, it has taken away the mystery. For example, up until the mid 1900's, very little was known about the Mayan empire. Their language was lost and their hieroglyphics practically unbreakable, until a young student just seemed to have a knack for understanding them. He seemed to be able to think outside of the box with a mind perfectly attuned to the style and foreign meaning of those hieroglyphics. Now of course, many scholars agree that he had probably been a Mayan priest in a past life and that for some reason there were still trace elements of memory in him, even if only as a pattern.

With the code of Mayan writing broken, many elements of Mayan society came to life, further fuelling interest in an advanced civilisation that suddenly died out. Their knowledge of the stars, calendars and mathematics were in stark contrast to their barbaric bloodlust. How could a civilisation that was so advanced for its time and so organised, suddenly, almost overnight, disappear?

Of course a lot of questions were finally answered over the following sixty or seventy years through traditional archaeology. War and famine had killed a huge amount of Maya and led to the destruction of their oldest cities. With some cities reaching a population of 50,000, water supplies were hard to control and their methods of farming were too basic with inadequate slash and burn techniques for land renewal.

By the time the conquistadors arrived, they were already a diminished society. The Conquistadors slaughtered a lot of the Mayans, but also brought diseases that the Mayans had no immunity over. The surviving Mayans fled to the mountains. They were great traders and thus had a good knowledge of trade routes many hundreds of miles in all directions. With this dispersal though, their numbers died out as even the last few survivors were absorbed into other ethnic groups. The funny thing is, they have survived genetically, and can be found all over the Americas and Spain, especially Madrid where most of the international flights from the Americas land. Now the Mayan descendants live in the land of the conquistadors.

So what is my point? All these answers were suppositions, theories put together by very clever academics who didn't mind spending lots of time with dusty books or digging around hot sweaty dig sites in Mexico. They theorised (many with their own political or personal agenda) and told the world. The general public accepted the ideas, but never completely as there was always a little room for that element of mystery. What if they got something wrong? What about the things they are not certain about? Why would they sacrifice so many people? What were they so afraid of? And, most importantly, could they really predict the end of the world?

Ah, the end of the world. That really is interesting. Of course, you may remember that they had predicted that the world would end in 2012. But, we were still here in 2013 so people wondered if their mathematics were a little wrong. Unlikely. Then, more accurately, we wondered if our interpretations had been wrong. Did they mean the end of the world, or just the end of things the way we know them? Did they just mean it would be the end of that particular calendar cycle (they had seventeen different calendar cycles, all mathematically linked)? So the romanticised air of mystery survived, until Awakening of course.

With Awakening came the memories from all sections of Mayan society. Farmers, soldiers, builders and priests. Information came flooding in faster than it could be handled. Don't forget, they were also getting information about the time of Christ, the ancient Egyptians, the gardens of Babylon, Constantinople, Aztecs, the Chinese Ming dynasty etc, etc, on and on the steady stream of information was being offered. It all had to be logged and it had to be verified, which was very difficult in the early days.

However, as the information settled down and began to stream into the general consciousness of everyone in the developed world, the mystery of all these ancient civilisations and societies evaporated.

We were all a lot more aware and probably knew someone personally from some such period that we could talk to. In the end, it just became facts. Facts like any other fact that you might find in a book.

Yes, people are still interested in certain periods of history, either because they have a connection themselves or maybe because of the exact opposite. Mike loves the Victorian era in Britain both for their achievements and for their suffocating emotionally stunted behavior, as if one needed the other to happen. The fact that he missed out in having a Victorian identity only makes him want it more.

Human nature always makes us want what we don't already have and that also relates to knowing about our past. In general, the mystery was disappearing and most people were not interested in reading (or viewing) about past events. We are all interested in our own past points, but then we 'see' and absorb most of the information we need or want. Only those with a keen curiosity keep going back to their favourite past life so that they can be expert G-historians of that period. If you happen to have had a body in a key point of history (without actually being a G-celebrity) and you take the time to really investigate it, both in terms of your own experience and that of others, then you can make a good wage as that historian, especially in the tourist industry.

Whilst I might sound like I am contradicting myself a little by saying there is a demand for historical facts, it is because it is all on a much more personal level. People want to hear it from the soldier's mouth as it were, not read about it or watch a documentary.

I found that out last year when I went with my parents to Hampton Court, former palace of King Henry VIII. I was a little bored if I'm honest, even though it is a very impressive building, but then King Henry VIII turned up. Yes, it was a special appearance by the great man himself, and my first encounter with an A list, G-celebrity. This man had previously been an estate agent in Scunthorpe, probably selling mock Tudor houses, (wikipedia.org/wiki/Henry_VIII_of_England/Tim-g) and like a lot of top G-celebrities, he soon quit his job for a short lived, but profitable round of press junkets.

By the time I saw him, he had made quite an effort to look like his former self, although I'm guessing he had been a little overweight anyway. He had the beard, and of course on this occasion, the full dress and I have to say, he was very interesting. Talk about bringing history to life! As he led us through the great hall, he regaled us with stories of courtiers tending to his every whim. He subtly touched on the subject of his various infidelities to his six wives and how he had had to deal with the numerous court cases brought against him by three of those six wives.

"All with no success" he added with a smile.

He had all the character you could ask for, with none of the nastiness you might expect from his fearsome reputation. While in the huge kitchens, he joked that he knew less than the historians about this area because he had seldom stepped foot into what was essentially the work area of his palace. What he did know though, was that "the foods produced in these kitchens were unmatched by any other, in my humble opinion," for he had enjoyed many a meal here during his royal life.

As part of the tour, we were all invited to the king's privy chambers. A fire was set, burning dried out logs of wood from nearby Richmond Park; his old hunting grounds. With the crackle of wood keeping us warm on this bitter autumnal evening, we were further treated to hot spiced mead and a more personal audience with his majesty. He then proceeded to give us a short summary of his life, from his point of view of course.

A potted history of Henry VIII in his own words

"Let me start by saying I am certainly not proud of my actions during my life as Henry VIII. Yes, I am here before you in my old identity, chatting and joking about key aspects of my past and this wonderful palace, but I feel I must give you my side of the story."

"Although I grew up in the most privileged of settings, my father saw me more as an addition than a son. Arthur, my older brother, was to one day take my father's place, and with that he held the majority of his attention."

"I was quite happy for Arthur to take that responsibility, and a life in service of my brother and the church seemed to suit me, they were happy, simple days. Father had Arthur married to Catherine of Aragon, even though he was only fifteen, and was not the least bit interested in her."

He paused a moment, a chance to gather his thoughts and signify an important point in his life, one that shaped his destiny and his character. A point in which one path had closed, and another opened up.

"Unfortunately, only five months later he died of tuberculosis. You could say marriage had not agreed with him. With that seismic shift, I was suddenly the next in line to the throne, with my father mourning for his firstborn and having to deal with the politics of his nation. He was determined that the Tudor line would be in power for a very long time. That determination in him distilled an absolute resolve in me to one day have a strong male heir to keep with my father's wishes. If only I had known what trouble that was to lead to."

His fists clenched a little, as if trying to grasp his past.

"As you must be aware, I had six wives during my life, and am more famous for that than any other achievement as king. Through special papal dispensation, I was allowed to marry my dead brother's bride in order to maintain a good solid relationship with Spain. I did not love her, but we grew to be fond of each other. She bore me six children over twenty-four years of marriage. Alas, all but one died a few weeks after being born, with Mary the only survivor. It crushed my very being and brought much sadness to Catherine."

"My father died when I was seventeen, so I was very young when I took power, and to be honest was out of my depth, which led to an over reliance on power hungry advisors and myself shirking away from my responsibilities through the distractions of sport and song. It was only with a realisation many years later that I had not produced an heir with Catherine, and never would, that my life really changed."

A small smile swept across his face as he looked into his mind five hundred years earlier.

"Catherine's maid of honour at the time really captivated me. Anne Boleyn was a good musician and a talented singer. She was also extremely intelligent and her time in the French court provided her with a great deal of interesting conversation. She was everything Catherine wasn't, and before you judge me remember this, Catherine, although a fair woman, was married to me as an arrangement. We had been married a long time at this point and though I'd had… certain distractions, I'd effectively remained faithful to her as my queen."

"History would have been very different had I just been content to live a life as a dutiful king and played to the wishes of the Vatican and the King of Spain, but life has a way of becoming complicated. Under advice, I approached the pope to recognise that my marriage to Catherine was not valid as she had once been wife to my brother."

"The King of Spain was furious and protested to the pope, threatening war over this now seemingly silly matter. The pope, caught between two powerful kings decided to just sit on his hands. He went quiet, knowing either answer would be politically awkward. A few years later, our patience had grown thin; Anne and I finally became more… intimate, with the result that she was now carrying my child."

He let out a huge sigh, eyes looking up to the ceiling. Now I could see the man behind the myth, someone holding a very heavy burden.

"It was a hell of a mess really. Catherine was understandably furious, even though she was well aware of my relationship with Anne, but I could not have my next child, hopefully my male heir, born out of wedlock. I took matters into my own hands and broke away from the church. The Pope, seven years after being asked to annul the marriage, now said that my new marriage to Anne was invalid, to which I retorted that the Vatican had no power in England and therefore I did not recognise his authority! It was the beginning of the end really."

He grew louder, his recital faster, betraying his emotions even after all these years as his mind stormed back to the 16th century.

"I had already felt the taste of power by having several advisors executed as traitors, and with a few, I honestly felt they were, but the sense of power took hold of me. With taking charge of my religious affairs, my power grew and grew."

"Anne was very religious herself, and had changed my view on the world. It had been her incredibly strong character and religious conviction that had led me to believe I could break away from the Catholic Church and become the head of the Church of England. A few years later, this would lead to my excommunication."

"And after all that, Anne gave birth to Elizabeth;

yet another daughter. I was mad with her, mad with the world, mad with the pope, mad with everything. For all my powers, I still could not produce a male heir. Three years later, Anne did give birth to a boy, but he was stillborn. Worse, it was deformed and I cannot begin to impart on you the ramifications of that poor child."

Then his voice began to slow down and tremble, pushing through this poignant point.

"In those days, deformed children were unfairly treated as proof of their mother's guilt for something wrong. It soon became talked about that this child was the result of my relationship with the church and my leaving Catherine. The political implications were too great to ignore and my relationship had waned with Anne anyway. It shames me to say it, but you must understand, I was a different person then with the weight of the country's legacy on my shoulders, that type of pressure will change any man."

He stopped for a moment, either for dramatic effect, or genuine reflection, but it illustrated remorse and an uncomfortable detail of your life that you are pressed to tell to complete strangers. Then he started again, looking me in the eye, making the hairs on the back of my neck stand on end.

"I had her executed under the guise of being unfaithful, which haunts me to this day. It was the simplest way to get out of this very damaging situation and I had to do it for the salvation of the Tudor monarchy and quickly find a new wife for a male heir. I married Jane Seymour soon after, and at last I was given the male heir that I had craved for so long. Jane unfortunately died during child birth and Edward was a sickly child. Maybe I was cursed after all."

"During all this time, I had broken away from the church more and more, seizing control and seeing my place in history as one of the greatest Kings of England. What folly was playing in my mind, how blind can a man be? I had bankrupted the country in doing so and robbed it of its monasteries. The wars that were to erupt in the future over these choices were not foreseen but I do wonder if it would have changed my resolve had I known."

"The rest is more of the same. More wives, more political and religious unrest, more mistakes. My final wife, Catherine Parr was a good stepmother to Mary and Elizabeth and so maybe I was lucky enough to have found the right person in wife number six. More likely though, she was lucky that I died five years later and thus she survived."

With that he gave the audience a wry smile from behind empty eyes, his short potted history over.

I know he has probably said these words a thousand times at venues all over the world, but here, in one of his favourite palaces, I think it was just that bit extra special. He'd had an amazing life, with its own difficulties and triumphs, and ultimately it was sad to see how his life had ended, but then he had ended many others' lives before him. He opened up about his remorse in how he had led his life consumed by power, illustrating how addictive that power can be. In the end, the power took control over him, rather than the other way round.

An Irish woman asked about his decision to break away from the Catholic church. It wasn't the first time he had been asked that, and therefore knew how contentious any answer would be. He looked up in the air, recalling his decisions and said that it had been a break away from the Vatican, not one from the teachings of God, as they held so much power over Europe. He conceded that his reasons had generally been selfish, but that he could never have imagined the religious carnage that his actions had led too, and for that he was truly sorry.

That illustrated the fact that the bigger a part you play in history, the bigger your responsibility. Any small action left over a period of hundreds or thousands of years, can lead to huge losses of life, especially when it involves religion. If you were aware of the implications of your actions on future events, would you make any decisions? Would you take any action? It's a scary thought and one likely to make you run away and join a monastery to lead a life of inaction, but then some people are thrust into history without any choice.

So even though we have lost a certain amount of historic mystery through Awakening, history can still be made interesting in a very different way. Now it can be on a very personal level and the history of lost civilizations such as the Maya might never be fully recovered without it.

The Mayans still have one trick up their sleeve though. They have managed to hold onto a mystery that still captures our imagination through its unanswered questions. What is the meaning of their most sacred calendar and could they really see the end of the world? A later Awakening was to change my viewpoint by taking me to one of those periods of history that seemed to have no sense of time or place. All I knew was is it involved the crystal skulls and those skulls somehow knew something of our future. It is probably my strangest Awakening and finally began to tie in with the skulls of my past.

Chapter 10 - The Dreaming

During the initial Awakening foundation, we do not get much time to re-visit the same lives over again, as we are trying to unlock as much of the past as possible whilst balancing it with school studies, family life and some semblance of a social life. Certain sessions warrant a re-visit, usually looking for a different period in that generation's lifetime to clarify something or just to complete a picture of their life.

Occasionally you will come across a life that you really enjoy and want to visit again and again. This might be due to an interesting period in history or maybe because you meet someone you really like there. Observers like Mike have to keep a close eye on this, as those periods in your life can become quite addictive, making you prefer the time in the past, to the time in the present.

For this reason, we are usually restricted to the number of times we can go back into that life for our own good. Some people try self Awakening to bypass any observers, but this can be quite dangerous, sometimes leaving you in a state of limbo or in extremely rare cases a coma; stuck in the past reliving everything again but with no control to change your destiny.

Time behaves very differently in Awakening, with days sometimes played back in what seems like real time, but in actuality, it is all happening within an hour or so during your session. This makes it very popular, as if giving you the chance to get a few days off in your lunch hour. Of course, you never quite know what you are going to get until you are in the zone, another reason why I need Mike.

However, the rules are flexible enough to let you have a few areas of your past used for leisure, as long as they are deemed safe against addiction or emotional involvement. Therefore ex loved ones are out (yes I know, some people get away with it) as are times of great achievement or drug taking. In essence, any time in which your life was bigger or better than usual. Makes it all sound boringly restrictive doesn't it, but it is a good safeguard, and one that you are allowed to slacken with experience and a higher level of training.

For me, I have a place I can go for total relaxation when the stress of everything is getting to me, and although I don't have as much time or money (sessions cost of course) to visit as much as I would like, I get into that life a couple of times a year. You might be surprised to find out that it is not as some multi millionaire or premier league soccer player, nor film star or astronaut. It is something much simpler than that, which is why Mike readily agreed to it as a chill zone.

Kemarre

My favourite place to get away from it all is in Australia, in a small tribe of aborigines somewhere along the north of Australia. I know little more than that, not even what year I am in, and somehow that all adds to the charm.

My name is Kemarre, and I have seen several different parts of his life, from very young, to very old and my life is lived in peace under the stars away from the madness of the world.

No mobile phones, no computers, no wars, no government or king, little greed, lots of kindness and a huge amount of spirituality. No money, no job, no school, no landowners to bully, no slavery, no guns, no murder and little crime. No TV (that just acts to divert your attention away from the drudgery of life), no taxes, no police.

Ok, it also means we have no doctors, or electricity or transport. We have to hunt rather than buy, have a short life span and water is bloody hard to get sometimes, but I have never felt so relaxed and in tune with the world. Plus we also have "The Dreaming."

The Dreaming is a state of mind in which you can visit your ancestors with stories of the creation of sacred places, land, people, animals, plants and customs. It is a complex network of knowledge, faith and practises that derives from stories of creation. It pervades and informs all spiritual and physical aspects of our life in Australia.

I love the Dreaming, and although it sounds just like Awakening (ironically an opposite word to Dreaming) in terms of seeing past lives, it is completely different. Through the Dreaming, your relatives come to see you, not you them. It is a state in which the mind wanders through the harsh but beautiful landscape in which we live, and we can share those dreams with each other. Our lives are told in stories to each generation, so it is only fitting that we should be able to dream those stories too.

It is a place of extremes. The hot, arid waterless desert may seem like a landscape of death to most, but through the eyes of Kemarre, it is a land that holds its treasures close to its heart, and shares those treasures with my brothers and sisters. We know all the hiding places and how to squeeze moisture out of the plants (and frogs) and find lizards under the best rocks for food.

I have spent countless evenings by the fire looking up at the stars and chatting with my friends. We have known each other all our lives and we have no external influences apart from the stories from our elders. Under these difficult living conditions, you come to trust your friends with your life as that trust has been tested many times over the years.

Describing life as Kemarre is quite tricky. When compared to life in our world, it seems very pedestrian, as if nothing ever happens, but everything is relative. With life being so much slower, we are able to see the smaller details that get overlooked by the modern world. Through the small details, comes the big picture of life.

Watching the wildlife around us teaches us how to survive as they do. Having the time to watch small plants grow tells us many things about how to cultivate them and eat what we need, but leave enough for tomorrow. Many civilisations in the past have come to an untimely end through their lack of understanding in this area. Over hunting or eating off the bush without replenishing the land and not leaving anything for the future just leads to empty scrub or desert.

My most memorable time with Kemarre was when I went “Walkabout”. This well known tradition is a time for Aboriginals (we prefer “Koories”) to find their spirit in the land around them. By going out by themselves, they learn about their different environments and the animals and fauna that inhabit it, all with the benefit of solitude to truly become one with their surroundings.

Not a lot happens obviously, such is the nature of walkabout, so I will try to condense the several Awakening experiences of my walkabout into one joined journal, as if written at the time with both the conscious awareness of Kemarre and me now as Adam.

Walkabout

It has been three days since I left my family. The first time away from them for so long and I miss them more than I ever thought possible, but I was warned about this and told it is all a part of the separation needed to embrace the world. My reward on my return will be the strengthened love borne out of separation.

I am using the spirit “Songline” of Nbaruto to guide me on my spiritual path to Uluru like so many before me. This song is unique to the path I am taking, its words describing the scenery with all its landmarks. It is a map, and will take me on the long journey to our most sacred ground as it was taught to me by my father and his father. I have seen Uluru before in my dreams, with my forefathers singing the song with me in my head.

I do not question the Dreaming, nor do I question seeing the spirits of our loved ones, for everyone I know has seen them too, you would be mad not to believe in what is so real.

This is in stark contrast to how we see things in the modern world. We question everything, thus stripping it of its magic, throwing the bare bones to the dreamers, loons and naïve people who admit to believing. Has this made it a better world? Yes we understand the pragmatic, logical elements of our surroundings, but have we lost touch with the intangible? Has belief been eradicated? And if so, is that a good thing?

Day turns to night; I now have the stars to help guide me and marvel at the fact that they are exactly as they are back home. The Milky Way is more than enough to convince me of the magic of the universe. Nothing is more beautiful or more awe inspiring. The thousands of sunsets and sunrises, delicate bush flowers blossoming, the desert sands, cool fresh water dripping off our faces in a sudden rainstorm, all pale in comparison to this majestic display, out of reach, out of harm's way.

Sitting by a small fire, as much for company as for warmth, I listen to the tiny sounds around me. The crackle of flame licking the dried twigs hungrily as it gives up its stored energy, a last gasp from what was a living plant. The drone of small flies is normally filtered out by their familiarity, otherwise it would drive you mad, now it feels reassuring on this lonely night. It is otherwise so quiet in this surprisingly empty wilderness, that I start playing with my breathing, just to change the noise in my ears and turn it into song and meditation, yet again tapping into the magical energy of the universe.

It is these moments that so clearly illustrate the mad, frenetic pace of the world I live in as Adam. Yes, I sometimes have the space to sit and think, but there are always so many ideas rushing through my head. Any time I get for meditation is limited and I have to remember a few rough guide tips on meditation to just try and come close to any form of connection with the universe.

Awakening is as close as I get to a full meditative like state, and that is whilst being assisted and monitored as I escape the current universe around me, living my past lives again. It is ironic that I should need to use Awakening to connect to the universe through another life in another time. It feels second hand but is my best option for now.

Sunrise, the birth of a new day and I have already been walking for a little while, making the most of the cool morning air. I experience day after day like this on my walkabout, to the point that I sometimes worry that I might have lost my way. The song line confirms my place though and I am now close to the end of that song, meaning I can pray on my people's sacred land soon, as my father did before me.

I have been finding roots to eat and rob of water, insects that dance on my tongue and crawl down to my belly. For treats, I have wattle seed, dried remnants of kangaroo, emu and possum, all prepared by my wife; I miss her and my son. I also find a snake for fresh meat or pick out the wichetty grubs from the bush.

My final sunset before I reach Uluru and I can make out a dim silhouette in the distance and my heart leaps as I know I am close to my spiritual goal. That night I look up to the stars again but see something different emerging from the Milky Way. My heart quickens, wondering if this is a sign from my ancestors. It is hard to make out at first, so I slow down my breathing, concentrating on two new fixed points of light.

I realise then that it is my face drawn out in the sky, but much harder to recognise as some of my features are not quite right, as if borrowed from other people's faces. The galaxy seems to be swirling now, something I have never seen before, then the face changes to a skull.

The eyes light up, but as Adam I am no longer filled with horror, I am growing used to this apparition haunting most of my Awakenings, but this time Kemarre sees it, the first time any of my bodies have been aware of this strange skull. Kemarre wonders if this is a sign of death and worries whether will he make it back to his family.

"Pos-chuh-leyt" A voice enters our minds, every syllable forced out, with neither of us understanding.

Now that it is affecting my host, I wonder if some of the original memory could be leaking into his consciousness or maybe Kemarre can see it because he is more in tune with the universe.

As Kemarre, I look in horror as the skull subtly

dissipates into the milky cloud as if my eyes have just gone blurry, leading me to wonder about the sign I have just been given. All the best signs come from our ancestors don‘t they? A special message just for you and no-one else? I slept restlessly that night trying to interpret the message, full of fear and wonder for what tomorrow would bring.

It was difficult waking up on that last morning as I had hardly slept, my mind racing over the implications of my vision. Rubbing my tired eyes, they pulled into focus and gazed upon a huge red rock, glowing on the horizon. Uluru, sacred ground in the land of the Anangu and inhabited by the creators known as Tjukuritja. Their spirits inhabit this strange land and I hope to see them in my dreaming when I reach the rock.

This whole journey along the songline to Uluru to see the Tjukuritja is my meditation through the eyes, ears and mind of Kemarre. If I did not have Awakening I would never have had the chance to feel this connection to the earth that Kemarre did. Whole lifetimes are presented as rich veins of experience, to live, to love and to survive in this harsh but beautiful landscape.

Kemarre spent three days on Uluru, that unique natural wonder you might only know as Ayers Rock. He saw his spirits, had visions of his family and those loved ones that had died so many years ago, but had never left his side. He had only seen Uluru through the words of others before. Now he would be able to return to his tribe and tell the young and old about his adventures. He would dig deep to find inspiration in his story and frighten the children with his description of the skull in the sky. Hopefully he could inspire those around him to make their own journey.

8-8-8-8-8-8-8-8

I like my life as Adam, but nowhere in it comes close to the feeling of community that Kemarre had. It is a simple life with simple pleasures and it is all the better for it. That is why out of all the lives I have experienced so far, I choose to return to my former self as Kemarre. I miss my old friends, I miss my family, I miss my tribe and I miss the feeling of belonging to something really good.

So when I get disheartened about Awakening I use these memories to correct the balance between whether it is a good thing in my life or bad. Few people have experienced living in an aboriginal tribe, but they have experienced life before it got really complicated, and for that reason alone, we should thank our lucky stars. Never has the saying, "it wasn't like this in the old days," been truer.

Not long after the session, I Googled the words I'd heard from the skull. I wasn't even sure if I had heard it right, but after some switching of letters "poschuhleyt" became postulate. I admit, I still had to look up the word, but one example sounded true.

VERB

Pronunciation: pos–tu-late

1 Suggest or assume the existence, fact, or truth of (something) as a basis for reasoning, discussion,

It sounds like the skull was asking me to acknowledge or believe in him, but for what purpose?

Chapter 11 - Addiction and retribution

Awakening can be seriously addictive for a lot of people for a lot of reasons. Let's face it, we all like to escape from reality once in a while, that's why we go to the cinema or on a luxury holiday. Awakening offers an alternate reality, one that has already been lived and therefore frees you of having to make any choices. Who says we are in the best of our lives now anyway.

Because Awakening is so addictive, there are strict controls on what you can and can't do, but as usual there is always a way round these things and plenty of people offering alternatives... at a price. Whilst it is easy to argue that we should live in the here and now, it cannot be denied that spending long periods of time in a different time zone also has its benefits. A language, if a new one to your current list, can be perfected. You learn a lot about the history of the time, and, whilst not perfect, it is probably better than a lot of other pleasure alternatives.

Lunchtime in paradise

One man in Italy would constantly go back to his time as a Roman governor in the town of Ephesus, Turkey. His life as a governor was one of opulence and sexual adventure. He had lots of money, lots of slaves and lots of women to attend to his every whim. No wonder he wanted to go back so often! His present day wife was not happy about it though as he was coming home from work exhausted and vacant. At first she thought he was being overworked, and then she thought he was having an affair. It was only after a friend had heard him blabbing about his seedy adventures that she learnt the truth and she eventually alerted the authorities to the illegal Awakening centre in the city of Bari in southern Italy.

He had spent most of their savings in a six month spree, spending lunch breaks tapped into the past. With the right observer, your one hour session can seem to last a day or more. This meant that his normal everyday life as a freight distributor at the local port was constantly at odds with his life in 83AD as the then equivalent of a playboy.

This is a perfect example of how your past life can be infinitely more interesting than your current life and therefore drag you away from the predictability of your normal life into the past. Hell, I know I would have been tempted and my life is pretty good as it is.

These illegal Awakening centres are nothing more than people's homes, with only the most rudimentary equipment and observers who are more interested in your money than your safety. Stories occasionally make the news in which their subjects have become stuck in their past, their bodies entering a catatonic state as their brains deal with all the information flooding in as best as they can.

Lost in time

One such subject, Rajit Khan from Bombay, went into a coma for two years. When he finally came out of it, his time as a rich merchant in 18th Century Venice was far more real to him than his present life. His two years had equated to roughly forty years in his past, only coming out of it when he had died in his past life. Can you imagine living a whole lifetime and then going back to what you were before? Which would feel more real? He was quoted as saying that his life in Venice felt like his real life and his time now in Bombay as an Awakening experience. Time had just twisted things around.

After a couple of attempts on his life, Kale came in to help Rajit come back to terms with his life now. It took another two years for Rajit to face reality, helped by Kale's advice to find a writer and co-write an autobiography of his time as the merchant. His unique exposure to that time period, in one of the most amazing cities in the world offered great insight into life at that time. His moderate success gave him the sense of purpose he needed in the here and now to re-embrace his modern life.

Since then, official Awakening centres around the world have specialist counsellors to help people rationalise their place in modern society. It certainly is a thorny issue, as without Awakening we would not have this problem. People are always wondering if the grass is greener somewhere else. Well with Awakening, you now know it bloody well was once! This plays into the hands of those dissenters who see Awakening as the Devil's work.

With a growing movement of people convinced that we lose our memories for a reason, they have lobbied for stricter controls and even advertised against taking the life choice that is Awakening. You can see their point, as Awakening has fundamentally changed the world in which we live at a phenomenally fast rate.

Perspective has completely changed, many new laws passed, inventions re-discovered, history re-written, religions destroyed or amalgamated, all of which add to the fear of where this might lead. And through this idea of immortality through re-birth, our value on life has lessened in terms of our bodies, thus affecting our life choices.

Of course, it can also put your life into perspective from your bad past lives. Lives spent as slaves, or crippled through disease or war. Lives lived in poverty or fear, sometimes again and again, one after the other. With these types of experience, we realise how far the modern world has come in terms of being more civilised. Yes, we might be busy all the time and stressed, we might have lost touch with our sense of community, but we do have a greater global awareness now and with that more work is done to help our fellow man.

So what would you do in your current life if things were not going well and you found yourself aged fifty, still single and without that family that you had wanted so badly? Then one day during a session you tap into a life whereby you had that perfect family. You feel the warmth of family love that you crave and wonder what your next move should be. Suicide is an option, or escapism through illegal Awakenings, or re-evaluation of your needs.

It is rare, but it does happen. Some people take the wrong path and do anything they can to go back and feel that way again, and some people use the experience as a swift kick up the arse to make those changes to their current life. Sometimes we all need a little push, so with the guidance given by an experienced observer, a guide and a counsellor, we pretty much make the right decisions.

Apart from illegal Awakening centres and a completely new branch of counselling, a whole batch of new services have been born to cater for the effect that Awakening has had on our modern day world. G-Eyes are a very good example. G-Eyes are basically just like ordinary private detectives, but hired to look for people who have affected their clients in a past life.

Jason Ives

In 2057, individuals who had lost their lives or family by the actions of the Khmer Rouge in Cambodia grouped together to hire Jason Ives to find Saloth Sar, better known as Pol Pot to bring him to justice. He had been able to just pass away in his sleep in 1998 without any retribution or account, thereby destroying any sense of karma or fairness. Jason Ives had become well known through his Nazi investigations for the Holocaust society of New York.

Two years it took him to route Pol Pot out, finally finding him as a hotel owner in Thailand. As you can probably guess, if Sukdee Chongmankhong had not gone through the Awakening process, then he himself would not have known he had been Pol Pot and thereby make this type of investigation very difficult. This situation also makes some people naturally reticent to find their past. Pol Pot was charged for his crimes and also sentenced with losing 10G's (Ten lifetimes) just as Hitler had been, but of course they will have to find him every time to be able to carry out his punishment.

It is theorised that if you lose a couple of lives this way, you may subconsciously never go for Awakening in the first place, therefore guarding your past identity; the survival instinct will kick in. Some people do not go for Awakening for many reasons, so again this makes it hard to investigate.

Jason Ives used to be an Observer himself, particularly adept at recognising thought patterns of his students. Ives was able to eke out as much information as possible, usually steering them in a way as to get the most from their experience in as short a time as possible. His skills gave him the ability to read into reports little snippets of information that would build up a character profile. He became known by his colleagues as “The mind reader”.

It was with this uncanny ability that Ives was able to find Julius Otto Mueller, a previously unfound Nazi criminal, living in France as Pierre Leconte, based purely on building up a character profile from Mueller’s wartime biographies. Ives was pretty certain he had his man, but Leconte had not undergone any Awakening sessions.

Ives posed as an Awakening professor looking to open a new academy in nearby Marseilles and offered him preferential rates to get the academy up and running. Given the chance at getting cheap Awakening sessions from such an established professional, Le Conte fell for it hook, line and sinker and signed up as quickly as he could. seven months later, Ives proved himself right, and handed Mueller over to the Nazi war crime investigation agency in Berlin.

This was the first time ever that someone had been found without them having gone through the Awakening process beforehand. There was a lot of praise, but also a level of condemnation that Ives had effectively taken someone who was unaware of his past, then made him aware of that past, and then arrested him for the life he had previously been oblivious to. It was seen by some as a new strand of entrapment and gave the law courts a huge headache.

Within three years, policies were drawn up in consultation with Kale and Ives to set up guidelines in cases like this, before they come to light under an investigation. With this high profile, Ives became the number one G-eye and is always in demand.

With cases like these come books, TV shows and movies, all as popular as the cop shows they used to show before. One character known as Vincent Vitae seems to have been every influential figure in history if you were to believe his story. The programme makers have to bear in mind that one day people from history, such as Leonardo Da Vinci, may turn up and not like the TV version of their life, so they have to be quite careful what they write.

There have also been several movies based

around G-eyes like Ives, adding psychic abilities or dark magic to give them their edge. One of my personal favourites was "Return From Hell" with Holly Holster playing a G-eye called Emma Hunter (I know, seems a bit obvious calling a G-eye "Hunter", but that's Hollywood for you).

Return from Hell

It starts in 2016 with Emma (then called Joan) and her family being murdered by a violent drug addict in New York when he breaks into their house for some money. He ties them up so he can raid the house, then sets fire to it when he leaves to burn the forensic evidence, but it also leads to their painful demise.

As she dies, a blinding light picks her up and offers her the chance to escape but her family cannot be helped. On refusing the help on those terms, she dies but stays within this blinding light. It is so bright that she cannot open her eyes at any time, thereby rendering her blind. She is looked after by people she cannot see and wonders if this is what her death will always be like. A year later everything goes pitch black and she is offered the choice again, does she want to go back and escape or stay where she is? She is so tempted by this that she breaks down in tears, wracked by guilt and pleads that her family be given the chance to escape instead of her.

Everything turns to white again, cleverly blinding the audience in the cinema so we know how she feels.

We come to the present day and find our heroine alive and well and in a body very much like her old one. She is now a G-eye but with the amazing ability to be able to see into people's past just by touching them, an added sight after being blind so long. She can also see into their past by touching objects they have touched. The longer that item has been touched, such as a piece of jewellery, the further back she can see. This makes her the perfect G-eye.

You can probably guess the rest. Yep, she finds the drug addict, who is now a powerful politician in the US senate and so he has a dark ops agency hunt her out to cover his tracks. After several battles and a lot of car chases, she overcomes adversity and finally wins in the end with the help of another government agent working undercover. She has only been in contact with him by mobile phone and messages left like a paper trail to the final scene. During these moments, she has flashbacks of her time being helped by her "guardian angels".

Tracking him down to a seedy apartment kept for his mistress, Hunter confronts the senator with the truth. Using her psychic abilities she projects images of her family's painful death into his mind to try and make him show remorse. Instead he taunts her, bragging about how he was never caught. Of course, she never expected him to give himself up, but is really using it as a chance to record him talking about his past.

He tires of this game of cat and mouse and drags her into the bedroom where he locks her in and sets fire to the apartment to repeat the past because he is a sadistic bastard. Eventually she manages to get the door open but is cut off by a wall of flames and has to fight off her demons. Flashbacks of the searing pain and dying in her last life roots her to the spot but then she hears her children whisper "close your eyes and run." A bright light in her mind leads her to safety through the wall of fire, just as the police arrive to arrest the senator.

The film ends with the senator being carted away by the police; our heroine battered and bruised but victorious. She picks herself up using her last ounce of energy and touches the door handle to get out. She "sees" the rather good looking officer who had arrested the senator and is able to see that same guy forty-five minutes earlier talking to her on the phone. He was the undercover agent! She traces the path to try and find him, only to discover he has left behind his wristwatch where his car had been – a continuation of the paper trail and a symbol of time lost. She "reads" the watch and sees a fleeting image of herself in her previous life looking into her own eyes. This shocks her, but then makes her realise it must be from an Awakening he has had.

Yep, he could be. It's Hollywood, so it should be. Let's hope it was, because that is where the film ended, and we all like a good ending with a little twist at the end, even when it's obvious. The sequel is out soon, so maybe I'll know for sure if it was her murdered husband or not when I see it, and maybe they will find their kids.

As you can imagine with so many amazing real life stories coming from people's Awakening sessions, it is getting harder and harder to separate the real from the fantasy. Alongside the TV dramas and films, there is a steady stream of documentaries charting the history of some of these people. People who find they were a famous person from history (G-celebrity) or knew someone from history or were an unknown cog in the workings of history. All this adds to people wanting to be famous, or at least be someone who had been famous.

This is another reason that Awakening is addictive. Everyone used to be happy with just fifteen minutes of fame, now it would seem they want a lifetime of it. A question that gets asked quite often is:

"Does the memory of having been someone famous give the same sense of fulfilment as actually being famous?" I'll explain what I am getting at.

Do you ever get that feeling in your very being that says you are missing your opportunity to fully achieve what you are capable of? You know, that feeling of being lost under the mass of chores you have to do just to survive in this world. Where you are so busy just making ends meet and bringing up a family that you take a break from trying to be successful at whatever you may have set your heart on when you were younger and freer, but you have not yet returned to those ideals.

Is that one of the reasons we crave fame, as an easy option to say we have made our mark in this world? Well, what if you have already made that mark in at least one of your previous lives? Is the pressure off, or does it just raise the bar that you set yourself, so that you feel you have to be even more successful than you were the first time? If that is the case, there will never be any respite or peace in your heart.

Along with the fame of any G-celeb, expectation will also be placed upon you by the rest of the world. Shakespeare to write more classics, Einstein to finally figure out time travel in a reachable way, Dali to paint more surreal paintings, Wordsworth to touch our hearts with his poetry just one more time. Socrates to makes us reflect on our modern day lives, Churchill to lead our country and, just maybe… Jesus to lead our world. Can you imagine that kind of pressure? I used to think I could, but as I was to find out later, I only had the smallest of inklings. When greatness is thrust upon you, your life is never your own, the responsibility is too great.

Chapter 12 - Philosophical moments

"All are lunatics, but he who can analyze his delusion is called a philosopher."
---Ambrose Bierce

The extremes of my past personalities never fail to amaze me. I understand that nurture plays a huge part in the personality of the time, as do chemical balances in the brain and its natural IQ. Our souls may carry innate abilities just waiting for the perfect combination to set them free, so that we can fulfil our potential and set our place in history, but for the majority of our lives we have to make do.

It is with these huge character elements that I struggle to find who I really am. From life to life, body to body, place to place, and from having nothing to having everything. Where am I in the middle of all these influences? Does my subconscious overwhelm my personality, or is my true personality expressed and controlled through my subconscious, bypassing my nurture when really necessary?

Now, after my initial few years of Awakening, it makes me think about the Jewish girl again, who found out she was Hitler. She was executed on the grounds that we cannot hide behind the different masks we wear from life to life, but if her upbringing was within a loving family, with the best ideals taught to her from the minute she was born, does that not count for anything?

I know very little about Hitler, but surely if he had grown up in different circumstances, possibly in a different country under different economic conditions, maybe with loving Jewish parents, would he still have grown up as an evil despotic leader? If not, can we really justify her execution? Sadly I think not, it's just not that simple. If we truly are a reflection of the life in which we are brought up, who is guilty, the individual or the people who have influenced his or her life?

As you can see, the more we learn, the more questions are posed. Maybe trials will have to be judged on the character traits experienced through a selection of life times, to try and find the real character behind that mask or the person who made it.

The more I go through this process, the more I wonder if I really have lived these lives, such is the difference in my character traits, or that my collection of lifetime memories is purely a record of an energy that passes from body to body, like the stories passed from generation to generation of tribesmen all over the world.

One such character of mine that seems at odds

with my current personality lived in ancient Greece and he fought against depression throughout his adult life using philosophy to get through it, or rather he used his depression to shape his philosophy.

Methodius, the pessimistic philosopher

"The optimist thinks that this is the best of all possible worlds... and the pessimist knows it."
- J. Robert Oppenheimer

Athens around 120BC

The first time I visited Methodius, it was like putting on a very heavy coat. As usual when settling into a body, different things come to you at different times. Memories can be richly detailed or skit all over the place according to the person or the situation they are in. I slowly begin to sift through the language, with English echoing in my mind until I suddenly forget about English and just... Understand.

Pain: Pain comes in many forms. With Old man Kirk it was his arthritic knee, Cabel was pure physical exhaustion from working the fields and finally feeling the noose around his neck. With young Sophie, there was no pain, just the vitality of life, mixed with the passion and sexual intensity she felt for her boyfriend. I have held all sorts of mental and physical pain over the years and it is always a relief to return back to the present, into my young adolescent body that is growing and getting stronger, rather than dying cell by cell as we do when we get older.

With Methodius though, I felt this incredibly heavy coat of apathy. The world just seemed to be against me. Everyone seemed to be blind to the stupidity of their lives and somehow I had been cursed to see through the fog of banality, to see the world for what it really was, a place of constant struggle, stumbling through it with hardly any sense of direction to achieve almost nothing, or maybe even leave this world in a worse condition than when we had started.

With that kind of outlook it is difficult to motivate yourself to do anything. What is the point of trying to make your way in the world if fate can throw her hand at any juncture and completely destroy all your plans? In those days the goddess Fate was known as a goddess that took no sides. She would make or break your life with any whim that might take her fancy. That might sound odd now, but how often do we still talk about fate or chance?

That was one of Methodius' chief irritations in life. On the one hand, Fate had been kind from the start, and ensured that he had been born to a rich family in one of the greatest cities on the planet.

With such riches he had been afforded a good education and an allowance that meant he would never have to work, but where was the fun in that? What could you work towards, where was the challenge?

But I'm starting in the middle. Methodius hadn't always felt like this, his childhood had been good up to a point. His mother was loving, his father strict but fair, and he felt secure in his surroundings. As he got older though, he wished for a brother to play with and would ask his mother why he had to sit alone when he saw friends play with their siblings.

This always saddened his mother, who just would say "Fate has decided that you should be the only child in this family". His mother was of course unable to bear another child, but could not explain it to him. As such, Methodius took it literally that Fate had singled him out on another one of her whims, and that he would never get an answer to why he had to grow up alone.

Then his mother died when he was nine. His father cried in front of him for the first and last time in his memory on that day, leaving Methodius torn between crying himself, and trying to stay strong to consol his father. Again Fate had played her hand and Methodius was beginning to think that true happiness would never come to him.

The following years were pretty difficult for me as Methodius. Father threw himself into his work, leaving me to be brought up by a nanny of sorts. Amynta had been a family slave since childhood and grown to know her place within it. Her biggest responsibility was to ensure that I was educated to the highest level, with instructions to employ some of the best teachers Athens had to offer.

Thus my life became all work and no play, and to what end? As I saw it, Fate could come in and take your life, or the lives of your loved ones without notice, or ensure financial ruin or debilitating disease, so what was the point of learning to try and improve oneself?

That is when my first philosophical thought came to me:

"To truly prepare for success, one must prepare for failure to stay one step ahead."

In this scenario, if Fate should take things away, you would be prepared for it and weather the storm, but if, as has been occasionally known from Fate, she decided to make amends for past abstractions by bringing good fortune, then it would only ever be a bonus. You would never have to be prepared for fortune, as surely that was the easiest of states to exist in?

It all clicked in my young mind, the loneliest of moments spurring me on to find an answer to the riddle of life's twists and turns. I pushed Amynta to employ the best philosophy teachers of the day, most of them spouting the usual Plato, Socrates, Epicurus and even Seneca to try and see what these experts of life had concluded.

By this time I, as Methodius, was beginning to notice girls. I was about the same age as I am now writing this book, but far more awkward. I had not been graced with any good looks and had the social skills of a village idiot. If a girl even walked in my direction I would turn red and lose the ability to talk coherently.

As the years passed, my inept manner only fed my insecurities towards the fairer sex, giving me the impression that maybe it would be simpler to live alone. By the age of twenty my philosophical studies were gaining momentum and, through my father, I was able to secure a small teaching post.

This is where I met Diantha; a pupil in my class. She was attractive, in a gentle, meek sort of way, but intelligent and kind. She saw past my clumsy exterior and loved me for who I was. She loved my intelligence and my viewpoints on life and we took our first kiss whilst talking of the world around us.

Unfortunately for me, my father had different plans to who my suitor should be and arranged a marriage the following year to a comely girl, the daughter of a general, and like her father, she looked built for war! Protestations had no effect on my father, it had been written in stone as far as he was concerned and he was definitely not a man to argue with.

Marriage under these circumstances did not suit me. We were not attracted to each other in any form, and apart from a few drunken fumblings out of a feeling of duty, sex was definitely off the menu for the first year. Pressure was later exerted for grandchildren and so we both reluctantly tried for a child. I found that I had to drink so much wine to get "in the mood", that I was no longer able to perform. This only served to heighten my feelings of inadequacy and strengthen her disdain of me.

So, yet again Fate had seen to it to ruin my life; my only love had been banned from me, and added the joke, much to Fate's eternal amusement, of giving me a woman who I could not even screw. My heart sunk to an all time low, setting me off on a depression that I was never to recover from.

"A pessimist is never disappointed."

I fell back on my theory of planning for the inevitable failings of life, and searched through the works of my philosophical peers but could find nothing that really dealt with matters of the heart. How could this be? Why would they omit such an important element in the potential happiness of man?

I sought out lesser known philosophers from further lands, but with no success, they all seemed to find love too far beneath them to deal with emotional issues, rather than matters of the mind. Affairs of politics, money, war and health were far more relevant to leading a useful and productive life.

So with no love in my life, a wife I tried to avoid as much as possible, a father who seemed more remote than ever and a comfortable, but ultimately boringly secure financial status, I set my attentions on trying to teach the obviously blind, ignorant populace of Athens their emotional errors by forming my own philosophy of the heart.

Philosophy was both revered and hated in Greece. Socrates and Epicurus had both irked their colleagues so much they had been ordered to commit suicide, with statues later built to honour their name when their viewpoints were better realised. For such a gentle occupation, if indeed you could call it an occupation, it was also quite dangerous politically.

That only served to spur me on, as it added a little excitement into my sedentary lifestyle. I resolved to fill this gaping hole in the heart of man, to teach how to deal with unhappiness in love after Fate had taken these things away from him.

What better starting point than in my own life, to record every sorrowful moment of my miserable existence so that I could look for some remedy in the maelstrom of events. I also realised that I needed to pull myself away from my introspective maudlin so that I could ask others about their lives.

I was soon to learn that I was not as alone as I thought. Through the thin veneer of the people's public personas, nearly everyone had some complaint about life. Getting them to talk was easy, getting them to isolate the fact from fiction was not so. Their perspective had become so skewed by their experiences that the stories became almost fantastical.

If it was to be believed, everyone's bad experiences were the result of outside forces. Yes, they admitted that they made mistakes, but the consequences had not been proportionate. Nothing seemed fair and if anything was going to go wrong, it would always go wrong with them, not anyone else, as if they alone had been singled out by Fate.

There were exceptions. Men of power were confident that they had built their own successful lives; that they were truly the architects of their own destiny. Does this mean you can control your fate, or just that those in power choose to view themselves in a more positive light? If we lose at something, it is too tempting to blame someone or something for that failure, but if we succeed, we want all the glory for ourselves.

Here are a few of my observations as Methodius and his philosophies. I must add that whilst he might have latched on to a few good points, his summations were never that eloquent. In fact he held little poetic imagination, which is why we have probably never heard of him. Even so, I'd still like to think he had some success, but that his work had been lost in one of the many fires that flashed through Athens, thereby depriving him of his place in history.

"Is Freedom an illusion that we all accept in a bid to blind us from life's inevitable choices?"

As Methodius, my dour character irritated some and brought out the moaner in most, thus adding fuel to the fire of my miserable soul. People complained about their wives, their lovers, their job, their inability to get a job, their health, their lack of wealth, their lack of possessions, their lack of freedom.

"Possessions are a curious thing, as they usually end up owning us instead... and yet we want more."

Very few seemed to know what they wanted out of life. Yes they would spout the same old rhetoric of money, love and a good family, but those who had it didn't seem any happier. In fact, those who had less money, and thus fewer possessions, seemed to feel freer, as if it meant they had less to worry about or tie them down.

"Love stirs the heart; lust stirs the loins; alas only without these distractions can we stir the mind."

Men wanted a wife to come home to and a lover to satisfy their sexual needs, but social convention prohibited this, as it still does to this day. Women wanted a strong man who would provide and protect, but they also wanted to be able to take control and wanted him to be loyal.

"For man, sex is full of political and social dangers, leaving us to procrastinate every move. But a dog in the street just has to sniff a bitch, takes her as he wants, and walks away – Simple mind, simple life."

This imbalance of needs and wants nestling within polite and "normal" society only served to create tension and madness behind closed doors. It was true people did want love though, in spite of any sexual need. They wanted a partner to share their lives with and thus they would blind themselves to the complaints and experience of others. This fascinated me as Methodius, as I'd come so close to having that with Diantha.

"Love is a device used to distract us from the banality of routine and yet war seems to be a device used to distract us from the banality of love."

If so many people sought love, found it, started the family they so dearly wanted and set themselves into a successful routine of work and family, why did so many men run off to war? Why do people who seem to have it all, take huge risks with the scandal of affairs?

"If love can turn even the greatest intellectuals into fools, what hope is there for the afflicted?"

The more I looked into people's lives, the more I became confused. Logic and lust could not share the same bed, that was quite clear, so where does love fit into this? Do we need love without lust or love without logic? The latter sounds the most fun, but the former makes the most sense for a long, successful and peaceful marriage, if a little dull.

"Why make life difficult by trying to succeed? Instead we should try to enjoy the gifts and torments that Fate delivers by going with the flow, knowing that death will inevitably come and tally the balance in the end."

And so going back to my original ethos, I advocated apathy in the form of total submission to the Goddess Fate. "If you can't beat them, join them," wasn't one of my quotes, which is a shame, it would have fitted in well.

"That which doesn't kill me, will eventually kill me."

As I got older, my coat of apathy grew heavier. I never found anyone to reciprocate my affections, so I closed that avenue of my heart off forever. My health was not good and I could not have lived much older than fifty or so, probably dying alone in my chamber.

"Death is nothing to us, since when we are, death has not come, and when death has come, we are not."

- Epicurus.

8-8-8-8-8-8-8-8

Looking back at the feelings of Methodius and his coat of apathy, it makes me thankful to have been brought up within a loving family in enlightened times. His problem didn't seem to be chemical, as happens with some sufferers of depression, although I'll never know that for sure, more that he was a victim of misinformation when young, combined with some unlucky breaks.

In some ways he tried to make sense of the world around him by finding a vocation that would validate his search for sense. Goodness knows we all need people like him to experience all the highs and lows of life and write them down for us to interpret into our own lives.

Oh, and as for the skulls? Nothing, or at least nothing that I saw in my Awakenings. For a man who almost welcomed death with open arms it seems ironic that I could not see any memories of him having the skull visions as in my other lives. Maybe it was his attitude towards life and death, as if existing on such a low emotional level took away any need to fear what he might see. He did not fear death, he practically longed for it.

After my time as Methodius I inevitably picked up ancient Greek as a language, a very useful tool in this modern world as it gives an insight into the etymology of so many words still used. Unfortunately I was also handed over the coat of apathy. For several weeks afterwards I felt this dark cloud over my head. Millie sympathised as she had once suffered manic depressive tendencies in one of her lives and so had been through the same process. Toby and Max were not so supportive, often calling me "Mr gloomy head" until I would re-surface with a stupid grin on my face, their old mate restored. Every now and then though I still feel that darkness touch my very being. It is scary; a reminder of what my life could be like under different circumstances. Of course, it also lets me understand what some people still go through every day of their lives.

Chapter 13 - G-Dating

The feelings I had felt for Ada as William Umpleby Kirk were still with me. The sense of understanding between us was something I'd never felt before. Far beyond lust and much more than friendship, it was as if we had a mental and spiritual connection. Yes, I was only Fifteen at the time, but now, a couple of years later, I look back at that and realise it was more than special.

By the age of seventeen I'd had many Awakenings in which I was in love with someone, or married, sometimes both at the same time, and though that had felt special too, it never seemed to match what I had felt for Ada. If a soul mate truly exists, then Ada is as close as I have experienced so far in my Awakenings.

For a while afterwards I considered G-dating to see if I could find Ada, but was too young to register and knew that was for a good reason. I have to learn all about relationships as I am now, not as the persons I had been. Yes, deep inside my soul is my true everlasting identity, but love is borne of what or who you are now, with the entire positive and negative character traits of your current identity.

I knew I would also be studying till at least

twenty-one, so not a good idea to be searching for the love of my life so young, better to just concentrate on studies and if I meet someone in the meantime, just let it happen and enjoy alternative relationships before finding my soul mate and settling down with her.

For those who are in a position to look, G-dating is now very popular. G-dating is the equivalent of the usual online dating but with added search facilities to find lovers from your past. In addition to the usual personal questions asked by such sites, you can set up a time-line, whereby you can state all that you know about your personality now and for previous lives. This “Time-line+plus,” as they like to call it, also includes photographs, maps, aerial photos of places lived, worked etc, and can be linked directly to Google generations.

Be wary though, if it hadn’t been for the privacy lobby of 2054, these sites probably wouldn’t have given you the option to remain private, as sites were popping up everywhere with the sole aim of enabling anyone to find you for whatever reason they have. Understandably some people don’t want to splash their lives online, and pressure was exerted to stop this invasion of privacy. There is so much digital snooping online, such as using hidden cookies in general software to watch your surfing patterns, use of mobile phones with GPS data, streaming accounts, credit cards, film/game club accounts, or even news international data points; it is very hard to stay off the grid completely.

Six years ago, a big scandal developed regarding remote medical services. You might know the private health monitoring company EverGen in which for a monthly fee you can have your body completely monitored 24/7 by their computer medics via a digital chip implant. If your body becomes low in any mineral or vitamin, it will send recommendations to your phone for you to top up. It monitors your BMI (body mass index), salt levels, sugar levels, heart rhythm, pulse, etc. Any early stage illness is readily discovered with a new system of cell mutation detection to try and anticipate the earliest possible signs of illnesses such as cancer. At this point, a human doctor is sought and you are asked to come in ASAP. Apparently it has already saved many lives, and added years to those able to afford it, but… they got greedy and started selling personal information anonymously. Clients started receiving cold calls from all the usual companies plus life insurance, health clubs, lifestyle gurus etc, all with seemingly accurate information about their wellbeing. It caused a huge stink when they were found out and put EverGen into receivership. Never say ever, EverGen.

The facility to store multiple personality accounts with a clear timeline under your current G makes it a very useful reference and organisational tool, as well as enabling you to link up your Awakenings with other people from your past. It is not always past loves that people are interested in finding, family members are very important too. Imagine the Christmas list you would have to make if you had been foolhardy enough to reconnect with all of your previous parents, children, aunts, uncles etc.

Ironically in a period of history where so many people have so few real friends, we are surrounded by virtual friends, the constant chatter of their personal lives in news feeds flashing across your mobile or personal RetVid. Call me old fashioned, but I like to turn it all off once in a while and see the real world around me.

As mentioned earlier, with Awakening we are given the opportunity to remember what it was like before all these modern intrusions. Don't get me wrong, I love gadgets, but I do get edgy, maybe even a little paranoid at the thought of always being connected to the Net. My retreat to Kemarre perfectly illustrates that.

I remember life as a carpet salesman called Peter Smith, using public phone boxes with a glint of nostalgia, even though in reality they were a pain to use. Invariably you had to queue up for them, or someone had used it as a toilet. I would never have the right change and that beep beep beep sound it made, hungrily nagging at you for more money. It would only serve to interfere with what was left of the conversation... but at least I could walk away from them and melt anonymously into the crowd afterwards.

Going further back in time, I remember the warm but almost claustrophobic feeling of living in a small village. No electric lighting, no cars or computers, just horses for some, and your feet for the rest. We were happy in the fact that we felt part of the community, but nothing could be kept secret and your reputation was known by everyone, and therefore guarded with your life. Gossip really could ruin lives.

That did make people behave themselves, in public anyway, so maybe it was better that way. Plus the feeling of community is like an extended family, you didn't need a thousand friends all over the world that you had never met. Time was used more wisely because we had less of it.

As usual I digress. G-dating is the next stage in internet dating and is a very popular distraction from life with some heart warming stories of reunion. It also has some cautionary tales.

Master and servant

Thomas Dent spent many Awakenings exploring his life as a wealthy Victorian barrister named Arthur Munby. He found this past life to be much more exciting, filled with forbidden love and passion, so Thomas became more interested in that life than his current one.

Although doing very well in his working life, Arthur was battling with a strange fascination. Stifled by the rigid social hierarchy of 1850s England, he was finding himself increasingly drawn to lower-class women.

He wrote in his diary: "My interest in social balls is dying out. But always to be among the sparkling froth atop of society has one sad delight in that it keeps vivid before me that gentle misplaced creature who lies grovelling among the dregs: that toiling maid of all work who might have been a drawing-room belle, but is a kitchen drudge."

He began looking for these forbidden women, searching the filthy backstreets of London to find them. Their grimy demeanour only served to heighten his interest, as if he was rebelling against society through his desires.

In 1854 Arthur had been appointed solicitor for the Ecclesiastical commission, thus taking his personal life and putting it in stark opposition to his working life. It was at this time that he met Hannah Culwick, and she was to become the love of his life.

Hannah was a servant girl, twenty-one years of age and it was love at first sight. He described her as:

"A robust hard-working peasant lass, yet endowed with a grace and beauty and obvious intelligence. Such a combination I had dreamt of and sought for, but I have never seen it, save in her."

His feelings toward her were richly reciprocated; she became besotted by him as both her master and her lover. Thus began an unusual romantic partnership that was to last for the rest of their lives, through good times and bad. Just after their first kiss, Hannah wrote in her diary,

"I kissed you when you asked. I wanted to see what your mouth was like. It was hot and warm. I knowed you was good and soft by the feel of your mouth."

It seemed they loved the fact that they were playing with fire. There was the very real possibility that they would be discovered and that would have been the end of Arthur's career and reputation. This only served to unite them further, fuelling that fire and placing them both against the world in which they lived in.

By the 1860s, the relationship had taken the master / servant role to new levels with Hannah wearing a secret lock and chain around her neck, and Arthur holding the only key.

She wrote: "I am his slave and he is my master freely given and freely received only for love, and while I have the chains on I am sure nothing can part us and that it is the same as marriage is to other folks."

And whilst this may seem a perverse love in most people's eyes, there can be no doubting the commitment that they had made to each other. This strange twist of love is what highlighted it from the many other stories, all with their own ways of displaying their ultimate love for each other.

But what keeps love alive? Is it the simple core values of trust and respect? Is it pure physical attraction, slowly replaced with convenience and comfort in each other's company? There are many different reasons and love is one of the few subjects more complex than the process of life after death.

In Arthur and Hannah's case, it was fighting against the restraints of society that kept their relationship strong. After 18 years of living apart, Arthur moved her in with him as his new servant, giving their relationship the veneer of respectability they needed and wanted.

At last life together was much easier, with less snooping of eyes into their private life. Arthur wanted to take it further though and live openly as a couple. Hannah fought against this but Arthur took charge and proceeded to try and educate her in the same vein as Eliza Doolittle.

He wrote: "Someday I may perhaps be able to do justice to her devotedness and to my own scheme of training her."

It was the beginning of the end, finally driving them apart by exposing the utter differences between them. Hannah revelled in her role as maid, wanting nothing more than to serve Arthur as her lover and her master, and yet he was taking that away.

It's hard to imagine anyone thinking like that in a relationship today, but if you had been brought up (conditioned) to believe that you were of the lowest class, then a job as a maid in a big house would seem a lot more like a dream job and something to be desired. Arthur was taking away the excitement, replacing it with respectability and removing her programmed desires in one fell swoop.

He made her his wife, thus adding more respectability and boredom. Four years later she suffered from a nervous breakdown, made worse by drink and Arthur had to banish her from their home under advice from his doctors.

Unbelievably they both lived for another twenty-eight years, but apart, both dying within six months of each other. They may have been forced apart physically, but their obsession with each other lasted till the end.

Now Thomas Dent had a dilemma. Should he just continue going back into his past to visit Hannah, or should he seek her out in his new life, away from the restraints of an emotionally suffocating Victorian society? He had tried before to be openly in a relationship with her and it had driven them apart. All the pain was now being relived in his heart through his Awakenings.

For two years he resisted the urge to find her, but one night after a bout of loneliness and too much drink, he registered with a G-dating site and found her; simple as that. She had registered a few years earlier, but had not wanted to push it any further.

She was now a checkout girl at a large supermarket in Madrid, Spain. Her parents had always worried about her shyness and hoped that the then relatively expensive Awakening process (the cost has gone down since fairer access to all was instated) would draw her out of her shell.

As it turned out it helped a little, but Hannah, now Maria, was naturally shy and reclusive. Within eight months of meeting, William and Maria were married, this time in front of a full family audience and with the acceptance of society. It would seem from their impatience to tie the knot again, that their passion had been well and truly re-ignited.

Life found its routine, as usually happens in committed relationships, and they hankered for something more. Joining an online BDSM club, they re-learned the skills of dominance and submission. The master and servant role had been restored but it was never enough. This time Maria held the key during one of their sex games and handcuffed him to a lamp post in the street in a show of public humiliation. Passers-by started shouting abuse at this outrage and Thomas started pleading with her.

"Please, for the love of God let me go."

A strange smile swept across her face, "I have been waiting for you to say that for over two hundred years," she uttered.

Then promptly pulled out a gun and shot him in the head before handing herself in to the police, claiming mental cruelty.

Shares in G-dating sites went down for a little time after that. Relationships are complicated enough without adding in events and partners from countless other lives, but still we register and search.

Sometimes love becomes lost over money.

A billion reasons for divorce

Marcus Schmidt was a self made multi billionaire after making his fortune through property investment. He thought he had it all; money, big house, beautiful wife and bright healthy kids. His mind was changed when he was contacted by a lawyer from San Francisco acting on behalf of four of his ex-wives from previous lives. The sneaky lawyer sniffing a potential pot of gold, had used G-dating as a way of building up a potential case. He had tracked down these four women and convinced them that he could make them incredibly rich.

The four women claimed that they had made him the man that he is now by making him a better person in the past.

Wife no. 1 claimed: She had taught him the values of being a good person through religious guidance. Through God's will comes good fortune.

Wife no. 2 claimed: Through being such a devoted wife in their time together she had taught him the value of love and that he had vowed to always be by her side.

Wife no. 3 claimed she had turned him from a meek and mild man into the strong character he is now. Without her input he would never have had the strength to build his business.

Wife no. 4 claimed that when they had been married all those years ago her father had given him a huge dowry and she had taught him how to spend his money wisely. Plus he owed her back from the dowry, with interest.

The press loved every moment of it, making the

women rich just from the rights to their juicy stories of when they had been married to him. This joint litigation held a lot of sway and was gaining momentum.

His current wife, on seeing the stress her husband was under, decided she would take advantage of the timing and joined the other four wives in their legal challenge by also divorcing him, stating she had helped him build his business up from scratch and that he had always sought her advice anyway. His money had been made by her decisions.

The courts were under scrutiny. The result would set precedence for future cases, thus opening up the floodgates to a tide of claims.

The wives had not counted on one fact though. There were many other rich and powerful men watching this case, trembling through fear of what might happen to them and trembling with rage at the way they were being targeted.

Marcus Schmidt could of course afford the best defence team money could buy but he was offered much more subtle assistance from his new wealthy and politically strong alliance. To mix my metaphors, a lot of fingers in a lot of pies can get a lot of strings pulled when the legal system is under threat. As such he walked away by paying minimal allowances. Now some would say that having friends in high places pulling those strings is unfair or unjust, but in these circumstances, with the legal profession being both used and abused, most people think it had the correct outcome.

"Timing is everything" is one of my most important mottos in life. It is the difference between winning and losing or life and death.

Pompeii

Harry Bennet searched for three years to find his lost love. They had been dramatically parted when Mount Vesuvius erupted and covered them both in a blanket of hot ash in Pompeii almost two thousand years ago. He had obviously had many other lovers during those two thousand years, but the memory of Sulpicia was the one that struck him the most. They had died in each other's arms that night, realising there was no escape from the anger of the gods. Then one day he received an e-mail with restricted information, only containing the message, but with no clue where it had been sent from.

It just said "I am missing you now, and have always missed you since we were cruelly parted. I still fear we cannot be together but I need to see you just once; to hear your voice and see if I can recognise you from so long ago." It was signed Sulpicia and gave an address with a time to meet.

At the requested time, Harry turned up at the tiny

pub in a small winding London city street, almost missing its location, so hidden was it from general view. His heart was pounding from the fear of going somewhere like this alone and his mind was mixed with trepidation and excitement. He was willing to risk everything to see where this adventure would take him.

It would be better to describe it as an inn than a pub, so old was it. This one had been popular over two hundred years earlier for weary cloth merchants after a hard day of peddling their wares on the streets. It had a long narrow bar as soon as you entered and a small, but welcome fire roaring in a nook towards the back. Even further back though was the "snug," an area that had been set aside for quiet cosy chats with women eager to ply a little trade of their own with those weary merchants' profits.

Nodding towards the solitary barmaid, he made his way towards the snug at the back. The lighting was low, atmospheric and reminiscent of its heydays. Harry could just make out a slim, feminine figure sitting on a leather bound bench, an elegant hat covering half her face and long lace gloves covering her hands and wrists.

She looked up, a smile just visible on her pale face.

"Stop there please Gaius" she asked, using his old name. "I just want to see you in what little light there is in this miserable place."

It was a strange request and a strange comment seeming as she had chosen the venue, but he complied anyway, not wanting lose the opportunity to see her. He stood there a full minute, being silently observed until he could bear it no longer.

"For God's sake Sulpicia, let me sit down and see you," and without waiting, he sat. It had been the longest minute in those two thousand years waiting for this reunion. At last he could feel whole again, be with the woman who had haunted his every waking moment since finding her again in his Awakenings.

He then noticed the lines on her face, and she saw his mouth open slightly.

"Sorry Gaius, time has not been kind to us."

She lifted her hat so that he could see her face.

Indeed, time had been cruel once more. She was now seventy-one, he was only twenty-five and even though they were in love with each other spiritually, the physical imbalance proved too much to bear. They say beauty is only skin deep, that the real beauty, the attraction, lies deeper within, but how would you cope with the situation?

He wanted to hold her, kiss her, make love to her, but he could not overcome what he could see. She told him that this would be their only meeting as it would be too traumatic to meet again, but he begged to stay in contact with her and she didn't have the strength to say no.

A year later they were both found in her apartment lying on the sofa, together in each other's arms. They had taken an overdose, hoping that when they would find each other again, time would be a little kinder. Awakening had opened up those memories and led to their deaths, but now it was their only hope of being together in a complete and physical union.

So as you can see, Awakening can cause many problems and G-dating can exasperate differences in ages or sex. Many people have found their loves, only to find they are now the same sex (or for some, a different sex). Some still make it work. Some commit suicide, some have sex changes. All in all though, it has created a problem that was just not there in the past. Yes, we might feel there is someone out there, that there is someone who truly makes you complete and that person may be someone you have had a very deep and passionate connection with in the past, but then maybe that is why we were designed to forget.

To forget is to forgive. To forget is to be released of all the pain we amass over a lifetime. To forget is to make room for more memories. To forget is to find excitement or pleasure in things we have not done for a long time. So what is the lesser of the two evils, to forget, or to remember everything of any importance in your previous lives?

There are some happy reunions:

Queen Victoria is famously known to have mourned the loss of her husband Albert when he died of typhoid fever in 1861. She went into a deep mourning that was to last the rest of her life, dying forty years later in 1901. Her stoic attitude may have helped to shape the suffocating emotional restrictions of her age, but that might in turn have helped drive them to be so inventive and productive. If he had not died, would the Victorian Empire have been subtly different? Maybe even enough to change the course of history of Great Britain? Any answer is speculative.

Now with Awakening, they had found each other again and were lucky with their timing. They were still man and woman, still heterosexual and still suitably attracted to each other. They were also both A list G celebrities, and so had not needed G-dating.

The amazing thing is that they both had their relevant Awakenings pretty much at the same time. It is very rare to have this level of simplicity when picking up on old relationships.

I have said it before, and will say it again; **Timing is everything**. If all we could do was learn to synchronise our personal timings for maximum effect, it would be the most powerful force in this universe. Everything would work out right at the best possible time.

So for Victoria and Albert, their time together had been tragically cut short, leaving Victoria alone for forty long years; bad timing. Now everything was in alignment, at least in their personal lives anyway. My time with Ada had been cut short too, so maybe things will also work out for me in the end.

Victoria and Albert's wedding was aired by the BBC and their photos in magazines all over the world. Their vows were uploaded to YouTube and became the biggest download of 2056. Everyone loves a royal wedding.

After hearing a lot of these stories I decided now was not the time to look for Ada. There will be plenty of time for that later in life and who knows, maybe another soul mate will turn up. Who says you can't have more than one soul mate? What really is a soul mate and what makes them different from anyone else anyway? Some questions may never get answered.

Chapter 14 - The Alchemists

I have had many other lives not yet described in this journal. Most of them are pretty ordinary, with perhaps only a few highlights to describe, so there seems no point in including them or building up a picture of their complete life. Think of your life so far, could you build up a chapter that captures how you feel? Would it explain who and why you are? Certain events give the opportunity to pick out an interesting segment but sometimes it is a pivotal point in that person's life that is worth re-visiting and recording, or an interesting aspect of their personality.

Through the minds of artists, philosophers and clerics, come visions seen through a very active mind, all with their unique view of the world, and through Awakening that view is re-absorbed into my current mind and becomes a creative part of my outlook on life. Through beggars, farmers and slaves, I gain a very humble side to my nature and the world becomes a better place to me.

The appointment

I was late for my appointment with Mike thanks to a flat tyre on my bike. Running in grubby and sweaty, I didn't really feel ready for another session and was wondering if it was really worth it anyway. I had learnt quite a lot already, felt like I'd worked out the benefits of Awakening to sufficiently coast the rest and was up to my eyeballs in my other studies. I knew Mike would not be happy if I dropped the appointment and I so didn't want to disappoint him. The flat tyre was the final straw though, and had put me in a foul mood.

The mood you enter an Awakening can affect the character that you discover, putting us closer to their personality as our minds merge. Nothing wrong with finding a cranky "you" but it can lead to some dark experiences, so usually better to avoid if at all possible. Sometimes though it seems we have little choice.

Mike was okay with the delay, but keen to get started as soon as possible, thereby forcing me to change my breathing and state of mind as fast as I could.

"Okay Adam, you are getting pretty good at this now. Forget the last hour or so and just use your breathing exercises to concentrate your mind on the rhythm of your heartbeat."

I sighed, too wound up to want to suddenly lie down, adrenaline still running through my bloodstream released by a stressed mind. As I closed my eyes, the now familiar image of a skull filled my mind. I had been doing this long enough to accept its presence without fear, and as asked by Kemarre's skull, learnt to believe it is trying to get a message across to me through all my lifetimes, I just hadn't figured out what it was yet. Slowly I managed to turn it into Sophie's tattoo of a skull, reverse time and turn it back into her original butterfly; its small delicate wings flickering to my heartbeat, rapid at first as it came in to land on my hand, then slowing down in line with my breaths as I gained confidence in what I was doing, leaving the wings to merely vibrate in an imaginary breeze.

Then I followed Sophie's butterfly to a window; tiny, glassless and bare as I hovered to its dark entrance looking for more of my forgotten past. I could hear a lot of shouting as I entered the ill lit room, more of a debate than an argument, a different entrance to this Awakening from the usual and I was glad of the change.

The great debate

"I'm telling you it doesn't exist, yet more foolishness that just captures the minds of idiots and drags them away from serious work."

These words were spouting from my mouth and followed by spittle, not an attractive first sight into this new body; my mind full of frustration and anger losing any sense of self awareness in this environment.

I had dropped straight into a heated conversation without any chance to see who is who. I made a mental note not go into Awakenings so riled and resigned myself to what would probably be an emotional session.

A man opposite me reflects my mood. An agitated face, red cheeks, tatty beard and scruffy clothes, 14th or 15th century by the look of things (I have been swotting up on period markers to make it easier to place a time point in my Awakenings) and we seem to be sitting in some kind of inn. A large bare floor with straw scattered over it, a cumbersome, crude wooden table and two tankards of ale separating my sparring partner from me as if in some verbal boxing ring.

***Round 1**:*

His turn; "Gabriel you have to keep your mind open. Do you really think we have discovered nearly everything in this world? Do you think God gave us a keen mind just so we could admire his work, or wise enough to realise that he would want us to use it to grow, as a child learns to walk and talk? We are his children, of course he would let us find a way to escape the boundaries of a short life."

I wish I knew what he was talking about, my host's mind is too busy thinking of a reply for me to tap in.

"Yes yes, of course I believe we have the ability to grow, but everlasting life is a step too far, a privilege only for the gods themselves. Do you really fear death so much as to cling onto such dreams?" I say it with almost pious eagerness, amazed that my friend Nicolas can be so intelligent and yet still hang on to this ridiculous notion of a magical stone that promises immortality. I must admit, this conversation beats the one I was having with my friend Toby last night, but then that was about retro gaming.

Nicolas just laughed, spluttering his foul smelling drink over that scruffy beard. "*And the meek shall inherit the Earth*; do you know the literal translation of that? The Greek translation from the bible shows *meek* as a person who channels his fear. It does not suggest weakness; rather it denotes *strength brought under control.* The ancient Greeks employed the term to describe a wild horse tamed to the bridle. I do not fear death, instead I use it as an impetus to spur me on. Think of what we could achieve with immortality, where time becomes an asset rather than a restriction?"

He was definitely winning this bout and had just delivered a right hook straight to the jaw. Picking myself up in this imaginary ring, I fought back as hard as I could.

"Nicolas, you are probably the cleverest person I know and certainly the most dishevelled, but you waste your time hunting this Philosopher's stone which is intangible, it is of the air; invisible, untouchable, improbable. Keep to the basics as I do, with solid base metals that are made of this earth and get them turned into gold. With you and me working together we can be rich and enjoy the life that we have now and make our names immortal by our endeavours. Don't you see how much more reachable that dream is?" I was pretty pleased with myself, a true comeback if ever there was one.

Nicolas just sat there, groggy from the ale, stuck in contemplation. Had I really beaten my old friend in one of our customary debates, our entertainment fuelled by alcohol and vivid imaginations? Ten, nine, eight, the countdown ran through my modern mind enjoying this sudden unexpected intrusion into their intellectual scrap. Three, two... And before the final count, Nicolas suddenly came back to life, the fire in his eyes brighter than ever, his mind in some far off place feeding his soul and energising his haggard body.

"But the prize is so much higher Gabriel. Why only reach for the sky when you can see the heavens? Yes we could be rich, and famous, but before you know it old age will set in and rot our bodies from the inside out. Our bones will become brittle, our blood become thin and our minds become mush until we are but an empty husk buried in the ground. People will remember us, maybe even for a few hundred years, but is that immortality, will that comfort you when the worms eat your flesh?" He had a point.

"Better to grow old rich than grow poor chasing an impossible dream" I countered weakly.

He dodged that effort easily, feigned to the side and delivered another painful punch.

"Turning lead into gold is just as much a dream as immortality Gabriel, but imagine if you were able to find the philosopher's stone, you could either be rich by its secret or hold the power to making as much gold as you like. You would have an eternity to spend and enjoy it rather than another paltry twenty or thirty years. Think of the learning and the time to go through all those Latin and Greek scripts. Think of the application of our minds and the geniuses of history that would lay their knowledge at our feet just for a sniff of our power. We could rid the world of disease and poverty. We could orchestrate a global community to work in harmony, to feed and nurture each other rather than fight and steal."

And then I saw the link. Here I am, Adam Capello listening to these two men talking in some French inn over seven hundred years ago and yet they are talking about the same hopes and fears that we think of through Awakening, the dream of solving all the world's problems through immortality and enlightenment, as if everybody would want the same things in life. In this context, with these two drunken alchemists huffing and puffing through fat cheeks and bloodshot eyes it seems absurd that we still hold the same fantasies after all these years. Are our dreams any more reachable? Has Awakening finally provided the link needed to take those steps? Is Awakening our philosopher's stone?

Now we can create artificial gold in particle accelerators or nuclear reactors, although the production cost is currently many times the market price, which gives it a sense of irony, as if to dangle that yellow metal carrot in front of our noses by still being practically unreachable. Gold from lead, the symbolic goal of alchemists throughout history, is still a dream, and I'm comforted by that.

Gabriel saw his way back in.

Round 2:

"Do you really think we would be granted that power? Do you think people would work together for the greater good, ignoring their primitive instincts of survival through selfish acts of greed and lust? Imagine the treachery to try and learn our secret. We would not be able to trust anyone lest they torture us for their gain. An eternal life of pain is far worse than any death imaginable. We would be waiting for death's sweet release but it would never come. We would be victims of our folly, punished for believing we could control this god like power."

Nicholas' eyes began to glaze over again, the fire quelled through reason, his heart suddenly much heavier as reality set in.

"That is why we would have to keep it a secret my good friend. It would be a power too great, too attractive, every few decades moving on with a new identity before people wonder why we had not aged. We could include our wives and children, but that would have to be the limit. The smaller the crowd, the harder we would be to spot."

I laughed out loud, instantly feeling guilty by the pained look on his face. He actually meant it, he really believed he was capable of discovering the Philosopher's Stone. I quickly changed tact, mirroring his forlorn expression, as if to pacify a dotty aunt.

"Sorry Nicolas, but even if this were possible, I wouldn't want to live in hiding. I'll keep to my more mortal objectives if you don't mind, happy to help and always ready to drink with you over the matter."

I had gone into this Awakening a little frustrated and fed up, tired of the hurt and pain unearthed through these sessions. I just wanted to get on and enjoy the life I have now without having to go through all my other lives as well. Is that so bad? Would I really be letting down the human race if I were to just selfishly give up and get on? Why should I care? What are the nagging voices inside me that say I have to do what everyone else expects of me?

Nicolas might be chasing a dream but at least it is his dream and not someone else's. At least Gabriel was making sense and was living in the now. Yes, he too had mad ideas of getting rich, but somehow it was more real, more human, as if he knew his limitations were more physical. Gabriel reflected how I was feeling, as if my soul's memory bank had latched onto the perfect point in my past that illustrated how I felt and I would actually enjoy talking this over with Mike and Millie, creating a heated discussion of my own. Maybe it is time to take control and start doing a few more things for myself.

Meanwhile Nicolas was looking a little worse for wear, the mixture of alcohol and overexertion proving too big a challenge for him on this late evening. He went very quiet; looking from side to side as if to make sure no one else was listening and whispered to me, a stark contrast from our conversation only a few minutes earlier.

"I have found some notes from Mesopotamia that may bear some fruit."

My word, there is still some life in the old dog yet! Mesopotamia, the fabled land of the ancients, the 'cradle of civilization', this would be a logical location for any ancient scriptures. My curiosity was suddenly ensnared once again, could Nicolas really have found something so important? Now it was my turn to sit down, mouth open, mind racing. "What notes?"

Round 3:

He looked me straight in the eye, as if to convey his utter conviction. "You know I am always on the lookout for ancient manuscripts, any texts that might give me a clue to unlocking the secrets of this universe. Can't say too much; I found a small book written in Hebrew with twenty-one pages of complex symbols. Perenelle (his wife) and I have been working on it for the last six months and have been able to decipher certain portions; it is only a matter of time before we find something."

I'd heard this kind of talk before from Nicolas, but never seen him so serious, so quietened by the gravity of his conviction. I was beginning to believe him and could feel my heart beating wildly as directed by my excited mind.

"Are you sure? You have chased many wild dreams in the past, how can you be so certain this time?"

"Because the symbols are affecting our sleep, making us both draw the same answers whilst dreaming. Look at this."

And with that, Nicolas pulled out a folded piece of parchment, again looking round as if the walls had eyes. As soon as he opened it up, my heart froze as that damn skull appeared in yet another one of my Awakenings. This time though it was covered in symbols, as if trying to convey a message either to Nicolas, or to me all these years later.

The skull was pictured beside a burning candle, as if to symbolise illumination in these dark ages, glimpsing shapes scrawled out across the top that looked human or spirit like.

I was floored in both time zones. Me by being taken by surprise yet again by this now familiar shape, and as Gabriel, purely through some dark feeling emanating from his own fears.

"Nicolas, I have seen this skull in my dreams too" I croaked.

Knockout!

The conversation became quite stilted after that, Nicolas had suddenly become quite cagey, as if he had said too much and yet I only wanted to ask more questions. He quickly finished what was left of his ale, mumbled an apology that he had pressing matters to get back to at home, and paid the bill.

"Have a good evening Monsieur Flamel." The inn keeper said thankfully.

Unlocking the code

I have revisited Gabriel a few times, curious to learn more about his dreams and conversations with Nicolas. As an alchemist I had followed the same path as everyone before me by not finding any secret to making my own gold; yet another dream unfulfilled on yet another one of my many death beds. I didn't see much of Nicolas after that. He said he was going to Spain to see a man who claimed he could help with the symbols in his book and was gone for quite a long time.

He and his wife became very wealthy in the following years, although no one knew how, and he seemed to avoid me, as if spooked by sharing the same dreams. I died before he did, even though his constitution when I had known him would never have indicated this was possible; he just seemed to get healthier as time passed by. Had he really found the philosopher's stone?

Online research showed that he had designed his own tomb in 1418, covered in arcane alchemical signs and symbols. Was that just showmanship or part of some ritual? Whatever the case, he would have been well into his late eighties by then. He then died soon afterwards, as if he knew of his impending death. Well, it says he died, but he was spotted many times after his death, thereby giving him at least one form of immortality through his reputation as one of the greatest alchemists in history.

He is a mystery, a legend from the early middle ages when quite frankly anything could have happened, but it is the kind of story you want to be true. If he really had discovered the stone and I had been part of his small trusted group, then theoretically I would still be alive as Gabriel rather than Adam now. How strange to have lived all this time in one way or another.

Is this proof of what I was thinking though? Is Awakening just another dream of immortality and all the possibilities it offers? Yes of course immortality has become a reality in some sense, but in truth we have always had it on a subconscious level, just never been aware of our other lives, the different sides to our core nature, crafted through life's experiences and environment.

As I left Gabriel, I began to doubt the path I was

taking yet again. I'm really not so sure if this is the right way for me; to unlock all these sides to my personality. I AM ADAM CAPELLO! I like who I am, do I really want to risk the chance of losing myself any further?

Chapter 15 – Quasimodo

I was getting really frustrated, and my confusing, albeit interesting visit to the alchemists only served to fuel my discontent. I was beginning to lose touch of who I really am. By this point I had just turned seventeen and like any normal teenager, had chemicals running through my brain playing all sorts of tricks. I would swing between sullen lonely days where all I wanted to do was stay away from everybody as if licking my wounds and then return the next day to my normal chirpy self.

But what wounds? Not only did I have to deal with my growing body, maturing, shaping, metamorphosing into what would one day be a fully grown man, but I had to deal with all the new feelings and emotions encountered and released through Awakening.

In what other era has any teenager had to cope with the memories of being beaten or hung, with scattered memories from unsuccessful Awakenings leaving flashes of burning pain, searing guilt or total despair. Remnants of lives on the edge of my subconscious, too frightening for me to confront; hidden as deep as my mind can manage.

What happens if one of those memories breakout

like some lunatic from an asylum, with madness in his eyes; wailing, thrashing, screaming, crying, butchering his way out, his sanity lost forever? What if that madness could infect me? I shudder just at the thought of it, making me nervous at the start of every Awakening.

Mike says it's normal to have these fears, the great unknown coming back to haunt you in its many forms, and that is why he is trained to recognise any sign of unusual behaviour in my scans or body signs during a session. That is why Millie is there to reassure me in a friendly informal way, someone who has been through the whole process themselves to guide me through the rough and the smooth. And that is why we have a counsellor on call at every centre to deal with any concerns that the trio; me, Mike or Millie, have.

It reassures me a little and I know the fact that very few people have any long term side effects from Awakening, but it does happen. Logically I know that I am statistically safe and that the reward is worth the risk, but I'm still not really sure what the reward is. What really is in it for me? What do I owe to society, or what more could I offer to it just because I have opened up my past?

Admittedly I feel so much more aware than I think I have ever been. The world seems smaller, more familiar, and with that I feel more informed in what I do, but I'm wondering if the choices I make are from my present or my past. Am I as Adam making the choices or are my past lives taking control and thus beginning to shape my destiny?

I don't want to appear negative when it is obvious that Awakening can offer so much good for everyone, it is just that I am genuinely afraid that by the time I finish looking into all my past lives, I, as the person I am now won't be around to see the results, that I will be lost in a cocktail of my previous personalities. How ironic that I view the process that offers immortality as the same process that would effectively kill me off, but from the inside.

Sometimes I wake up in the middle of the night, my fists clenched over the duvet as I feel utter despair at losing someone I love. Brothers, mothers, lovers, all gone as I knew them and oddly, I sometimes grieve for shadowy faces, people I don't recognise because I cannot get a firm fix on them. I pity myself as I see my life cut short as Sophie or Peter, at least Caleb felt freed through death!

I know I am not the only one, we all go through it and we all deal with it in different ways, I just wish I could build some form of emotional detachment so that I could take from these experiences what I want or need, rather than the whole package lumped together, waiting for me to unpick the good from the bad.

And so, by age seventeen with all this

enlightenment, all these new skills, all this hindsight and experience to draw back on, I was more lost than ever in deciding what I wanted to do with my future? Do I tap into my skills and become a lawyer, a doctor, a priest, a banker, an actor, a fisherman, a photographer, a policeman, a human rights activist, a tour guide... All these ideas, remnants from my enlarged past and yet I don't think any of them are right for me.

Of course I know at seventeen it is quite common not to know what you want to do at that age, but it just kept nagging at me. How can I go through all this and still have no idea?

Just over a year later from this point, I was fully resigned to not knowing what I should do, and thinking about falling into anything that would catch my fancy like everyone else around me. Then the goddess Fate stepped in and showed me that my destiny had been staring me in the face all this time, with clues laid out by the skulls and selection of lives I was encountering. Just as well I didn't know what I wanted to do, I never had the choice anyway.

So after all these doubts in my mind where I am genuinely afraid of losing myself as I am now, and trying to figure a way of dealing with the emotional impact of it all on my life, Imagine my disappointment to hear two old fools drunkenly debating the same immortality issues from seven hundred years ago. It makes all the dreams we have for a new and better world through Awakening sound so foolish. Yes, at last immortality has been realised in a roundabout way, but the hopes and fears remain the same and seem just as unreachable. Kale was killed when he first unveiled Awakening to the world and has to live under close guard to this day. Of course he could always come back again if assassinated, but the time lost and the chances of him having a unique brain for the third time in a row seem all too unlikely. He is too valuable to take the risk.

What if I go through this whole process just to get run over by a bus in a few years? How long before I get a new body? Would I be in an area of the world that has easy access to Awakening? Would I have the courage to go through it all again? One thing for certain would be that all my friends and family would have moved on in my absence, leading their lives without my presence, only to have to get used to a newer, younger version of me trying to re-assert itself.

With these ideas running through my mind, I came to the conclusion that I would finish my foundation at eighteen years old and call it a day. I would have unlocked a good portion of my past and be readily accepted by everyone else who has gone through the same process.

Those few in British society who are young but have chosen not to follow the herd are still accepted, but socially seen as a second class citizen (unofficially of course), or rather more accurately, as half a person, someone who does not truly know who they are. It is a light layer of prejudice that forms around anyone or anything that does not fit in with the norm, and no one wants that do they.

So I'll do enough to fit in, like so many others and then quit the Awakening foundation to try and retain the personality that I feel comfortable with. I can still visit Kemarre for rest and relaxation sessions, and who knows, as I get older and my current personality becomes more secure, then maybe I will try a few more, but at my own pace, following my own instinct.

Writing down all these details seem to be my only consolation, a reminder of what I have been through, all the illnesses, deaths, heartache, poverty, loneliness and desperation... and yet I am still here. I'm living and breathing now as Adam Capello and although sometimes it feels like I get stuck in my past, I know I have moved on and am completely at ease with the 21st century in which I live.

Sometimes I lose a little faith and I wonder for how much longer I can hold onto me as I am. I know I have to grow up, even if I don't want to, but just let me grow up as I want to grow up, without the baggage of a millennia chattering in the background. At the end of my Awakening I was given the minds of thousands of my lives.

Cafe Sorbet

Millie just laughs when I tell her of my worries, and God knows she is proof of the whole process working. She admits that it completely changed the way she views everything and everyone in this world, but to her, she has recovered who she really was, not lost who she is.

It was about this time that Millie could see I was not my usual happy-go-lucky self, so she invited me to join her for a hot chocolate at Cafe Sorbet, her favourite haunt, situated just five minutes from the Awakening centre.

The coffee shop reminds me of Sophie as I walk into its French decor. Metro station signs denoting different seating areas and even the toilets. We sat in St-Michel Notre Dame, a wall painted with a view looking over the Seine showing the Gothic cathedral in all its majesty, and for the first time, I noticed a small figure lurking near the bell tower; blurred, mysterious, hidden from sight, a reminder of my personalities lurking within.

I had ordered a Café au lait as it seemed a good choice in this setting, but was soon regretting my decision when I saw Millie's large marshmallow laden hot chocolate, sprinkled with dark chocolate flakes.

"A penny for your thoughts? She offered.

"Jeez, do people still say that?" I countered, half

joking, half defensive.

"They do now and you heard it first right here. So what's up Adam, something seems to be bothering you?"

"Ah, it's just stupid really." I felt embarrassed by my doubts. "Wow, is that Quasimodo hiding in the bell tower?"

"Adam! Do not try to change the subject, you are forgetting how well I know you and your tendency to try and dodge certain topics." She changed tact, adding warmth to her voice. "Come on, there is obviously something on your mind and it is in danger of turning you into a miserable git."

I let out a big sigh, breaking down my barriers so that I could talk freely about this seemingly modest issue. "Okay you got me... I'm just finding it more difficult to carry on with this whole process than I thought I would. I feel like I'm losing touch with my real self sometimes. I see photos of me only a few years ago and it is like seeing a completely different person. Ironically then I couldn't wait to get older to move on in the world, but it has all happened too fast, I've lost what was left of my childhood and I miss it. I'm genuinely afraid of losing myself."

"That's not stupid Adam, just common sense. Of course you are worried, most of us are, it is a huge, mind expanding experience, so of course it's going to change you, but believe me, you would have changed during this period anyway. You are a teenager with the whole world at your feet. You are lucky enough to live in the right place and time to be able to claim back what is rightfully yours. Don't shun your past experiences, embrace them, and fill the gaps in your soul that have been missing pieces of your personality all these years. You are not losing yourself Adam, quite the opposite, you are finding yourself."

Her eyes were wide open, letting me see into her personal space, her memories sitting behind those beautiful brown pupils; contained, structured and completely at her disposal. I had to admit, she made a good point.

"That's easy for you to say, but I ended up having all sorts of weird feelings for Toby after being Sophie. Took about a month for me to stop thinking he had a nice bum." I laughed out loud, embarrassed by my admission."

"Perfectly normal, I've had several crushes on some of my girlfriends after some Awakenings." She countered.

My mind wandered to places I cannot repeat.

"Ha, now you are the one distracting me from the conversation." She thumped me on the arm. Hard. "Ouch! Okay, if that is not weird enough, what about waking up some mornings with feelings of complete apathy because my dead wife from two hundred years ago is not there with me?"

Millie was suddenly touched by this comment, a

flicker of recognition running through her mind.

"So you lost someone too?" I asked, but it felt like a clumsy enquiry into her private life.

"I have lost some people so special that I don't think I will ever meet someone like them again" she answered. "But I am still thankful that I have seen them after all these years. They were such an important part of my life, why would I want to lose them? Yes it is painful at times, but again, they are part of me. Sometimes I feel they are part of my soul."

"Oh, sorry, stupid question, I guess everybody goes through that." I mumbled.

"Yes, a bit." she smiled "but don't worry Adam, you will meet her again one day, I promise."

An awkward silence presented itself, broken by Millie sipping her Hot Chocolate and me slurping my coffee a little too loudly. So I changed the subject.

"So you still think we should all go through Awakening?"

"Pretty much, there is so much to gain from it all."

"Then why do I keep getting these warning signs from the skulls? Throughout many of my lives I seem to have dreamt about them, and now the bloody things are affecting my dreams here in the present. Last night I dreamt that I was Kemarre, but in Egypt instead of Australia. I was sitting on the top of a huge pyramid, so big I could see around the world, like the little prince on top of his little planet. Scattered all over that world were skulls, one right in front of me by a sphinx, illuminating a path to the rest of them, their eyes glowing, creating a big number 8 across the continents".

"Okay weird boy" she said, pulling a funny face as if I was crazy, "that's some imagination you have there, any idea at all what eight could signify?"

"No, not at all, could be the eighth wonder of the world hidden somewhere I guess, or eight of my lives hold some kind of significance or that I only have eight more years to live! Only clue, if indeed it is a clue, is that the eight was on its side, horizontal as if I was sitting in the wrong position to see it, but I could only have ever seen it from the top of that large pyramid so it does not make any kind of sense". I threw my hands up at a loss to explain my warped dream.

"Or maybe it could signify that you are seeing things from the wrong angle, so that you need to see things from a different perspective." She looked pretty pleased with herself on that analysis.

I nodded, impressed, "Very good Doctor, but why the number eight?"

Millie pouted, she always does when she thinks about something difficult, and is yet another distraction to me. I sighed internally, when, would this schoolboy crush ever end?

"Hmm, so the eight was on its side... was it like this?" She took her lipstick and drew a horizontal eight on a paper napkin so it looked like this:

∞

"Yeah kind of."

Adam Capello, if ever there was a reason for you to continue with your studies this would be it. If you are too dumb to recognise the symbol for infinity then you need to keep learning," she mocked.

Of course I now recognised the symbol, although it had been lost on me when illuminated by the lit skulls, acting as eerie shaped candles with spooky symbolism clouding my reason.

"Oh, er yes of course, I knew that." I laughed, a little embarrassed. "But what can it possibly mean?"

"Who knows, dreams are usually a way for your mind to work things out through different scenarios but, as you can see, they can be really cryptic sometimes. Thing is, your subconscious plays a very active part in it, as if it is the only way it can push certain ideas to your fully conscious mind, and now of course your subconscious plays host to a lot of your past lives. Somewhere in all of this is could be a very important message."

I looked at her incredulously. "Great, so now you are trying to tell me that my past selves are grouping together to give me an important message. You were meant to be calming me down, not worrying me further. Surely it could just be a dream made out of mishmashed ideas?"

"Yes of course it could, I'm just saying that theoretically this could happen. I'm not saying your past lives are working together consciously as if still alive, I just mean that their essence could produce something organically, an idea evolved through your experiences.

I took the last sip of my coffee, wishing there was more. "So how do I find out what it all means?"

She took my hand, a serious look on her face. "I honestly don't know Adam, but one thing is for certain, if you don't carry on with your Awakening sessions, you will never find out."

I looked at Millie and then glanced over at Quasimodo hiding in the bell tower too afraid to come out and show his face. I knew she was right of course, we cannot hide from our fears, we need to open them up, expose everything to the light so that we can confront them before we finally put them to rest. It wasn't going to be easy, but then life is not meant to be easy. The more we test ourselves, the more we grow.

Serious decisions were needed.

"Do you fancy another hot chocolate?"

Chapter 16 - Death of a salesman

You will probably like this chapter gramps, as it is set in your era and in England. Apparently we tend to gravitate towards certain geographical regions, just as we tend to stick to a certain sex or sexuality.

Peter Smith is an interesting case, even if my character was to most people a little dull. A salesman in a carpet store gets little credit for the skills he possesses and little do people understand the importance of finding the right style for the right setting or choosing which material is best suited for the room in question. Juggling these requirements under a tight budget can be tough, especially when you consider that it is one of the most visible features of any good home and needs to last a minimum of ten years or more. Try doing that in the fashion industry.

It is interesting because I saw his memories through his time in a coma, and even though he didn't go into a past life, his / my experience in the coma was very much like an Awakening before its time.

I am going to try writing my experience in the third person in this chapter, as it gives me the freedom to describe him within his surroundings as an overview, which adds to this particular story in my humble opinion. At the start of this tale, Peter thought he had died.

April 6th 2007

This is the story of a forty-three year old man called Peter who led a very ordinary life. He was of average build, average looks, average height and average intelligence. In effect, Peter was your average... Joe. Life has a funny way of leading you down the domesticated path. Children dream of growing up to be astronauts or film stars but end up being assistant managers at a carpet store and being married with two kids and having a dog called Lucky. That was Peter's life and it could be used as a description of "Average life" in an encyclopaedia.

Every now and then though, life has a habit of shaking things up, almost as if life was getting bored of its own little paths of destiny, and today, April 6th 2007 at 7.26am, it decided to shake up Peter Smith's life. It would never be the same again. Actually, it would be the same again and quite often, but in the big scheme of things, his life would never be the same again. It's a bit complicated but you'll see as this story goes along.

At precisely 7.26am, Peter closed his eyes and waited to die. He felt his body lift up, a crackle in the air, his ears pop and a charge run through his limp body. It then went quiet as his senses went into hyper drive. He could feel the moisture in the air, smell a mixture of blossom, dog hair and grass, taste the coffee on his tongue from earlier that morning and then landed on something very soft. Everything was still, but the hairs on the back of his neck were on end. Too afraid to open his eyes, he reached out to feel his way around. Strangely enough, the softness underneath was smooth and springy. He was covered with something slightly restrictive, almost like crisp sheets and blankets. Curiosity finally got the better of him, thus replacing his fear. Peter opened his eyes and it was dark. He started to panic, his heart racing like an express train and beating so loud it made it hard to think. He began to make out some detail and saw that he was lying on a bed, in a bedroom that was strangely familiar. It was his old childhood bedroom, he hadn't seen it like this for over twenty-five years and it dawned on him that he really must be dead or dying.

It also occurred to him that maybe this was a random memory thrust out of his sub-conscious and left to dwindle in his dying brain like some kind of screen saver. Again he found himself waiting to die. Maybe this is what they mean when they say that your whole life flashes before your eyes. Well, this was hardly flashing, in fact it seemed to be moving in a painfully slow fashion. He had a horrible feeling that he might have to view his whole life over again like some trapped spectator for the next three decades and watch all the mistakes he had made in his life. Was this some kind of atonement, a way of confronting his failures and misdeeds before he could move on to the afterlife? Had he really been that bad?

It took him about five minutes to actually think about getting up. During that time, he went over in his mind about what had just happened. He had just been struck by lightning! Walking his stupid dog like he has to do every bloody morning in all kinds of bloody weather, he had sheltered from a storm under a tree. What a chump. Only a fool takes shelter under a tree. Peter realised he was that fool and probably deserved everything he got. He then felt a little remorseful over Lucky and then turned it around and blamed Lucky for being in this situation in the first place. If the bloody dog didn't insist on going walkies every bloody morning, he'd still be alive. Yes, it was Lucky's fault.

With that established Peter felt a little better about the situation and began to explore his new but familiar environment. Cautiously he lifted up the blankets and swung his legs out. Oh for the love of God, they were covered in Womble pyjamas. He was dumbfounded. He'd prepared himself for a shock, but nothing like this, remembering that he'd pestered his mum for ages to get them, they were his favourite. Illustrated all over the PJ's was Great Uncle Bulgaria standing on the common with his walking stick whilst talking to Tobamory and Madame Cholet was in the background looking for something to cook. She had a strange and hairy, but still feminine expression that had always bothered him. That's it thought Peter, either I'm dead or mad. He'd worn those pyjamas till his knees were almost sticking out of the bottom and must have been about fourteen when his mum had finally packed them away. Then he remembered that they had been stuck in the attic for years after, and rashly thrown them out when he was having a massive clearout upon moving into his first flat, probably a collector's item now, available on eBay.

Peter could not believe that only five minutes ago he was preparing himself for death and now he was lost in nostalgia for his Womble pyjamas. This was going to take some getting used to but at least he'd calmed down. It was time to look into the mirror. Holding his breath, Peter walked over to the wardrobe and peeked through half open eyes too afraid to see what he was beginning to suspect. Sure enough, standing there in front of him was the image of himself as a twelve year old boy. Peter was transfixed, like a rabbit caught in some weird time machine headlights. This went on until he realised he hadn't been breathing for a little while and exhaled, gasping for breath. How skinny he looked, how pale and scared. Actually, as by all rights he should be dead now, just looking pale and scared wasn't too bad.

The radio alarm clock kicked into action:

"By the time we got into Tulsa Town,
We had eighty-five trucks in all.
But they's a roadblock up on the cloverleaf,
and them bears was wall-to-wall.
Yeah, them smokies is thick as bugs on a bumper;
they even had a bear in the air!
I says, "Callin' all trucks, this here's the Duck.
"We about to go a-huntin' bear"

What the?!!

'Cause we got a great big convoy
Rockin' through the night.
Yeah, we got a great big convoy,
ain't she a beautiful sight?
Come on and join our convoy
ain't nothin' gonna get in our way.
We gonna roll this truckin' convoy
'Cross the U-S-A.

Convoy!

This was the ultimate wake up call. Peter realised that now he was standing there as a twelve year old geek wearing Womble pyjamas and listening to "Convoy". There really was no doubt, he must be in Hell.

Or maybe not, there was still a chance that he was just in a coma. He had to find a way to wake himself up. He tried all the usual things, slapping his face, pinching himself and banging his head on the wall with the result that now he was in Hell, and in pain.

"Come on Peter, concentrate, think your way out of this" he thought to himself.

With this, he sat cross legged on the bed and started humming like a Buddhist monk he'd seen on the Discovery channel. Alas, two things that monk had had that Peter didn't, was inner peace and eternal patience. Peter's not so eternal patience lasted only a couple of minutes. This was not going to be easy.

The music had improved though, with T-Rex in the background telling him to "Get It On". A huge wave of nostalgia overtook him and he began to feel good about the situation. Laughing out loud, he decided that he would just enjoy himself until he either woke up or finally died. There was no point in trying to rush the process, and with that he decided to get dressed.

Looking in the wardrobe took the nostalgic

experience to the next level. Amongst this strange collection of clothes he found denim flares, Birmingham bags and brown shirts. This was just too much. Peter knew he should probably embrace this experience, but wasn't sure as to laugh or cry. Could he bring himself to wear this stuff again? He knew he should get washed first but he didn't want to venture out to the bathroom just yet.

He quickly jumped out of his pyjamas, too afraid to look at himself and threw on a pair of Y-fronts. Next, the Birmingham bags with their ludicrous three buttons on the waistband and trying to do up those buttons was made much trickier by having to get used to his younger, smaller limbs again. He was all fingers and thumbs. Peter got off the bed to get a shirt from the wardrobe and with that he promptly fell flat on his face. The flares on his Birmingham bags were so wide they were flapping against each other as he walked. He was tripping over his own legs! The brown shirt had a collar big enough to match the flares but by this time he was resigned to the fact that he was going to go outside looking like John Travolta in "Saturday Night fever". He then realised that the film wouldn't be out for another year so no one would even know who John Travolta was and then it occurred to him that for the first time in his life, he'd be fashionably ahead of his time.

Dressed but still too afraid to go out, Peter just stood there looking into the mirror wondering what to do next. This might have gone on for hours but the situation came to a head with a knock on the door.

"Peter, come on dear, time to get up". His mother's voice.

Peter had known that this was going to happen, a part of his old routine etched into his mind. Not for the first time since this bizarre experience had begun, he took a deep breath and stepped out into the world of 1976.

Walking down the floral carpeted stairs and looking at the swirly Artex walls, Peter felt like he had never been away. It was incredible to think that he had forgotten all these details (his parents had moved from the house when he was fourteen) but now they were flooding back. The David Shepherd elephant painting in the hallway, the dimpled glass panel in the front door and…

He stopped dead. There before him was his mother looking younger and healthier than he could ever remember. It took his breath away. She looked amazing. Tears welled up in his eyes and all he could think to do was to rush over and give her a great big hug. It was the best hug he'd ever had, making him truly feel like a twelve year-old again as he nestled his head into her generous bosom without an ounce of self consciousness, and could hear her heart beating. He wanted to stay like that forever, and realised that he still hadn't really come to terms with her death six years ago.

"Wow that's some hug darling but it still doesn't mean you can go to school dressed like that".

And with those few words, the golden glow of childhood disappeared; replaced by the stark reality of being a schoolboy once again.

"Mum you don't understand, I don't feel... right."

"Come on, I don't want you pulling a sicky today, it's Wednesday, half day, I've only got the morning to do my shopping before all the shops close."

He didn't know what to say. He tried protesting a little further but to no avail.

"Come on Peter put your school clothes on and no excuses."

Experience had already taught him that there was no point in arguing with his mother, she had heard every excuse in the book, although admittedly he hadn't tried the one in which he had woken up with the mind of a forty-three year old man.

Moments later he was back in his bedroom putting on his school uniform and trying not to think of the day ahead. School had been bad the first time round, going again would be insufferable. How was he going to know what lessons to go to? Should he care? He fretted over this while getting dressed, wondering what move to make next when suddenly the whole situation dawned on him that all this must just be a temporary experience. He would more than likely go to bed tonight and wake up to real life the following morning.

"This can't go on, people do not just get struck by lightning and go back into their past, I'd know, I would have read about it." He muttered to himself.

And with that simple line of reasoning, he was suddenly looking forward to school. Thinking about it, he could do anything he wanted and the next day not be there to pay the consequences. It would be a bit of a gamble but he had to believe in it to keep his sanity, if indeed he hadn't already lost it.

His school uniform consisted of the following:

A pair of grey polyester trousers
A white cotton shirt with stiff collar
A tie with maroon and royal blue stripes
A scratchy maroon jumper.

All ill fitting.

After a quick breakfast of Golden Nuggets, he was running down the road, late for school as usual. Nothing had changed. Upon entering the school he was instantly hit by the familiar smell of floor polish. No, not polish, wax. This pungent, thinly smeared wax that would scrape under your nails if scratched, gave the floor a strange kind of shine. It was very glossy, giving on quick inspection the appearance of cleanliness, but when looked at properly, did nothing to hide the grime created by years of schoolchildren running over it with their muddy shoes.

The architecture of the building was mid 1960's, something that had never occurred to him as a twelve year old living in the mid 1970's. It had felt quite modern then, but now it looked so dated. It had been designed by a new generation of architect trying to forget the still recent struggles of post war life. Instead, they favoured the shape of things to come; in the birth of the new "Space age". Any decorative character enjoyed from the previous fifty years was ignored in favour of clean lines, simple geometric shapes and glass. As a fairly new building it didn't look too bad, but now Peter had the hindsight that told him it would quickly age. It would reveal its soulless corridors and classrooms, hidden only by its newness. Like the Emperor's new clothes, everybody believing what everybody else said about it.

Peter finally found his classroom, more through luck than anything else. The name "Miss Williams" officiously displayed on the door above the meshed glass viewing window. He recognised the name but wasn't sure if he had the right year. How much we forget he thought, and yet when he walked in, everything came flooding back, he even remembered

where his desk was, right next to Higgins.

Miss Williams was none too pleased at his la arrival as she was halfway through checking t register.

"What's your excuse this morning Peter?" s said with a tone that indicated she would nev believe a thing he said.

He had thought about an excuse but wor suddenly deserted him, leaving him floundering li a fish out of water. He'd always had a habit of bei just a few minutes late into class, could never ge into his head that the register was called at 8.55 and not 9am. What a stupid time anyway, h pedantic, how anal, how just like school. He had c particular teacher (a couple of years later as it turn out) who found him quite amusing as long as could think of a different excuse every day. He s Peter was just like Reginald in a comedy series "T Fall and Rise of Reginald Perrin". He remembe watching the repeats a few years later and laugh out loud at some of his excuses.

"Sorry I'm late..."

'My wife threw the key to our house into the to and flushed it... we couldn't get out.'

'My dog has diarrhoea.'

'The train driver got out to have a fight with the driver of another train.'

'My train was hijacked by evil terrorists and they wouldn't let us get out. It all ended peacefully, that's why you won't have heard about it on the news... they kept it quiet for legal reasons'

'Well, I was having breakfast, and the orange juice container said concentrate'

'I got mistaken for Bruce Forsythe, and had to spend ages signing autographs.'

Instead he mumbled an apology and took his place at his desk. It was the old wooden traditional type with a hole in the right hand side where you would put your ink pot for filling your fountain pen. He lifted the table lid to look inside and to his relief had some of his books, an old scratchy pen and a lesson planner; he might just get through all this.

In fact Peter managed to get through the first few lessons quite easily, marvelling at the juvenile attitude of his classmates and realising why he had learnt nothing in all his years there. He hadn't banked on Mr. Thompson's history class though.

Ten minutes into the lesson, Peter had used all the tricks he had for staying awake in a desperate bid to fight against Mr. Thompson's lethargic monotone

delivery about Roman Britain. Pinching his wrist was still having no effect, holding his breath, pulling his hair, nothing worked. Lower and lower his head went until it rested into the comfort of his folded arms. He peeked above his wrist with one eye until it hurt trying to stay open.

Sleep, such beautiful sleep, finally envelopes Peter, a short but peaceful escape... instantly followed by an explosion of colours behind the eyes and a severe pain to his left ear. He could only guess that Mr Thompson had done his infamous "smacking the child across the head" routine.

Blackness surrounds Peter, leaving him cold and frightened as he hears his heart beating louder and louder, pronouncing the arrival of a skull made of glass. It is looking straight at him, a slight glow emanating from the centre this time. Peter is petrified. As far as he is concerned, death has come for him and he is not ready.

As if from nowhere, a beautiful Asian girl takes his hand, pulling him away from the Sea Devils stumbling out of the ocean, but his legs feel like lead, dragging him down to the ground, removing any chance of escape. His last view in this surreal landscape is a Sea Devil reaching out and touching his leg, sending a shock through his system, his spine rigid for the second time that day. Now he really must be dead!

Beeping noises.

Out of focus figures surround him in different shades of light and dark as a buzz turns to a murmur.

Had he really been smacked that hard?

Those figures turned out to be his family. He was back in 2007 and had never been so happy to see them. Somehow he had found his way back. His brain had gone into emergency shutdown when he had been struck by lightning, putting him in a coma for two days. Why it had chosen to take him back to his childhood was a mystery, but he was very thankful for it. It made him appreciate his life and his family more, it even made him appreciate Lucky more, and it made them appreciate him more. The threat of death does that to most people. Most of all though, he was thankful for that one last hug with his mother and maybe, just maybe, that is why he had gone back.

It was just as well that he learnt to appreciate his life more, as tragically he died of a heart attack just a few years later, but those few extra years afforded to him and his family were the best he had ever had.

8-8-8-8-8-8-8-8

Going into some of my past experiences has really taught me how lucky I am to be where I am here and now. At a time of relative ease, where most people abide by the law and society looks out for the weak. Yes, it is not perfect, and a lot of people might argue that we are ignoring millions of people in the world less fortunate than us, but we are in an era of greater public compassion than any other I can remember.

On a personal scale we may have lost the feeling of unity, and we might get lost in our careers or selfish plans, but nothing about that is new. We have had selfish, cruel, despotic people throughout our history. Power attracts and power corrupts. Through greater awareness given by Awakening and heightened global communication I am quite hopeful for a bright future, but then I am a glass half full type of guy, when I'm not being Methodius.

Some unity still exists, but it is spread thinner and thinner through the virtual networks of our lives.

Somewhere deep inside me though, is a nagging feeling that we need unity more than ever, and that our very lives could depend on it.

Chapter 17 – Mistakes

I have made some huge, life changing mistakes in the past. How does the old adage go, to forgive and forget? Sometimes it's just as important to forget, even if it only gives the impression of forgiveness, and that, as I may have mentioned before, is one of the major benefits of death. To forget those you loved so much because life is difficult without them and to forget those you loved only for it to go tragically wrong. Death also lets you forget your wrong doings and your mistakes, but that luxury is rescinded if you open the Pandora's Box.

There are many types of mistakes in the past, but to me the ones that I remember with the most pain are mistakes made with someone you love. Love is so closely attached to all the most powerful emotions of guilt and hate, along with the pluses of happiness and jubilation. So often to love is eventually to lose, and to lose is to hurt. No wonder we sometimes give up, building emotional walls around us in the vain hope that we will never hurt again. I will describe one simple, normal tale of love, in which it was all a mistake. We have all been there in at least one life.

I don't want to go into exact details, even though they are from my past lives, as it is too personal and painful to think about yet again. Too many books have been written describing their relationship with someone famous from history and there are too many people who pay good money to read them. Some have even been made up, with lengthy court cases just to correct history, or at least the version of history that the plaintiff wants to be accepted. Love is complicated enough with just the two of you involved. Add another one or two people to the mix, and lies have to follow. I guess some people walk away with very few battle scars, but for me… I am always wounded.

The other man

In this past life I had just moved into a small village in Bulgaria because my wife had died and everything around me reminded me of her. I was still fairly young and wanted to start life all over again, being afforded that one small mercy as we had not yet started a family. Although things should have been fairly similar, the small details seemed to overtake the more obvious larger details, so the move seemed much bigger than you would think and left me free of those places I had shared with my wife.

I quickly found a place to live and decided that I

would just take my time in setting up my new life in this new village. Everybody knew each other, as it used to be like that in most places in those days, so I as a stranger really stuck out, but it didn't bother me, I was too lost to care.

Outside my lodgings was a pretty flower covered bridge that I could see from my bedroom. It arched over a fresh water stream, its waters constantly replenished by the rain falling off the local mountains and scurrying along its meandering path until it passed under the bridge. Being free of family or friends or a loved one, I had plenty of time after my work to stroll along that stream marvelling at how peaceful it all seemed. I had only been there a couple of weeks when I met Yana. She was out walking with her two boys enjoying an unusually warm and bright spring day.

They were making daisy chains and playing hide and seek, so, being quite good with children I joined in and we soon got talking. The attraction between Yana and me was instant and palpable. Have you been in that position where you are observing the niceties of conversation but you can't take your eyes of each other? This meeting had been so unexpected and my desire so obvious that it took me completely by surprise, leaving me unguarded.

I reminded myself that my wife had passed away just over a year ago, and it was clear that this woman was married so nothing was going to happen. So, with the distraction of her sons, we both turned our attention to playing their games. Maybe in hindsight it was just us beginning to play games of our own.

Soon after, the boys invited me over to join all of them for a picnic nearby. I met their father, who turned out to be a charming and intelligent host who knew a little about my old village so we had plenty to talk about. I remember sitting in his garden thinking I shall not pass any line. He is a decent man, as indeed so was I, and that I would not even look at his wife any longer than is polite. Fate has a habit of twisting intentions though.

Over the next few weeks we saw each other many times, as they were practically my neighbours and the glorious weather continued to surprise and delight us all. Oddly, the husband would never stay around very long, always finding reasons to go off and do other things. I never argued with that as Yana's company was also very good. She was tall and slender, large brown eyes and shoulder length hair, incredibly intelligent, funny and well read. What was there not to like?

We would have long conversations in the garden as the children played, getting to know each other better than we ever planned. She would let out little snippets about their marriage that showed they had problems behind the charade of happy families and it turned out that he was quite reclusive, finding it difficult to stay in people's company any longer than an hour or so, which answered in my mind why she was left alone with the children so many times.

Through mutual friendship and desire we found ourselves sharing our first kiss, even though we were both fully aware of how wrong this situation was. We both had something missing from our lives and we seemed to fill that void with each other. It wasn't long before we shared a bed together and the guilt pulled me apart. Using that guilt for moral strength I tried ending the relationship but to no avail. She pleaded their marriage was broken, and that seemed to make it a little easier for us both, but it was short lived.

For over eighteen months we saw each other off and on, but always wracked with guilt. We were feeding off the excitement of an affair, but starved of any kind of security. We couldn't tell him about us, things were just too difficult in those days and already we had taken much bigger risks than we should have.

Eighteen months is a long time to live a lie; to talk to people you know as if you are a single person and look into the eyes of a husband you are cheating; to be friends with him whilst sleeping with his wife. Eventually it gets to you, ties you up in knots until you think you will go mad. She tried convincing me to run away with her and her children, to start a new life again, but we both knew he would find and confront us.

In my mind we would never know peace if we were together, and shying away from the chaos of such a life I let her move away by herself, the only way she could part from her husband and me at the same time. I let her go, thinking that maybe we would find a way in the future of being together as this separation would give things time to breathe.

A year of love letters passed between us as my life settled into some form of peaceful routine, but one letter destroyed that peace in a heartbeat. She had met someone else. The news hit me much harder than I would have ever guessed. I couldn't work out why at first, but then I realised I was still very much in love with her, my feelings repressed to cope with the situation we had been in. The mind plays funny tricks on you in those circumstances and acts to protect your heart.

I also felt guilty. Not any more guilty to the husband than I had already felt, but guilt to her for not being braver. I felt like I had let her down when she needed me to be strong. All those times when she had burst into tears saying she could not cope with things the way there were, and I had just consoled her without any action.

She certainly wasn't blameless, but in her letter she had not been slow to point out many of the mistakes I had made while we had been stealing time together, with each mistake pointed out feeling like a dagger going in my heart. I started screaming to myself, "how could I have let this happen?" I had lost this beautiful woman, someone who made me think and lust in equal proportion. She made me laugh and cry and brought out a lot of the good things in me that I thought had died years earlier. How could I have let this incredible woman slip through my hands and into the life of someone else?

It sounds terrible to admit, but this loss seemed so sudden, even though it was inevitable over such time, and hit me just as hard as the death of my wife, maybe harder, as in this case she was still walking around somewhere but in someone else's arms. My pathetic attempt at protecting my heart was ripped to shreds.

So many sleepless nights were spent lying in an empty cold bed with my mind running over the different scenarios. **What if** I had done this or **what if** I had done that? I feared I was losing my mind from this lack of sleep and a head that had not had a calm moment in months. Stamping the floor, bashing my head with my fists, weeping at any given moment, knowing that I had screwed it all up! And all I could think of was finding a way to go back in time so that I could correct my mistakes.

Of course I knew that was impossible, so I looked to God to help me out, knowing I was so guilty and full of sin that I would be left to my own fate. This was all part of the punishment of having an affair with a married woman. I thought that my only solace was that I was not as guilty as her, as I had been the other man, not her the other woman, but it was of little consolation in the whole mess that we had created. In reality, was I really any less guilty than her?

It took me years to come to terms with everything and evaluate all the guilt that had been left at my door, some of it unfairly, and to deal with the loneliness thereafter. Sometimes that loneliness can only be cured by the love of another. Sometimes even that is not enough.This Awakening brought all this back to me of course, sometimes spilling into my consciousness and thus it still upsets me sometimes, as if it had all happened recently instead of a few hundred years ago. Awakening does offer some help though. It reminds me of many other relationships that I have had, some even more painful, many less so, and it puts it all into a better sense of perspective. So I might have had the memories re-opened, but I am now better equipped to deal with new relationships. Hopefully if I ever get to meet my soul mate, I will know she is my soul mate and won't screw it up this time.

Other examples include relationships with women (and men) that I should never have been involved in, but then isn't that just part of the rich tapestry of life? A good relationship is fantastic, but to be in a bad relationship... we are better off alone.

Other past loves

A girlfriend who suffered from anger management issues (no one knew what that was at the time) and therefore would take me through the idolise / demonise routine. She would be so loving, and tell me how fantastic I was, only to turn at the drop of a pin and find fault. She would become angry and jealous with the tiniest provocation, getting violent at times and driving me to retaliate physically and emotionally in the same fashion.

Why did I let that relationship go on for so long? Why didn't I realise that she would never change, no matter what she or I promised each other? Marriage would have meant murder as far as I am concerned.

I guess I had a few marriages like that, one or both of us unhappy but unable to communicate the important points to each other. How can we be so happy to marry someone and be with them forever, only to wonder a few years later how the hell we can get out of this bloody situation?

Some marriages were lovely for so many different reasons. Some of the best were made out of business sense rather than love. Marriages arranged for us could be good if the parents were wise enough to leave some room in the agreement for some mutual attraction. Enough to start a family, but not too much as to cloud the mind and affect any sound judgement. My arranged marriage as Methodious had no attraction built into the equation for me, which left me in a cold and empty relationship, but spurred me on to fill my void with philosophy instead, and thus shaped my life in that fashion.

I have no experience of a gay marriage yet, it being relatively new to our history, but certainly some experiences in Roman times were… eye opening looking back. Jealousy still seemed to feature highly and there is not as much mutual logic used as I would have thought, but at least we did understand each other's needs from the same side of the coin, so to speak.

Most relationships have become a blur when looking back, only remembered at the time of Awakening, complete with obsession, jealousy, love, hate, spite, kindness, cruelty, incredible patience, incredible sex, poor sex, no sex.

That is the amazing thing about Awakening, that the memory is just as intense as the first time you felt it. At least this time you know that you have no control, all you can do is witness the events and, unfortunately, the same mistakes over and over again.

Other mistakes

Not all mistakes deal with affairs of the heart of course. Huge mistakes in history that may have been made in business, or fighting in a war and losing the lives of hundreds of your men. Getting drunk and falling off a roof to my death. Seeing your child die from a misjudgement you may have made, whether it was because you felt you could not afford a doctor, or because you let them go out to buy some bread and they never came back.

These are tragic mistakes; when you are responsible for the lives of others, especially children. It can make you want to curl up and die, offering your soul for theirs so that they may come back again and relieve your conscience. Emotions can be far more painful than any physical wound, and yet we have relatively little sympathy for people who have lost someone they love and are losing their grip on reality as a result. Yes we show kindness and sympathy, but for how long?

There always seems to be some sadness around the corner. That is another reason why I like the life of Kemarre, with its lack of complications and a solid, firm family of loved ones surrounding me every day. He had no money, but his was one of my richest lives.

Ada

Ada was of course someone very special, one of the few that I remember so much about. Her strength of character was only matched by her compassion. She was a gentle, loving woman who somehow knew how to strike the right balance between parenting your children and policing them. Considering it was during the end of the Victorian era, she was way ahead of her day. Of course, as Kirk I didn't know that at the time, as I was conditioned to live under those rules of life like everyone else. I did know she was someone special though. She brought out the best in me.

I'd like to think I brought the best out in her too. I introduced her to the classics, as well as the best books written in that period. Books by Charles Dickens illustrating the differences between the classes, with hope shining through all the hardship and despair. The Science stories of Jules Vern and H.G.Wells adding a sense of marvel to both our lives, and Sir Arthur Conan Doyle with his wonderful detective stories of Sherlock Holmes. And after reading "Around the World in Eighty Days", we dreamt of adventures together on steam ships, and elephant treks in India.

When you have that connection where your separate hobbies become shared hobbies, where showing an interest in what they are doing is a pleasure rather than a chore, life becomes so much more interesting. We practically learnt to read each other's thoughts, so that just a slight nod of the head could convey my whole mood to her. When I could finally know what she meant when she said one thing, but really meant the opposite.

One of my hobbies as Kirk was stargazing with my trusty telescope. Fired up by tales of Martian invasion in H. G. Wells' new book, "The War of the Worlds", I even tried marrying my two interests of astronomy and photography by making a bracket to attach my camera to the telescope on its tripod mount.

One bitterly cold, but beautifully clear winter's night, you could see so clearly into the night sky that it was as if a veil had been lifted. Ada brought out a hot drink whilst I meddled with the film plates and we both caught a shooting star racing across the horizon; we made a wish to go travelling and see the world. With that we stood still with our heads pointed towards the heavens, our teeth chattering, wondering about beings from other worlds.

Just three weeks later, Ada died from a chill she had caught that night. Her beautiful presence in my life extinguished so simply (if only we had known of antibiotics she would have made a full recovery). It made me so angry with myself for letting her stay out. It made me angry that our sharing of each other's interests had led to her death. Where was the justice in that? Why should someone so good die doing something so innocent? With the loss of Ada, came the loss in my belief in God, for how could He let such a tragedy occur to such a good person?

I had to live as Old Man Kirk for another thirty years without Ada and never forgave myself for encouraging her to stay out. I never looked through my telescope again, even finding it difficult to look at the moon without fighting back the tears, guilt and rage. A few years later, another of H.G.Wells' books, "The Time Machine" gave me hope that one day I would be able to go back to her. Maybe Awakening is that time machine, reliving those moments through Kirk that first reminded me of Ada, and then gave me the chance to spend those times again with her; every minute replayed.

If only we could have new conversations though. If only we could touch. If, always if. Never when, and always so seemingly impossible. Mistakes, no matter how innocently made, can hurt like hell for an eternity. **What if** things could be different?

But what options do you have? Just to get out of bed in the morning can lead to death. Actually, just staying in bed can lead to death. Inaction can cause just as much hurt and pain as any visible action. So we make judgement calls all day, every day of our lives and all we can hope is that we end up tilting, and it really is only tilting, the odds in our favour.

To forgive and forget? To die and forget is the ultimate pacifier. Now we are resurrecting painful memories too, will we ever know any peace?

Chapter 18 - Carving canoes

We are always being told by people obviously wiser than ourselves that we never really appreciate what we have until we lose it. From my experience so far I have to admit that statement holds true. Why we become so blasé about things that started off by being so special is a mystery. Could it be that we cannot function properly if we were to become constantly appreciative of something? To look at the world with those wide innocent eyes and an imagination that knows no boundaries, open to any suggestion?

Love is of course acknowledged as the ultimate prize. It is linked in with happiness and a sense of completion. The corny line, "you complete me" illustrates perfectly, that to some of us at least, we feel there is something missing in our lives and in our souls without a soul mate. Yet we still grow accustomed to our loved ones; be they wives, husbands, siblings, parents or children, and show them less appreciation or respect than we might a friend or even a stranger. We truly do not know what we have until we lose it.

One Awakening quickly illuminated something that I took so much for granted, and now marvel at what I had without even thinking about it.

Honduras

Mike has just worked his own special type of magic and quickly puts me into a deep Awakening, the world has disappeared and I calmly leave my trepidation, to seek the past I had left behind so long ago.

Darkness surrounds me even though I'm surrounded by noises of everyday life. The juxtaposition of noise and darkness puts me on edge, even though I'm still under Mike's calming influence. I reach out instinctively, instantly remembering that I now have no control of this body. It is only my present day mind that is grasping into thin air.

My memory is now coming back to me in dribs and drabs as my body inhabits this dark environment. I am Stancio and I am blind. Blind since the age of eight when I had been bitten by blackflies in the Rio Tinto Negro while swimming with my brothers and sisters some two years earlier, the larvae slowly robbing me of my sight. River blindness is feared just as much as malaria and can end up being just as deadly.

So I am left with a slightly skewed child's view

of the world. Colours are all over the place, vibrant but not quite right, as if they had been over enhanced by some image software. I am twenty-four, but "see" everything from a child's height. Every visual memory I have has been played over and over again in my head as I have no new ones to take their place and my heart reaches out to him as I realise this.

Stancio feels no self pity though, just acceptance and memories of a life that has had to adapt to this dark world. My brothers and sisters have all made sacrifices to help me, and as such we are as close as can be. There is a lot of love in my life and I have been told this is one of the rewards for living my life this way.

And this is the strange thing. My memories, although visually skewed, are in some ways clearer than my present memories. I feel I can navigate through my mind a lot easier because I am less distracted by the world around me. These memories are obviously mostly made up from after my blindness, and consist of smells and sounds, touch and taste, my other senses coming into play with a more dominant role than I could ever have imagined.

Tastes of peppery semi-hard frijoles, sweet and savoury plantain and the lovely filling, fibrous, slightly buttery tasting yucca plant boiled in salty water. When we were lucky we had fish or spiced chicken to mix with the rice; always fresh, every bit used and eaten. My taste buds come alive just thinking of it, ordering my tongue to produce saliva so that it can maximise the taste and help with the conversion from food to fuel.

Sweet, tangy oranges, occasional pineapple and the strange but oddly addictive (to me anyway) flesh and juice of the Cashew fruit. This pepper-sized fruit looks like an apple and has a brown kidney shaped pod at the top which when cooked, produces the cashew nut that we all enjoy around the world. The fruit is strange though, as it gives a juice that furs the tongue, thereby refreshing your thirst and then making you thirsty again straight after. This combination of textures was like a mini explosion in my mouth and I could see every virtual colour it produced.

Music was another huge part of my life. Every note crystal clear in my mind's eye with a place and a purpose and the ability to mould my mood in whatever way the person playing wanted it to be. Tears of happiness and sorrow, mixed with stories that I knew so well, but still wanted to hear over and over again.

It reminds me of a short but very visual poem, and to Stancio would have seemed like another world. It is about Bourbon Street in New Orleans, the music and people that inhabit the old bars on every corner.

His eyes they glint as he waves a hand,
arms flowing, feet tapping, the old man is dancing to the rhythm of the band.

He stands on the corner of a Bourbon Street bar,
an attraction himself, displaying an attraction inside.
Some people stop and stare, some watch from afar,
this... dying character; alive in New Orleans!

Then we come to the music... Ah, the music.

It forms an image in my mind of shapes and sounds and colours unbound,
Then the music dies, and I go blind; I grope in the dark waiting for God's aural light...

1,2,3,4

Then the music is back; brighter, louder, better than ever!
The charismatic bar is a smoky paradise, filled with those holiest of pilgrims,
For that holiest of sounds... Dixieland jazz!

To me it completely evokes the energy of Bourbon Street and reflects the way in which Stancio saw music. "God's aural light" filling his mind with all his treasured memories of colour in a completely different pallet to every different tune.

Within the peaceful moments of Stancio's life, I am able to see into his character clearer than any other. Seeing into some of my other past lives feels like an intrusion in other people's personal memories and I have to constantly remind myself that what I see is me buried somewhere within that personality. It is my core identity, the real me that survives from lifetime to lifetime but diluted by the loss of memory and addition of our native nurtured surroundings. Only now with an improved understanding of Awakening are people saying they feel like they are able to retain more of their core identity, and build a longer lasting, further reaching identity that leads to immortality.

My life as Cabel was so different from Kirk or Methodius that I find it hard to believe they were all me, even though their memories are now part of me. Without feeling ownership of our past personalities, can we honestly say we are immortal through re-birth, or are we just the same energy producing a different wavelength in the story of life?

All we can say, and already a lot has been said, is that through total self discovery comes the answer to those questions. With Stancio (and some of Kemarre the aboriginal) comes a greater level of self awareness, and to me that holds the key.

It is all too easy to lead life without focus and without self awareness. Just take a look around you.

People are walking around wired into their akpods or mobiles without even seeing what is physically in front of them. Television acts as the soma of our generation, washed down by the Victory gin of routine that makes us all glaze over.

When my father was twenty, he had been lucky enough to go on a three month voluntary field trip to an orang-utan sanctuary in Borneo. They had no TV, and mobile phone signals were quite limited in the remote region they were staying. As a result, his group slowly disengaged themselves from the modern world, re-learnt the art of conversation with each other, and felt like they were seeing the world for the first time.

The conservation work they were doing was important and they were young enough to absorb every element of their strange surroundings to make the most of it. Their main aim might have been conservation work, but in reality it showed them all that there are alternative ways in which to live.

On his return, he watched the world as if it was through glass. The world seemed dimmer and detached and he had been wary about falling back into the trance of life again. Of course, life has to be led and before he knew it, he was back into all his old habits again, but the memory is still very strong with him and he will have that forever.

Now with Awakening I have extra memories of times like that. When the whole world was detached, held together only by the localised society in which I was living in at the time.

This time as Stancio gave me a chance to explore a more introspective lifetime, to try and glimpse a view of the real me without visual distractions. I saw a person who was morally strong, fairly independent, fair minded, if a little stressed sometimes but with an easy going sense of humour. Of course, these are the clearly marked character traits. Far more difficult to describe are the subtle blended traits that only come to the fore under certain conditions.

As I learned to recognise more of these subtle traits in Stancio's character, the more I recognised in other life time personalities. I began to see where the core identity stopped and started around the nurtured personality of that life. I began to see myself for the very first time.

With that knowledge came a confidence that the lives I was seeing from the past, are my past. They are traits that other people who know you really well would also recognise if they were able to view your memories. So much so, I have even recommended to Kale that more work should be done on getting people to share their Awakenings in depth for cross analysis, so they can be can be seen from a more detached viewpoint to highlight our character traits. I'm still waiting for an answer on that one though.

As Stancio, touch has become incredibly

important to me since I became blind. I see my mamma by running my hand across her smiling face, feeling the new wrinkles form over the years. These wrinkles act like writing, telling their own strange story about the hardships of life in the Honduran jungle, scraping a living every day just to stay alive and offer a better future for us, her children.

The calluses on her hand act like Braille across a leathery parchment, formed by digging and cutting and cooking and gutting and planting. Yet she still has creases around her mouth, which to me are evidence of her always smiling, always looking at the best side of life. Her feet are also hard, like built in moccasins protecting the soft flesh underneath from the small stones, twigs and bugs on the ground.

Ants run around everywhere, furiously trying to bury their head into your skin, giving a small but sharp pain as they bite. Children with softer feet are always complaining about the ants, but their feet have to grow harder too, so they have to go through the same process as everyone else even though we hate to see their discomfort. It seems a rule of life that you have to let the children experience some pain and hardship if they are to grow strong, even though you want to protect them from everything.

Using my sense of touch, I make money carving dugout canoes that we call “Pipantes”. These simple narrow boats are made by cutting out the shape from a single tree, scraping off the bark, then gouging and burning out the wood beneath. The heat forces the sap from the green wood to sweat through the bark and forms a natural waterproof layer. You then sit in it and paddle or push away with a large wooden pole, much as you would with a punt if you were in Cambridge. Some of the boats are large enough to let two people stand on small platforms at the front and back so that they can both use poles to push the boat along when full of supplies.

My apprenticeship was slow at first, patiently guided by my cousin as I learnt to cut the wood the right way, rather than cut myself all the time. Now I am a master of my craft, so as a sideline I carve small figures out of different types of wood which are very popular in the village, with small toys for the children, ornaments for the women and tools for the men.

With this skill I have been able to earn a good living and that gave me the ability to find a wife and start a family of my own. I have not seen Reyna with my eyes of course, but I know she is beautiful. The touch of her smooth skin all over her body just sets me alight. Her perfect breasts end with large responsive nipples and the small of her back curves perfectly to her generous behind. She is gentle and kind, and a wonderful mother to our first born.

So in some ways I am very lucky. I have a beautiful family that I can support with work that I enjoy but there is something missing and I don't quite know what it is. Sometimes I think it is because I cannot see, and therefore will never see my wife or my children. I will never see my mother or father again or the sunrise or the moon shine. Inside I know it is more than that though.

It is a feeling that I recognise throughout my different lives in Awakening. A feeling that there is more out there in the big wide world. A feeling that I should be doing more, that the world should offer more, that somehow I am missing something very important and without it my life is not finished, it is not complete. Somehow I know I have a purpose in this universe and I will remain restless until I complete it.

I think we all have it to a greater or lesser degree. When distracted by the everyday process of living it fades into the background, but when left alone too long, it re-appears like a deep, dull stomach ache. So we keep busy with hobbies and charity work or playing with relationships and adding to our workload by having families and volunteering to be a scout leader. Watching TV, reading and surfing the net all take us away from our everyday life, and transport us to someone else's.

The distractions that we crave so much, and yet find ourselves saying, "If only I had a little more time to myself, a little more me time". Ha, no wonder we are so confused, will we ever find what we really want? Would finding it, and I do believe it is an intangible “it”, would that fill the void? Is that the answer to happiness?

Stancio’s life was a lot better than some others of mine, and it makes me happy that even without the use of his eyes he was able to have a good life. Did he ever see the skulls that seem to plague my other lives though? Yes; in his dreams, from something he had seen when he was really young, the colours madder than ever, the symbolism of life and death lost on the child.

In his dreams, several skulls are alight and one of them is speaking about the end of the world!

Chapter 19 - Childhood memories

I don't always get a full recollection of a life. Quite often I'll be tantalised with brief glimpses into lives that I never see again. Snapshots into my distant past like a disconnected flick through YouTube. Images, sounds, smells and emotions add the extra dimensions to these otherwise featureless images.

For some reason most 'clips' are childhood memories, as if demonstrating a complete lack of concentration in my young head; my attention flittering like a leaf in the wind. But they hold the strongest feelings; all my senses alive, amplified through a young active brain in full imagination mode.

As such, it can be hard to know what is real and what is my imagination. It was once said that to exist, we need to be seen. Now that we can see into our own minds looking back, does that make these memories a reality or does someone else need to see them?

Night time terrors

I'm lying in a small bed with only the moonlight providing a night light. Huddled, slightly cold in the winter air and staring at a scary crack along my wall. Every night I stare at that crack, watching it grow bigger the harder I stare at it. Every morning I'm saved by the brighter, warmer daylight as it almost fills the crack, reducing it back to its original size.

One night the wall will fall down. One night it might open and gobble me up. One night eyes will appear, looking left, then right, as if there is a strange alien trying to get out, or another child on the other side, staring in just like me.

I hate this crack with its night time terrors, silently threatening and no-one believing me when I tell them of its powers. When I came out of that brief Awakening, I had tears running down my cheeks. God knows what kind of impact that creepy wall had on my adult life. Did I just forget about it when I grew older, or did it have such a strong influence on my life that it helped shape my destiny?

Talking of night time terrors, I better describe the dreams I touched upon with Stancio.

Stancio and the glowing skulls

I could still see when I was taken to my first burial, which tells me I must have only been about five or six years old. It was my grandmother being buried and she was loved by the whole community, so it was a big turnout. In those days we buried our dead in local caves and by chance we lived by one of the most famous of them all in the region of Catacamas.

Called the “Talgua Caves”, they bathed the dead with a magical property that made their bones shine or glitter in the light. To us it was a blessing from the gods showing that they favoured our people. In reality, it was the unique atmosphere of the caves that slowly placed a layer of calcite on the oldest of bones, thereby giving them their “glowing” appearance.

I had been told all the stories of course, of which there were hundreds, all told round camp fires on starry nights. No one feared the bones, they were our ancestors after all, but I was not so lucky when it was my turn.

I had been very excited about seeing the cave, but naturally sad at losing my grandmother who had been with me every day of my short life. Chattering away I stepped into the mouth of the cave, our voices reverberating as soon as we entered, a slight echo acting as a sign for us to be quiet in respect for the dead.

My father and his brothers carried the body into the cave whilst the women wailed in harmony with each other, as much part of tradition as from grief. The wailing bounced from wall to wall and sent a shiver down my spine. It was then that I saw my first glowing skull, sitting on a burial pile where it had probably been left undisturbed for centuries.

As you can imagine from my past experiences, the sight of the skull both entranced and horrified me, rooting me to the spot. I couldn't even close my eyes, I was sure the skull was looking at me, the wailing from the crowd and the beating of sticks on the ground all conspiring together to make me feel like I was dying. Apparently I then fainted and had to be carried out of the cave by my grieving father; tending to me now as his mother had to him when he was young.

Years later the images of that skull hung in my mind, but were skewed by my blindness and young memory. This led to a dream that I would have once or twice a year. It was always similar, always frightening; waking me up in a cold sweat and screaming that the sky is falling.

In the dream I am standing on a small desert island in the middle of the night and the mother of all storms is blowing through the palm trees. There is just enough light from the tiny sliver of moon in the night sky to create shadowy silhouettes on the ground. Mixed with the howling wind, they look like wailing banshees performing some demented dance.

All of a sudden, a giant glowing skull emerges from the ground, its eyes staring straight at me.

"You are on my island, you are on my island," it booms above the wind. "Beware the sky is falling but you are not ready. This is the end of the world and all for nothing."

I would never get further than that in the dream, as if the world in it had truly ended. There was nothing left to "see" until I grew older. By then I had learnt to keep myself calmer on that lonely island, thus giving me a chance to study the surroundings in more detail. On one occasion I noticed a tiny light hovering in the distance and could just make out the shape of a man. The hovering light had been him holding a lamp in one hand and a bible in the other, the only light in that god forbidden landscape and I wondered if he was trying to show me the way out.

Recurring dreams always make me feel odd. They seem to be offering some kind of message but it is always so cryptic. Peter Smith always used to have a beautiful oriental girl stand next to him in a house full of children running around. One touch from her and Peter would die. Only in his coma did it change, revealing the "Sea devils" from his childhood days of watching "Doctor Who" as being the creatures with the deadly touch. On this occasion she kept him calm and led him to safety. He thought that maybe she represented his fickle fate, this time saving him instead of killing him. Methodius would have approved.

My memories give me the benefit of being able to see childhood from all angles. I end this journal at age eighteen, and yet I now have the memories not only of many childhoods, but also of being a father and a mother too. It is like looking backwards and forwards and makes me wonder how it will affect me when I start a family in this lifetime. Hopefully it will give me the patience needed to deal with the demands of young children and give my wife the support she needs and deserves, as I will have had the same experiences myself.

As Adam, I remember when I was younger, say seven or eight, my father telling me off for fiddling with his new media centre and losing all his presets. He was really angry and yelling at me, but I felt it was unfair. I didn't really know I was doing any harm and it was only a silly gadget anyway. I had vowed that I would never forget what it is like to be a child and would therefore understand my own child's protestations when the time comes. I would be a better parent by remembering what it is like to be a child.

You may remember, in Ancient Greece I'd been a lonely little boy who would just sit and watch the other children play. I'd not really learnt to fit in as well with other children as they had, and thus I had plenty of time for questioning the world. Why was I different from other boys? Why are some things funny and other's not? Why are obvious tired old jokes, still funny to parents and children, but not to me? What makes everybody tick?

So as Methodious, when my mother died, my whole world as a child died too, never to be the same again. I could not make sense out of anything. Having to stay strong for my father had not allowed me to express my grief to him, robbing me of the need to mourn her properly and thus carrying her death with me for many years after.

Those formative years led to my fascination of philosophy at a time when it was popular but could also be politically dangerous. As I was growing up, I learned that Socrates had been tried in our law courts and ordered to take his own life by ingesting hemlock, a painful natural poison. Only after his death was his work appreciated and a statue built to praise his life and work.

In my observations of the people around me, I studied the children against the adults and would try to distinguish their loss of innocence in relation to the wisdom that accumulated through growing up and being schooled. We may have become better educated, but our thinking seemed to become more rigid, leaving less room for creative or inspirational thought processes.

My childhood as Kemarre, gave no formal tuition but I was completely surrounded by a loving family and tribe which gave me the most subtle transformation from boy to man. Even though we had to learn how to hunt and provide, our outlook seemed eternally young.

Kale's self-awakened childhood is unique of course, a complete loss of childhood from that point on. He speaks very little about his own personal experience of this, or the struggles to regenerate Awakening across the globe. Within months, he was whisked around the world for press interviews and was on the cover of many magazines and newspapers. Yes, he had the knowledge of his past lives and the unique, against all odds position of being born with the type of brain that can cope with that power of thought. To be a savant once is rare, twice in consecutive lifetimes… amazing!

Of course he wasn't the first person to be a child prodigy and thus lose his innocence. Leonardo Da Vinci, Isaac Newton, Mozart to name but a few. Pop sensation Michael Jackson, who fought so hard to preserve his innocence that he was accused of paedophilia by a society that just could not understand what he had lost and was trying to recover. One minute you are a child, the next a predator in the eyes of the press.

Children in Africa abducted and trained to kill lose their innocence in the most tragic of ways. Millions of children in India, so poor they have to scrape whatever food they can to survive, leaving little time or energy to think about running around playing "chase". Children all over the "Third World" in the same desperate situation, it makes me weep just at the thought of it.

Looking back over my childhoods they are generally happy. Even life as a slave child was ok. I was lucky enough to have my birth mother with me till the day I died. So now, as a child in the modern world where so much disease and famine has been cut back and systems are in place to protect children from all the harms in a big dangerous world, I feel very fortunate indeed to have made it this far in history.

Childhood is special, fragile and sweet, and to me looking back, one of the most important periods of our lives. Without a good foundation, we stand very little chance of surviving intact with the rest of our lives. This is one of the reasons Kale has set a limit of fifteen to be the youngest anyone can undergo Awakening. Sometimes I wonder if he wishes he could have waited until he had been older.

Then there is the flip side: memories of being old; the body failing us and learning to live with inevitable pain of bones seizing up, lungs too exhausted to breathe properly and eyes growing dimmer until the world around us disappears into a haze. These memories are foggy and uneventful though, thus fewer stand out to be remembered along the paths of time.

It illustrates the battle between our brain that manages our everyday existence, with the consciousness that holds our core identity from body to body. I liken it to being a Formula 1 racing driver. You can have all the talent in the world, but if you don't have the right car to drive, you are never going to win. Yes, you can change the set-up, try different tyres, fuel additives, software for the engine management system. You can adjust the suspension, re-design the chassis to hold the road better, but ultimately, you need to start with a new body from scratch.

Now that this is understood a little better, the fate of G-celebrities, such as Shakespeare, is better understood. Whilst he may have lost the ability to write anything decent now, he might hopefully find another life with another brain perfectly attuned for that innate ability to shine.

My childhood as Adam is drawing to a close and would have done with or without Awakening. I know that now. I hope I can hold onto my playful nature and keep a healthy level of curiosity that enables me to learn through experience. I hope I can hold onto many of the positive elements of a young mind which adds to a huge sense of fun in life. The one thing we can never hold onto though is our innocence, which is why we treasure it so much in children.

Watching the world through the innocent eyes of a child is like seeing a world of magic; everything new, everything waiting to be discovered and everything possible. No wonder we guard our children's innocence for as long as we possibly can.

Chapter 20 - The artist and the church

My exploration into my past life as Hieronymus was probably one my most difficult. Of all the lives that I have revisited so far, his is the most troubled and so far removed from my own character that again I find it hard to believe that we share the same spiritual energy. I am a bit embarrassed by his personality, even though he achieved so much and was only trying to make the best of his mind and his environment. In fact, he is so different I find it difficult to write him in the first person as that involves accepting him back into my head, but we need get into the mind of the man to see his torment clearly. I questioned myself whether I should include him in this journal of my Awakening, with Millie finally making my mind up, saying that to give a fully rounded view of my past I have to show both my good and bad sides; the Jekyll and Hyde of my personality.

He was not a bad person, quite the contrary, he was just someone living on the edge of madness trying to do the right thing. Unfortunately, the harder he tried, the more troubled he became. That troubled mind produced a creative genius, painting scenes that preached the teachings of God louder and further than any preacher could. To some he is probably a hero.

Genesis

The first time I entered this troubled mind, Hieronymus was arguing with his family over the way he should paint scenes from the Bible. Traditional views dictated that we had all been given our skills from God and thus we should reward this blessing by representing his love and devotion as we had been taught to do by our fathers and their fathers.

My father and uncles were all artists making a living in a small Flemish town in the mid-15th century. As such, it was my destiny to follow my peers, learning to paint onto panels of oak and mahogany under a long apprenticeship that felt more like being a dogsbody than an artist.

Only one subject was more important to us than our obsession with painting, and that was the church. How can I convey to you the turmoil our world was going through at the time? The mid-15th century was a very difficult period in time with the Roman Catholic Church in arms against dissenters; would be reformers who were frustrated by the workings of the Vatican. The printed press was introducing new ideas to those who could read, thus helping to erode certain principles by supplying alternate views to the Vatican.

This was a time when the Devil was strong. People everywhere were dying from the plague and witch hunts in every village were used to find some explanation for all this tragedy. Looking back to Hieronymus' earliest vivid memory, it probably won't surprise you to know it included the skull. This memory was to have a massive impact on my life as Hieronymus in many ways, as my mind had already been shaped by its surroundings; the skull just flicked a switch in my head and shaped my destiny.

My father decided it was time to take me to Traitors' Point to see the rotting corpses of dissenters, witches and thieves, their heads on spikes to warn everybody the consequences of straying from the teachings of the Vatican; religion at its worst using fear to trap and enslave, instead of love to invite.

The stench of rotting flesh hits you before you even see the bodies piled up on top of each other. Swarms of flies so thick they look like a sickening, pulsating black blanket, making it impossible to see through them. To the side of that, maggots were crawling out from the middle of blackened putrid faces as they gorged on the fetid flesh, finally stripping them clean to the bone.

Things were different in those days. No one worried about how it might affect a young boy to see such horrors, the most important thing was to teach them what would happen if they did anything wrong against God. I remember the feeling of bile in my stomach as my father pushed me towards the spikes. He was shouting out verses from "The Book of Revelations" to ensure I got the message loud and clear.

To the side I saw a pile of skulls thrown to the ground to make room for the fresh heads of new traitors. That familiar feeling of terror took over my body as several of those skulls lit up; my father's voice booming in the background masked the strange garbled unintelligible stream of words coming from their jaws.

I ran as fast as I could to the nearby stream and vomited till I had nothing left in my guts. As Adam, I was aware of my experiences in the past, but as Hieronymus, it was the point in which the Devil had entered my mind and I was never to be the same again. My father thought he had completed his duty by literally putting the fear of God into me. In reality he had pushed me over the edge.

Never in all my lifetimes have I felt faith like this; all consuming, unswerving faith in the almighty God. The perpetual battle between good and evil laid down on our beautiful planet and the Devil gaining ground every day. He sucked the soul out of any living creature foolish enough to stray into the shadow of sin and you would burn in Hell for all eternity if you were caught. And yet the world was full of sinners.

I grew up with this type of faith, trying to decide

upon a life in the church or to use my gift to show people the consequences of their actions. Puberty only added to my problems as chemicals filled my brain with new thoughts.

As I delved deeper into the heart of Hieronymus as a man, I discovered he had a secret that even he tried to keep from himself. In today's world, we might say he had a high sex drive, or at worst, an addiction, but to Hieronymus it was the Devil making him lust and want for female flesh. His desire to fornicate drove him to despair as he would become torn between his love and fear of God and his primitive desires.

Everyday would be a battle for me… wanting to concentrate on improving my mind by reading or painting, only to be distracted by a pretty shop girl or serving wench. My mind fogging up, unable to read the page as my aching loins would nag at me to go and sate my "hunger" as quickly and ruthlessly as I could. The sight of an ample bosom would completely disrupt my day, being solved only through self flagellation in my private chambers.

My only salvation was to paint in opposition to my thoughts; illustrating my fears of the world in which we were all caught up. I used this passion to warn others with beautifully detailed but frightening representations of our modern world. The louder I was shouting out people's sins, the louder I was shouting at myself.

My addled brain endured such terrifying dreams, all remnants of Traitor's Point and my father's teachings. In one such dream, I found myself walking through the woods watching an orgiastic mass of bodies writhing like the maggots from the corpse's face. They were too involved in their sin to see the monsters emerge from the trees with multiple heads and beetle limbs, their razor sharp teeth biting and ripping the flesh off their bones.

I fell backwards, unable to take it all in, and felt a chill that reached down to the very core of my bones. Through the screams I could see the souls of these people crying as they left their hosts; abandoned and cursed to walk the earth unaided. The body needs the soul and the soul needs a body, without each other they are nothing. It reminds me of Stancio's night time terrors and is the only link I really feel with Hieronymus.

Waking up with my bedclothes sodden in sweat, I would sketch out these dreams so that I could incorporate them into my paintings, holding back some of the images as they were too shocking to be used. To me this was the result of my conflictions; my soul was crying inside but at least it was still safe within me, and I would one day depart to a higher plane to enjoy the reward of Heaven. My time on Earth is a test, I knew that. If only Eve had not taken the apple from the tree, we might have been spared these tests.

I find myself apologising for this rather depressing chapter and maybe now you can understand why I was hesitant in including it, but that was how things were at that time. It was a period of great fear and ignorance, a time of death around every corner through plague or religious persecution. When we say things are not as good as they used to be... just be thankful we are no longer in the Middle Ages.

I painted my representation of the seven deadly sins

Lust

Gluttony

Greed

Sloth

Wrath

Envy

Pride

It attracted much attention to me and my town, its symbolism striking at the heart of all those who viewed it. The duke requested another in the same style, paying me richly and letting me take the name of my home town of Bosch as my own. It gave me some financial independence away from my father's money and at last I felt like I was making a difference by spreading the word of God through my paintings and high society connections. I now wonder if they just wanted my work for their shock value, like some apocalyptic ghost train to scare and excite their friends for pleasure.

I wonder what Hieronymus would have made of the world today, with all its free access to pornography. By flooding the world with sex completely, will it corrupt the world, or will it eventually just remove the "kink" of sex? If it is all out in the open, then surely it would just become routine like everything else. After all, human nature likes best to have what it is not meant to have.

When I married, I expected my lust to finally wane but if anything it got worse and those desires continued to find their way into my dreams with ever increasing regularity. More orgies, more fantastical creatures ripping into flesh, but now the creatures were raping women whilst the men just drank more ale, laughing and fighting but never defending. Man's decadence in plain view, the world a mess.

Surprisingly, the more I painted this distorted view of our world, the more successful my life as an artist became. To be on the edge of madness only served to promote my successful life as it went from strength to strength, thus making me a rich man, sought by royalty and gentry. I gave huge donations to the church in a bid to buy my way into Heaven. I am yet to find out whether I have ever been there.

These were people of high education, sophisticated enough not to be shocked by paintings of naked flesh and fantastical beasts. The more lust I felt, the harder I tried shocking them out of their complacency but with little effect. Judgement day would soon arrive and they would beg for forgiveness as soon as they were confronted by their sins.

How do you see your future? Do you believe in a god or some form of karma? Imagine how it would affect your decisions if you truly believed someone was watching you all the time. Every misdeed noted as a black mark in your book, even if it was just a thought, your mind is not safe if God can see into it. Any slip up, any negative thought would have to be quickly validated and penance planned to beg for forgiveness.

That seems like an incredible level of pressure to follow you your whole life. You could only hope that God was either too busy to see into everyone's minds at the time, or that he was full of love and forgiveness as long as you repented immediately. As Hieronymus I was constantly policing my thoughts, justifying every whim. No wonder I went mad.

I created one of my finest works after a particularly hot summer; the heat drugging my mind into soporific slumber, raising the temperature of my blood to breaking point. I contemplated castration, envious of the simple peace a eunuch must feel, but was too cowardly to make this sacrifice. Strange how my fear of the mortal flesh was greater than the fear of eternal damnation when challenged by this dilemma. Does this show a tiny inkling of doubt in my mind?

I attempted to capture the full story of man's downfall within a triptych (a three panel painting). As usual, I painted it on wood and gave it folding doors. When closed, it showed the earth as it was when first formed on the third day. It is an amazing view from the heavens, the globe of Earth fresh and new… looking so clean.

On opening the triptych, displayed on the first panel, Adam and Eve are seen in the Garden of Eden with God by their side and nature beautifully displayed all around them. The apple tree is out of the way to the side, overshadowed by a much grander, wonderful tree that bears every fruit imaginable, surely man could want for nothing more?

The middle portion shows life as it was being led

now in the 15th century. People with no thought for the future, just living for the present and enjoying everything a man could get, as quickly and easily as possible. The seven deadly sins all being practiced in what was left of paradise. We can still see this paradise in the background, but it is ignored in favour of more… physical things. Lots of naked bodies with eyes wide open to display an air of lost innocence.

There is no sexual act displayed, that would have been too much for people to bear, but I can feel the sexual energy curse through my veins with every stroke of my brush. I had justification though; this painting was in the name of God. This excess cannot be allowed to continue. The more flesh we see, the more we are tempted away from the path of righteousness.

Now that I can stand back six hundred years later as Adam, it makes me wonder what it was about sex that everyone was afraid of. Surely sex is a gift from God as given to all his most treasured creatures. Man is able to enjoy it for more than just procreation, to the point in which it becomes entwined with love. Yes, sex can be enjoyed without love, like some alley cat without a care in the world, but it also demands a level of trust to fully realise its potential.

Does this not elevate us as higher beings? If it were not for our incredible brains, we would not even be able to rationalise this or any other 'sinful' process. Why give us these desires if they are sinful? Is it as Hieronymus thought, set as a test just as the apple was in the Garden of Eden? Why give us abilities and emotions and physical needs if they are not allowed? Surely procreation could still have been achieved without lust if it was such a problem?

This takes us to the third and final panel. I let loose my nightmares as far as I dared, our beautiful planet being destroyed in front of our very eyes. Gone is the innocence of play, now is the time to pay our dues. This is no traditional view of Hell with fiery pits, this is Hell on Earth. The animals have become larger, more distorted but crippled by the weight of fat fools riding their backs, whipped and kicked to exhaustion. Some are learning to rebel though, taking charge and whipping their riders.

In the background buildings burn, reminding me of scenes from the blitzkrieg more than five hundred years later in World War II. The flames greedily remove the possessions amassed through the greed of man; punishing us and freeing us at the same time. Looking up, the sky is dark from smoke filling the air, making it difficult to see or breathe. It cuts off the light from the sun, as if choking the Earth to death - the final act.

Now we see the skeletons of dead giants, serving to act as prison cells in which people are trapped or hiding, the victims of their own misdeeds trying to avoid their penance. It is too late for salvation now, the ultimate price must be paid, and they must lose their souls. Are these souls let down by their bodies or their negative energy? Whatever the reason, the souls being ripped from their bodies are in torment with utter grief, akin to losing a child.

Could it be that an apocalyptic end means the end of a life for a soul, or the end of them being able to take a new body, thus forced to wander the Earth unattached, empty, lost with no direction? Could this actually happen now, just when we are discovering ourselves through Awakening, the dream of immortality snatched away from us so soon?

My fears as Hieronymus never left me, finally following me to my death bed, which I remember very clearly. I felt peace for the first time in years, feeling like I had finally done enough in my life to earn that place in Heaven. Which makes me wonder what my soul might have been thinking as it left this poor man's body? Would it have been bemused at the folly of this man, afraid his whole life of burning in Hell when there is no such place? Would it have been angry at how his whole life had been tortured by his faith? Or would it have been one of joy that somehow, in the grand scheme of things, this pious life is the right path to take, whether it be for religious reasons or the true path to a purer energy; a clear spirit able to go to another life?

Until we remember our time as spirits we will

never know. One thing I am certain of though, religion should not be used for fear or persecution. War should not be fought in its name, and power should not be gained through those who practice their faith.

Family values, fairness and love are the best elements in almost every religion and many parents display that devotion every day without fear of retribution. Even more amazing are those people, whether parents or not, who have a strong moral code built within them, showing kindness with no thought of reward. They need no church to preach from, or hierarchy to keep everyone below them, they just do it out of love for their fellow man, or woman or pet or creature or plant or planet. They are the people of pure spirit and I don't think I could ever reach their level of human kindness.

Unfortunately we tend to just hear about all the bad stories of human nature read to us on the news every day, but if you look around and look hard, something wonderful appears. People everywhere are showing kindness on a small and personal scale; unannounced, unclaimed kindness that holds human compassion together as a quiet energy.

One day we will need to come together and use that energy to turn it into an incredible force for doing great things.

Chapter 21 - The Awakening foundation

Awakening is still in its infancy. Kale would be the first to admit that there is still a lot to learn and improve on and for that purpose we have the Awakening foundation. Formed by Kale and a few of his original circle, the foundation was set up to give others the chance to add their thoughts and theories to the mix. As the years went by, research posts were set up and important additions to the process discovered and implemented.

My father had been quite involved himself, volunteering for new techniques and studying the effects of cognitive processes under natural and artificial stimuli. It was a very exciting time in this fledgling science and felt more like being part of a mysterious religious sect than an accepted scientific process as it is today. Kale had stipulated right from the beginning that all research had to be conducted under the same existing rigours as any other scientific body in a bid to separate Awakening from a cult-like status, or accusations of quackery.

Now it is a proven science and very much accepted into the status quo to the point in which it has completely changed the face of modern society. Many laws have been revised or completely re-written to accept the changes that Awakening has made to our very existence. I have already mentioned a few in earlier chapters that deal with murder and the complex decisions that have to be made with what we now know. Some of those decisions are still debated and could be overturned in years to come, but that is the flux of such a huge and consuming shift to our everyday lives.

When virtual immortality through Awakening was realised, our attitude to our time on this earth was revolutionised. Only a few hundred years ago, our life expectancy averaged about forty years, less in some parts of the world. By the end of the twentieth century it had risen to almost double that. Already this was changing people's attitudes to old age and how we would plan for it, but we were still thinking within the confines of one lifetime and thus thrusting our hopes and dreams, and hopefully some inheritance, onto our children. Their survival in this world was our immortality through our gene pool.

Awakening then gave people the chance to plan for their own rebirth inheritance, whether in terms of property and money, or through multi-generational self improvement, in terms of spirituality or self awareness in an unending education.

Attitudes to the life of our bodies changed and viewpoints on religion changed. Our attitude towards the universe as a whole became much larger as more was deemed possible; time is no longer a restraint to what we can achieve.

However there is still so much we do not yet understand and as such research has been split into several fields beyond the Awakening process itself in a bid to answer all the new questions posed every day by ordinary people in this extraordinary science. So I will pull out a few of the relevant fields of research that has so far caught my eye:

What are souls?

Why do we not remember being animals?

Do we choose the bodies we take?

What happens to us between bodies / lives?

How far back can we "see"?

Can we ever really communicate with the spirits of the dead?

Will we ever be able to see into future lives?

Do we exist in other dimensions?

As part of my father's specialised Awakening sessions, he found himself entering a life in the heat of battle. Not from some sodden battlefield dodging between bullets or charging on a horse with sword drawn, but from the sky in some form of aircraft that he had never seen before. Strange markings adorned the cockpit and he was relieved that his body knew what to do otherwise he would have crashed in a matter of minutes.

The sky was enveloped in a strange hue of unfamiliar sunlight and the terrain below had an arid but silk-like surface made out of some reddish rock. Images and sounds were bombarding him from every angle and he felt like his thoughts were being read by the helmet on his head, thus directing supplementary commands to the craft's onboard computer. He wondered whether it could read his modern mind too.

It occurred to him that he might be seeing a life from another world. He had heard rumours of such things happening, but not from anybody he actually knew. Could he really be looking at a life separated by billions of miles, or billions of years? Or was it in another dimension, indicating that our souls can migrate from one to another or through time itself?

This experience was short lived, ended by a blinding flash and he was back with his observer, trying to reconnect to an earlier point from where he had left. Death had probably caused the end, but he was frustrated to find he could not delve back in, especially as he had already done the hard work of forming a visual hook into that life, like trying to get back into a dream you have just had.

Broken static flashed before his mind; noises, smells, fears and disjointed images creating a wall of confusion that only served to drive him further away from what he wanted to see. He never did find his way back.

An investigation was quickly set up to research into what he had actually seen. His observer pointed to his charts, showing the different active parts of his brain and replayed the audio recording from the session.

Had he really experienced something extraterrestrial, or was it his imagination running wild under the influence of the light sedative he had been given to put him in a deeper trance? Could it have been a World War II experience but with everything altered by the drug, thereby making it look like somewhere else, a different time, a different dimension, a different planet or a different perspective?

It could never be verified in the end, proving to the foundation that however tempting it was to use natural or artificial stimulants for Awakening processes, the loss of confidence in what was seen made the stimulants redundant in their overall effectiveness.

My father is pretty sure he saw another world though and of course, occasionally reports do come in of experiences that we cannot explain within our own world. As such, the study of non-terrestrial

Awakenings is a very interesting but fully contentious field of research that captures the interest of only the most adventurous of academics, willing to bet their reputations on the Awakenings of a small number of individuals who give very credible accounts of where they have been.

The science of souls. How does anyone even begin to try and understand something so intangible? Theories abound and stem from countless religions and personal philosophies. Scientists have explored every avenue of "ghost detection" using radio wavelengths, energy fields, atomic resonance, magnetic pulse, photometric sensors, thermal imaging and human mediums; all with little success.

As ever, even with Kale's stipulation of rigorous scientific principles, results have been sketchy and nothing concrete has ever been found. Photos of spiritual energy have been taken, as have audio recordings been made, but everything is so… fuzzy. For every report, there always seems to be a reason for out of focus or blurred images, which damages its credibility.

So it would appear that the best answer will still come from someone remembering their time in the "Spirit world", as memories of past lives seem to offer conclusive proof that there is a link that connects our bodies to each other.

Some believe that there are young and old souls. The older souls do not need to find a physical form any more.Their task is to look after the new souls, as a parent would a child, and find them a body to inhabit. The time spent in a body is time spent to prove their worth. Some believe that there is a Heaven and a Hell and that the time spent on Earth is the in-between stage or "vetting" period; their time at the top or bottom determined by their behaviour on Earth. In that scenario, a mediocre performance would therefore constitute a short visit to either ethereal plane, thereby leaving it in the position of having to find a new body quicker.

If that is the case you would think that Hitler would burn in Hell for an eternity, but he came back as the Jewish girl after less than a hundred years. I think it is hogwash myself, believing that there has to be an answer that is less driven by religion that can give us a truer sense of purpose for our existence.

Karma feels more natural and one would hope that the fact that we have different bodies born with different good and bad physical levels, to good and bad parents and differing levels of poverty or luxury, allows plenty of scope for dishing out the penance without having to be born as a dung beetle, but who would administrate such a complex system? Could it be the older souls again?

Searching for a soul is the ultimate needle in a haystack. When you consider that 99.999999999% (not a made up figure) of an atom is empty space, it therefore illustrates that any form of mass is amazing in its ability to be solid but it also leaves a huge area for things we do not yet understand. To me, this area of conventional science could lead to an answer. It might not be the right one of course, but what might seem like hokum now could be scientific fact in the not too distant future.

Passing these memories from body to body seems to be such a small part of the jigsaw. We do not know where we have come from, and we do not know where we are going to, but the fact that we cannot tap into our memories in our spiritual state poses several questions:

> Do we have a consciousness when not inhabiting a body, or are we a source of energy that needs the human mind to give us the power of thought, symbiotic until one part of our evolutionary process makes the leap to become self aware?

> Is Awakening part of some cosmic plan to slowly give us the knowledge and ability to become truly sentient, taking us another step closer to enlightenment?

> Is the other side our real existence, with this side just a playground to exercise different ideas and setting tests along the way?

> Is our soul aware of our existence as bodies, or are we two completely different sides of a coin that goes through a metamorphosis, like a caterpillar when it changes into a butterfly? Does the butterfly remember being a caterpillar?
>
> How many bodies do we get? Are we limited to a number of regenerations like Doctor Who?

Now there was an interesting TV character and one that had worked its way into Peter Smith's coma through his childhood memories of watching from behind the sofa, because it was scary. Created well before Awakening, Doctor Who was a fictional Time Lord, a race of humanoids who hold the key to time travel and are therefore its guardians. When his body dies, it is instantly regenerated.

It is the perfect example of how we change. He was able to remember everything as if he had not died, but his character and even his accent would also go through a metamorphosis. Yes, he held some basic character traits but, in the end, he was someone new and exciting and holding his memories from all his past lives which he could delve into if he wished or needed. With these memories and regenerations, he could live to fight another day.

At last we are able to regain some of our memories and slowly but surely we can begin to unravel our place in this Universe. It is strange and frustrating, sometimes scary, confusing and interesting, but ultimately it is exciting too.

Other areas of interest look at our place in time. Are we really in the present, or is time running on many different parallels? When we look back into a past life are we really seeing the memories, or are we remotely seeing into the past through some kind of host?

Kale's re-birth was the first example of someone coming forward from a past life to the present life, with memories that were so exact, that people had little doubt that he had really returned. Since then, many people have been re-Awakened, thus changing our perspective forever.

Our greatest insight may come with the answer to why we never remember being animals. They all have obvious levels of intelligence, especially apes or dolphins, and there are millions who would testify to the intelligence of their dog or cat, but do animals have a soul? I cannot see why not. Maybe our souls use animals as a resting point.

Animals are more instinctual, with the basic principles of survival leading them to make sure they can eat, drink, sleep and reproduce. They do not agonise over how their actions might look bad to others, even if they do appear to show remorse when reproached.

Thus, as a physical host, it could be a much easier existence in which to recuperate. I know it sounds daft and in all honesty I am just throwing the idea out there, but in the context of the strange and wonderfully complex actions of the universe it doesn't sound that crazy.

Awakening type trances have been accomplished on apes in which a basic level of communication has been achieved, but like the fuzzy images of ghosts, the descriptions of their experiences are fragmented and unreliable. Without a clear level of communication, it is almost impossible to draw any solid conclusions. Which highlights Man's other unique ability; the power of speech and communication.

Is it a coincidence that we are the only living creatures that appear to have a soul and can live eternally from body to body and have this amazing power of communication that has shaped our world way beyond what it would have been if all we could say was "Ug"? Maybe animals do have souls, but for one lifetime only.

As you can see there are many questions raised by Awakening and still very few answers. There are departments of research and a huge army of talented individuals and groups conducting their own research and supplying their personal theories. I could go on about the different techniques used or the accomplishments made, but I think it would be easier to just lead you through to the next chapter.

This chapter begins to answer a few of those

questions (whilst creating new questions naturally) and leads us to where we are now.

In Hamlet, Shakespeare wrote:

"The undiscovered country, from which no traveller returns; puzzles the will and makes us rather bear those ills we have, than fly to others that we know not of."

Shakespeare was talking of death, but it could just as well relate to the Awakening process itself and make us wonder if we really do want to see what else there is to learn.

"And enterprises of great pitch and moment, with this regard their currents turn awry and lose the name of action."

Too late. We have already set off along the path and there is no turning back.

Chapter 22 - Yarkel and the Crystal skulls

One of the strange side effects of Awakening is the incredible amount of information your mind suddenly absorbs. Not only from your experience, but ironically, also from the research you carry out afterwards. Millie has been great at showing me different web sites to look at, and even took me to the British Library on one occasion to try and find out some more elusive details.

On that occasion, it had been about an experience that seemed more like an incredibly vivid dream than an Awakening. The "physical" experience felt the same, it's just that the story, if you can call it that, is very strange. It's one of those Awakenings that I could not place a time or location to. Unlike all the others I'd had before in jungles or deserts or some other God forsaken place, this was in a large city of unrecognisable architecture.

Mike had been quite agitated on this particular day; some kind of problem in his own life.

"What's up Mike, you don't look so good."

He grunted, gave an apologetic smile and just pointed to the couch. He wasn't in the mood for talking.

"You ok to do this? We can cancel if you want,

I've got homework to do anyway" I said helpfully.

"No, no, sorry Adam, just been a bad day, you know how things get."

"I guess" I answered, a little unsure of this strange behaviour from Mike. This was just not like him and I could feel the nervous energy fill the room.

He smiled again, a little better this time. "Let's start again. Good afternoon Adam, make yourself comfy and I'll get the equipment set up."

I sat down on the comfortable leather sofa, crossed my legs and started to relax. "I was thinking of seeing if I have any Roman experiences, Millie was telling me about a life she'd had as a priestess in Rome and it sounds like an amazing time zone to explore."

"Hmm, are you sure you were not more interested in thinking she might be one of the vestal virgins?"

Good, he was becoming a bit more like the Mike I know. A little humour goes a long way to get you in the right frame of mind. We were soon ready to begin.

As I've mentioned before, there are many different ways of starting your Awakening. Most commonly is a white light gaining detail, darkening until you see the world around you. Another is the false (although commonly debated) impression of seeing the whole room around you and the body you are about to enter. You draw nearer, entering the body until the eyes ”fit”. The experts hypothesise that this is the result of all the information flooding in, complete with our own self image and the memory of our surroundings, thus creating the impression of hovering above our body. Of course, some believe this really is our ethereal self, watching from above.

This experience started quite differently though. The white visualisation in my mind turned grey to black but I can smell the dank, dusty air around me and hear a strong rhythmic beat which seems to pulse in my head like a soft but persistent sonic boom as I find myself lying on a cold slab in a darkened room.

I'm calm, surprisingly, or at least my past body is. My present self is still in a state of shallow trance, as is usual when entering the Awakening state. Memories are flooding in, my former self using the time alone to let his mind wander into his personal past, giving me his memories within a memory.

With these memories come images of buildings the like of which I have never seen before. Huge buildings carved out of the surrounding rock with smooth, concave surfaces perfectly cast into them. They look both ancient and hi-tech at the same time. The ultimate in retro-tech architecture.

There are solid windows of what looks like glass, but there is something odd about them. They are thick, again very smooth and I'm guessing the refraction is slightly out of kilter, producing a beautifully subtle translucent quality to them. They are stunning.

People are everywhere, wearing simple garments in the early evening breeze, and I can smell the local fauna. It reminds me of when I used to visit my aunt in Cyprus when I was little; stepping off the air conditioned plane into the sun and smelling the unique smell of that beautiful country. I love that smell. Crickets complete the memory within my memory, their chorus soothing my mind.

"Yarkel, you are late, the moon won't wait for you." My mother looks at me with controlled patience. She has big brown eyes encased in a pretty but ageing face. The sun has not been kind to her copper coloured skin.

"Take the west side with your brothers in the Plage quarter. Your voice is needed there now. I'll be with Sarana at the Hepledex till the end."

"Yes mother." I say it with a little resentment as I'd prefer to be playing in the ball courts with my friends but duty calls and I know well enough not to argue with her.

I hear the words but do not recognise the language, only knowing what has been said through the echo of my mind. Then I follow my three brothers to a section near the front of a semi-circle of similarly aged boys. It looks like some form of outdoor choir, and my memory begins to blur, missing out the dull bits in-between, like a kid flicking channels. Now we are ready for the vocal projection, and you could be mistaken for thinking that I was dreaming this too, so strange are my surroundings and what happened next. We are in a gigantic bowl-like structure, formed by the buildings around us, perfect symmetry with precise, smooth, elegant lines, highlighted by the window-like blocks still shimmering in the early evening light.

It dawns on me that we are in an amphitheatre, the like of which I have never seen before. Where am I? When am I? There is no real clue to my geographic or temporal location, I can't even tell if I am still on Earth, then remind myself that this is a memory within a memory and thus reality always blurs at the edges as it is interpreted through an extra level of the subconscious.

When we remember things in everyday life, it is always as we interpret the events. Never is this more so than when you are trying to resolve an argument, as you both have different recollections of the same events. So, when viewing an Awakening memory where your body is caught in a moment of also looking back, the edges get even fuzzier, making it harder to determine what is real and what is not, but never to this extreme. Normally it is small details; who did what to whom? This was much stranger, it was so foreign and harder to drag details out of my mind as it was already preoccupied.

My attention was then grabbed by a priest-like figure walking into the centre of the amphitheatre, followed by a small entourage of men and women in much simpler clothes carrying skin drums. The priest is physically very different from anyone around him. He is much taller, and even from here I can see his piercing blue eyes looking out at us, offset by long blonde hair and pale skin. He looked like a Norwegian god; miles away from home in our tropical paradise. Curiouser and curiouser.

Yarkel's mind has long left any ideas of play time, it is now focused intently on the priest's eyes. Within my experience of being Awakened, I recognise the method of mass hypnotism being used here; the crowd was being lulled into a trance. Even those less susceptible to hypnotism will be caught in the trance, fed by a burst of controlled emotion and contained by our natural need to fit in with our surroundings, a form of mass hysteria being controlled and manipulated.

We began singing without words, just hitting notes in time with the banging of the drums as the sun was setting. With our minds focused, we are able to project our voices into the bowl at different pitches and the result is astounding. With the sound so perfectly focused and pitched into the acoustically crafted amphitheatre, the sound waves feel like a sonic ripple. Then the window-like structures grow brighter as if the sound waves are being further transformed into light waves.

With the shape of the building and its lit windows, it gave the impression that we are standing in the middle of a huge flying saucer, powered by our voices; it feels amazing.

Two more priests rise out of the ground from a carefully hidden staircase. Tall and blonde like the first priest and I begin to wonder if they are even human, so different do they look from everyone else, and I watch as they carry a small golden pyramid towards the main priest in the centre of the amphitheatre. In the centre is another window-like structure but horizontally placed in the ground, so that the light can emanate upwards towards the sky.

The two priests then placed the pyramid onto the lit square which fitted perfectly, thus blocking out the light. Our voices grow louder and higher, with static bursts coming from different sections of the crowd. This, along with the drum beats, makes the whole theatre vibrate and the lights grow even brighter. I couldn't wait to see what came next through my host's eyes.

They made quite a ceremony of removing a thin cap of triangular gold from the top of the pyramid, which released its thin walls so they could fall back, thus creating a four pointed star that shone like a small sun. It is very bright and takes some time for my eyes to adjust giving the impression of someone's head being projected into the middle of the star, for what reason I cannot even guess and my host's mind is completely fixed on its vocal projections.

When my eyes did adjust, I could see that it was a skull, and for the first time in a year or so, it sent a familiar shiver through my spine, as if my fear had been reignited. I'd been wondering if it was about to appear, but it still surprised me in this alien setting. It looks like it is made of glass though, rather than the shape being projected over the many different versions of skull from my past experiences, and again I wonder if this could be the point in time that has had such a great impact on me, thereby echoing through all my lives, and giving me this acute reaction to its image? I had not felt like that as Adam before my Awakenings though, so how can this be?

It resembles a crystal skull I had seen in the British Museum a few years ago. Widely acknowledged as a fake, it represented itself as one of the thirteen mystical crystal skulls said to have some influence over the planet. These lost skulls would all come together once more at a time of great change, maybe in our darkest moment. Could this ceremony be part of the mystery?

The Mitchell-Hedges skull is the most mystical of them all. Carved out of one solid piece of pure crystal, complete with a detachable jaw, experts can only hypothesise that it would have been initially cut with diamonds and then slowly sanded to sculpt it into its shape. When they say slowly, they are talking of a period of 150-300 years. Sometimes it seems easier to believe in magic than people sculpting a piece of crystal into a perfect skull over such a long period with such rudimentary tools. It could also have broken in the carving process at any time. Can you imagine having to explain that on your sanding duty?

The eyes of the skull lights up and transfixes us, just as the high priest's eyes had earlier and I can feel the hypnotic trance affecting me, even through the gap of time that separates us. All those lifetimes in-between with the skull apparitions, and yet I am still caught up in the moment, as if time is running concurrently in all my lifetimes. Time has changed from being a point in past and future; it has stopped counting the seconds, now all of time is in my present and inside my head. It is looking at me, and I am looking at it; a direct connection.

Maybe the skull needed that connection to communicate with me, or was I just one of the thousand or so people standing in that spaceship shaped amphitheatre under a mass trance, some religious charlatan trick to hold power over their subjects? Maybe it was real, who can tell?

The skull seemed to speak to me. Not as part of a group but directly to me and this time it was clear and concise.

“Welcome Adam to what you might call your fabled Atlantis. You are probably curious to know what or who I am and where and when you are. I am Sandris, eighth vessel to the Guardians of your Earth. We, as guardians have many names throughout your world but we are best known by your Native Americans. They have preserved part of our history through many generations. The time you see now is approximately nine thousand years before your Christ in your Gregorian calendar, before the great flood that took away everything that we had built here.”

His voice was soft, without any discernible accent, like so many people I know. It was not menacing or judgmental in any way, just calm and measured. I wanted to ask questions but didn’t want to interrupt what he had to say. I was also too shocked to say anything by the fact that he had called me by my name, even though my contact with him was apparently eleven thousand years ago. How can that be?

“We can communicate through time when the conditions are right,” he answered, obviously tapping into my thoughts as well as talking from the past, “and time is not just as you see it.”

”Are you reading my mind?” I asked.

“Something akin to that. Time is not always in a straight line from past to present to future, it is also in a much bigger circle, so big that we cannot see that we are in a circle. And of course, time is a circle, but all points are at the same juncture in different dimensions."

I think I mentally gulped.

"At this moment, we are communicating through the right dimensions. My dimension is temporally synched perfectly with yours and so it is not a question of forward and back in time, more simply a question of matching our energies, thus phasing our dimensional space. What seems like magic now, will one day be scientific fact, you have said so yourself, or will do one day."

"To what end?" I asked.

"Ah, now that is the relevant question. We want you to contact and work with Martin Kale so we can take the next step of Awakening. Kale is clearly instrumental in this part, but needs you to direct him onto the right path.

"What path?"

"That Adam, is still for all of us to determine, but be assured, it is for the good of mankind. We have been watching for an eternity".

"Then who are you?"

"We are many different things to many different cultures. In essence, you could say we are all part of God. Not as an omnipotent being, but as all part of the life force, the ethereal energy or even the Holy Spirit."

"I don't understand!" I blurted out. These ideas

were far too big for me to comprehend.

"Yes you do Adam, it is just that you are not quite ready to accept the ideas yet. Put simply, we are all from the same source. What your scientist might now call the original Singularity, the almost mythical, but theoretical source of the Big Bang. Our energy began dividing as our different elements wanted different things. This is where your "Big Bang" happened. Everything changed as mass grew and settled, suns and planets were formed and we dispersed into life; the latest "game" to involve our minds through the eons of time. Through life we gained bodies and through bodies we unexpectedly became trapped by the hopes and desires of those bodies."

"Trapped?"

"Yes Adam, trapped by the desire to procreate; to build new bodies through the pleasures of sex and the politics of love. Nothing that has ever been invented or created has been as addictive as these two forces. They lead to all the vices and strengths in this world, be it love of power or love of your fellow man. The brains that have evolved within your bodies have become so advanced, that they have made us forget our past lives. Kale has finally found a way to re-programme the brain in such a way that you can now remember your true self again, to realise that you are more than just a body, you are an energy that inhabits your own personal bodies. The True Awakening process is about to begin."

"But why? I like being me."

"If you like being you, then why did you undertake this process Adam?"

"To unlock my potential I suppose, but I don't want to let go of my core identity. I am Adam Cappello."

"No. You are presently Adam Cappello, but also William Umpleby Kirk, the Victorian photographer; Cabel the rebel slave; Sophie the Parisian; Adeline Piggott the innkeeper; Peter Smith the salesman; Kemarre the Aboriginal; Piet Hein; Stancio; Methodius; Gabriel; a thousand different people and right now you are seeing me through the dimension that inhabits your life as Yarkel. You are all those people right now, at the same time in all those different dimensions. So tell me Adam, who you really are"

"I…I don't know!" My soul felt like it had been sucked up, thrown away, leaving me with nothing. I thought I was learning so much about myself but now I realised I knew nothing. All those identities were just distractions, time spent in the game of life. Who am I really? What character traits are truly my own?

I began to weep, as you do in a dream. Utter despair without any kind of self awareness.

"Don't worry Adam, you are more of yourself

than you think. You have already taken the first step to true self awareness, now take what you know to Kale and come back to us once you have spoken. Also tell Kale to take the Mitchell-Hedges skull to Chichen Itza in Mexico for the summer Solstice on the twenty-first of June in two months time. We can communicate further from there."

Suddenly I felt water dripping on my head and I was enveloped in darkness. I wasn't Adam, and I wasn't Yarkel in the crowd of worshipers any more, I was Yarkel back in the dank dark room with water dripping from a bowl held by a priest, back to where I had started this particular Awakening. I'd had enough though. I willed my mind to return to my present day, or at least, what I assumed was my present day. With this new experience all I can know is that this is a point in time that I am currently fixed too.

For however long that may be.

Chapter 23 - Meeting Kale April 24th 2064

Mike was a little dubious at first, convinced that my experience had been a misplant; an idea that had formed in my head and somehow come out as a bogey Awakening experience. It does happen and usually with much odder outcomes than a standard experience. Mine certainly fitted that category but I just couldn't shake the idea off. Something about the way the skull had been communicating directly with me felt too real.

It sounds crazy I know, but one of the problems with going into light trances to instigate an Awakening is that it is quite easy to get lost, which is why we have observers like Mike to keep an eye on my brain activity as well as just observe me lying there and noting my body language; a bigger clue than you can imagine. My readings backed up my Awakening though. Apparently my brain activity had been very high, but in the logical area of my brain, not the creative. Also, my semi-conscious activity was at standard level, thereby not reflecting the rest of my brain.

Whatever the case, Mike thought it was at least worth notifying his manager and she could somehow let Kale know if need be. She probably hears reports like this all the time. Plenty of people have the "Jesus experience", not to mention Buddha, Confucius, Plato, Mahatma Gandhi, Muhammad, Lao Tzu, etc. It's a big world out there and it's filled with egotistical loons, maybe I've joined them.

Mike asked me to write as detailed a report on the Atlantis Awakening as possible, which was not too dissimilar to what I've written here. Kale is a stickler for the smallest level of detail.

It took just two weeks to hear back, and much to my surprise, Kale asked to see me as soon as possible. I couldn't believe it. Kale is a reclusive figure, not surprising after what happened in his last G, and yet he had asked to see me.

I could never have imagined at the start of my sessions that I would end up meeting the man who has changed our world so much through the power of Awakening. Never in our history has one person made such a difference in terms of shaping the social fabric of our modern day society.

Through his work, immortality has been realised through re-birth and recoverable memory. People are thinking in terms of thousands of years into their future as a result, and that has made them a lot more responsible in terms of looking after our planet. They have also been reunited with loved ones lost through war, disease, accidents, circumstance or old age and given another chance to live their lives together.

Murder rates have been drastically reduced and racial / sexual / religious / class tolerance has been greatly improved, as most people realise that they themselves have trodden the different paths of everyone else in their shoes.

As a result, the world economy has grown and become far more stable, with peace in parts of the world that had only known war for generations.

Somehow I had stumbled upon something that was to involve me meeting this incredible person, the creator of Awakening and still so far the only person to self Awaken. I was excited and nervous. I just didn't want to come across as some kind of idiot who was imagining things.

Within a week, I found myself in a cab being driven to his house in Godalming, Surrey. A huge house on the outskirts of town with sloping ivy covered gabled roofs and a flint stone exterior. These are set off with neatly kept wisteria plants that meet a beautifully kept, luscious green lawn. It is the chocolate box country house, neatly concealing its high security cameras and electrified fences.

I was shown to the drawing room, offered a drink and told that my wait should not be long. Apparently Kale was on the phone to someone important, offering help in the form of a new academy in the city of Tegucigalpa. The world is being converted in every corner.

"Mr. Kale will see you now Adam," said his

P.A, with that lilt in her voice that all P.A's seem to have. I'd been miles away, remembering my Awakening and trying to second guess any questions that might be asked.

His office was large, comfortable and, fashioned in a retro 1950s American style, it was certainly cool. A large anglepoise lamp in fire engine red dominated the steel and glass table, pouring light over Martin Kale's surprisingly young face, but then this is his second G as Kale, no wonder he looks younger than you think.

I have seen photos of him of course, and TV footage from both G's, but for some reason I always think of him as G1, Especially as he was only ten when he self re-Awakened as G2.

His features are fairly plain and it would be hard to pick him out in a crowd, but his eyes have an intensity of something far greater, giving me the impression of a mind that never stops working on things.

"Come in Adam" he said, indicating with his hand to the chair I could sit in. I was quite nervous, so thankful for the simple instruction.

"Thank you Mr. Kale" I squeaked. My voice had not been this high since it had broken four years ago. Come on Adam, get a grip of yourself.

"Adam, I have heard good things from Mike regarding your Awakening progress. It would appear that you have gone much further back in time than most manage, at least in explicit detail anyway; possibly eleven thousand years?"

"It's hard to tell when it was, Mr. Kale, there are so few temporal references."

He smiled. "Call me Martin, I hate formality. You are not the first person to mention a civilisation of this style, although rare, and the skulls have featured in some of them but never have they spoken so directly, or been involved in so many timelines. You are unique Adam, a young man in his time."

I didn't know what to say. Being called unique by someone who epitomised the word unique was an odd feeling but a great compliment all the same.

"Thank you… Martin, I don't know what to say. The skulls seem to seek me out, not me them."

"Yes, but it would appear that you are in the optimum temporal and geographical phase for whatever these beings want. In essence Adam, not only were you born for the job, you were born many times for the job, and always on cue; an astonishing achievement."

"I'm sorry Mr. Kale, I'm finding it hard to keep up with all this technical stuff."

"No you're not Adam." He said mockingly, "It is just that sometimes it seems easier to play a little dumb."

"That's what the skulls insinuated" I said laughing with him.

"Look at it this way Adam, you were in the right

city, at the right point in history to see a long forgotten ceremony performed by an extinct, very advanced civilisation, at a time that was perfect to implant ideas into your head. Since then you have nearly always been in the right temporal and geographical space to be contacted by these beings and at the perfect age to start your Awakening sessions here and now. And to top that, you are in the perfect place and time to meet with me on this matter. Admittedly, that point is easier in this modern age, but still part of an amazing set of coincidental points."

"I hadn't thought of it like that," I said, my eyes wide open, emphasising my surprise.

"No Adam, you probably hadn't. In all these past lives you have encountered these skull images and all at the precise times when you would eventually look back from where you are now."

"So why should the skulls matter, why should I need to see them?"

"Possibly to convince me of the enormity of the task that we could be undertaking. For them to be able to orchestrate such a complex set of time and geographical zones within your different temporal points, they must be very powerful indeed and they certainly have not done it for fun."

Kale then looked at me intently, studying everything as if to try and see beyond the eighteen year old adolescent before him. I just sat there, a willing subject to be scrutinised, speechless from what I was hearing.

"You could quite possibly be the infinite article."

It was time to look blank at him again. I was really feeling stupid in his company.

"You have probably heard of the infinite monkey theorem, which states that an infinite amount of monkeys hitting keys at random on a keyboard for an infinite amount of time would almost surely type a given text, such as the complete works of William Shakespeare."

"Er, yes, I think so."

"Good. Well it's a mathematical metaphor, it doesn't actually mean you would end up with a Shakespeare classic, although the way he is writing these days it would probably only take a few monkeys, poor guy. It means that given an infinite set of values or circumstances, anything is possible, and you are the common link. You are the point of contact where the infinite number of relevant conditions converge, thereby giving the impression of all the different times that you have ever lived in the last eleven thousand years running at the same time. As the skull told you Adam, time is not just straight, it is also curved and some hypothesise it as a single point. It all depends on how you look at it."

"So are these skulls alien, inter-dimensional or from some ancient civilisation?" I asked.

"Honestly, I don't know. Possibly they have the

power to travel dimensionally which, as you could imagine, if you had a machine to do that it would be practically impossible to navigate given the infinite choices. We are talking of some type of being or consciousness that is way beyond my understanding and I must admit I'm not really used to that." And with that he gave a modest little smile that indicated behind all of what he had just theorised, he honestly didn't know much more than he was saying.

I thought back to my time as Yarkel, meeting the skull called Sandris and what it had said about contacting Kale.

"The skull told me that I had to work with you in the Awakening process and that I had already passed the first stage, but I don't know what he was talking about. How can I help you? Awakening is your process and I know so little about it compared to so many others."

Kale calmly sipped his orange juice, taking the time to collect his thoughts.

"I don't think they meant you should develop anything new Adam, but maybe they are implying that the experiences you have been through in your lifetimes have some bearing in how we go forward. I have never said that the Awakening process is finished, new ideas come up all the time, influenced by other people's experiences. Yours seem to be from a pivotal point in our history and they seem to have some special connection with you. They also give you an insight to the different complexities of human nature."

I let out a sigh as I realised that maybe my role in all of this was to be the vocal connection between Kale and the skulls.

“If I truly were the infinite article in human form, then I guess I would be the easiest person for them to communicate with. That would be the reason they wanted to show me the skulls through history, to show me their ability to influence events in time."

Kale looked at me and nodded, this did indeed sound like the most logical explanation. His eyes lit up as a thousand scenarios flitted across his mind. I could see him watching me, reading my most subtle, hidden body language as if I were screaming it from the rooftops, looking for any information that might indicate I was making anything up.

It would be impossible to lie to this master of human observation and I wondered if he was married or in a relationship. It would be hard to live with someone who can read your mind and thinks on several planes higher than most people. His communicative powers were good though, completed unaffected by his savant skills.

Again he laughed, guessing what I had been thinking.

“Yes, I am seeing someone and no… it probably won’t last long, they never do.” And although he had a wry smile on his face, his eyes dimmed ever so slightly; it would appear I have some body language skills too.

"Right Adam, here is what we are going to do. I have already spoken to the Mitchell-Hedges foundation who didn't seem surprised by my request at all. They have agreed to lend me the skull for Chichen Itza in June, are you free to go then?"

I had a few plans over that period, but nothing as big as this.

"Yes of course, if you think I can be of any help?"

"Adam, from now on you will have to start believing in yourself a lot more, because if I am right, people are going to have to believe in you as much as they believe in me. That might sound scary, actually it is scary, but you are going to have to get used to the idea. Some are born great, others achieve greatness and some have greatness thrust upon them. Looks like you will be one of the latter."

My mouth was dry which made it difficult to swallow. I was beginning to see the enormity of what I had been asked to do, and quite frankly, I was bricking it. It just goes to show how quickly your life can change. All those worries I'd had of not knowing what I want to do with my future and yet it was being decided for me anyway.

8-8-8-8-8-8-8-8-8

The next few weeks were a frantic rush of completing parts of my studies, trying to spend some quality time with my family and many meetings with Kale.

On my last weekend before setting off for Mexico, I tried to free my mind of all the expectations placed on me by Mike and Kale, I wanted some "normal" time with mum, dad and Ben before stepping out into the unknown.

We went for a walk in the woods, the first time I had done that in ages, and I started chasing Ben along the long winding footpath, shouting and screaming, my childhood returning as if it had never left in this moment of fun. At one point Ben stopped dead in his tracks, looking forward towards the sunlight peeping through the trees, trying to decide which path he should take.

We have many paths to follow in life, some leading to joy and some to pain but we will never know what we will find until we set off. Sometimes, we have to make new paths of our own and hope others will follow.

That walk was so precious too me. It showed me that although I had recovered and relived so many of my past identities, my fears of losing myself had been wrong. With my family and friends around me, I am still Adam Capello. They are the ones who help glue my present identity, keeping me in the here and now. Without them I would be truly lost.

Now it was time for me to follow Kale on this new path ahead, as he took it upon himself to teach me as much as possible about the advanced processes of Awakening.

Somehow I had become his protégé.

Chapter 24 – Awakened

Kale didn't want to go into Mexico unprepared, so he suggested revisiting Yarkel to see if we could glean any more information. This time he would take me through the Awakening, with Mike observing Kale at work. The only logical point to revisit would be the same time period as I had been in before, to try and find out why I was lying on a slab in a darkened room in the first place and to see if I could re-communicate with the skull. As usual, I was a little reticent to go ploughing through what might be a traumatic Awakening, but very aware of the importance of our work.

I was mesmerised just by watching Kale, unable to really believe that I was in the privileged position of being Awakened by the great man himself, Observer to presidents, royalty and billionaires all over the world and now me, eighteen year old Adam Capello, from Tunbridge Wells.

This Awakening was going to be a lot more advanced, with Kale channelling my consciousness between present and past in a way that they are defined a lot clearer. He let my body go into a simulated paradoxical sleep (a deep stage of sleep with intense brain activity in the forebrain and midbrain) that lets my body rest by removing most of my body movement, but, leaves me with the ability to talk, although maybe a little muffled. In effect, this gives the person being Awakened more focus on their past by letting go of their body movement, but, as it is being channelled, it gives the ability to communicate to the Observer what they are seeing.

Suddenly I'm back on the slab, the sound of dripping water like echoes of the drums I had heard before, the priest behind me, as if we had never left, the moment recaptured after 11,00 years as if it was yesterday. The drops of water are being used to focus Yarkel's mind to his frontal lobe, the location of his body's personality, and I suddenly realise that this is no simple ceremony, this resembles a form of Awakening. I was incredulous, how could this be? But of course there is no reason why someone else or some other off-world civilisation could not have developed their own version of Awakening, and if it had come from Atlantis then that would explain a lot of things.

It would explain how an ancient civilisation could be so far advanced, and its disappearance could be explained by some huge natural disaster, thus wiping out the ancient Awakening until Kale developed it again 11,000 years later. Or it had been introduced by an alien civilisation and removed soon after, maybe because we were not ready at that point in time, mentally or physically. By all accounts, Atlantis may have been wiped out by a massive flood, possibly a Tsunami or global warming melting the ice caps, thus flooding great swathes of the Mediterranean or islands in the Atlantic.

As I link into Yarkel's mind, it confirms my suspicions. He is already in a state of deep Awakening, but this time there is something different about his experiences. I can feel him dropping into my consciousness. ***Now he is observing me.***

"Oh my God"! I shout out. My last words before I was changed forever, and how prophetic they turned out to be.

As described before, to go in a memory within a memory can be very useful, even if a little blurred on the edges, but this was to be an Awakening within an Awakening. Not unheard of in our time, but never using two different methods and with a gap of 11,000 years in-between.

Yarkel and I fused together, stronger than the bond before in which I was seeing myself within him, this time there is a shared consciousness. This time we are aware of each other. It feels like we are long lost identical twins, so similar, but still with our own personalities, linked by an invisible bond of sharing a womb together, of being identical in shape and form right down to our DNA. I cannot describe any conversation we had, as it wasn't like that. It was more a case of joined up thinking as if in conversation with your subconscious.

And with that we "jump" into the mind of a lady inn keeper serving weak ale. Laughing and swearing, always entertaining the customers with long stories as I persuade them to part with their money for another drink, to drink them into a stupor, to ready them for the press gangs as I slip a silver shilling into the tankard. That was how the poor bastards found themselves enlisted into the British navy around the 18th Century, and that's how I, as Adeline Piggott made my extra money with little rewards from those press gangs.

Our collective conscience sighed, ashamed that we could act so mercenary, before we jumped again.

Now we are aboard a vessel which Peit Hein's mind tells me belongs to 'The Dutch East India company' and I'm barking orders at my crew to make the most of the winds heading west. We have silver to steal from the Spanish treasure fleet. This means more than money to me though, it is also revenge for being a prisoner and slave to the Spanish many years earlier. Through adversity I have become strong, but at what cost as happiness seems to have no place in my heart?

Jump:

Experiences running faster now, details instantly available. Whole lifetimes of knowledge passed in an instant; returned, replenished, reinstated.

We revisited Kirk with all his dreams and hopes, his love of Ada and pride in his work. He had been my first Awakening. The poster flitted in front of my 'eyes' again, the skull recognisable now as Sandris, but not at Lake Timran, now it spells Martin Kale, the letters jumbled by time or language or just by the distance they had been sent. Kirk's achievements which had mostly been lost in time, are now recovered through my experience.

Stancio with his dreams on the stormy island and his blindness removed in his sleep. Now I can see the man holding the lantern revealed as Kale; Stancio had dreamt the face of someone from the future. His life that consisted mainly of blindness, had taught me not only to appreciate the human gifts we have, but to admire his ability to adapt to his dark world.

Sophie with her gorgeous face, innocent in a world that was already lost. She was full of love's young dream, passion heightened and a reminder of the skull's tale of the two strongest influences from having a body. Love and lust can be all consuming in their different guises. All before she died of Cancer, her life snuffed out before she could make her mark on the world. Her butterfly tattoo must have symbolised a transformation from one part of our lives to another, the skull indicating something about our future.

I see Methodious again with his heavy coat of depression, using philosophy to make sense of his life. Through intellectual reasoning we can overcome so many of the world's problems, but only when it is combined with compassion and common sense. Maybe it is time to place greater value in philosophy and incorporate it more into the modern lifestyle in our lives. At least we don't force our philosophers to ingest hemlock anymore.

Gabriel debating with one of the most famous Alchemists in history; Nicholas Flamel. Somehow the skulls had managed to influence our dreams and maybe even guide Flamel to his destiny. Is he really alive somewhere in the world, or is he, as more than likely, just immortalised by the illusion of immortality that he himself devised?

Hieronymus had lived his whole live with visions of Heaven and Hell, all contained within a religious fever that had been programmed into him by his family and surroundings. The souls of mankind ripped out of their bodies. Now it finally makes sense to me that it was a representation of our core selves battling with the desires of our bodies, but are we really enslaved by our own flesh?

And talking of slaves, Cabel's tortured soul is now as free as a bird.

All my old selves are reappearing in front of me, as if in a hall of mirrors that is reflecting my past personalities, until they form a circle around me and close in, with Yarkel willing me to embrace them. Then, from the corner of my eye I see what looks like another hall of mirrors, but this time reflecting people I don't recognise.

"This is your future my brother" Yarkel whispers.

The mirrors shimmer in the eerie light then dip down to form a tunnel and I fall down and through, like Alice in Wonderland's rabbit hole, absorbing elements from all my future selves. The faster I pass my future selves, the less I see and absorb from them, until I land with a thud and darkness grabs me.

"What's going on?" I scream.

And then I see Yarkel, dimly lit in front of me and crying with joy. "This is it Adam, we have arrived at our future to the point in which we have returned to the stars".

I was going to say I don't understand again, but

then the oddest feeling of "remembering" some future events flickered into my consciousness, thus furnishing me with an answer of sorts. We have all come from the big bang... in fact, everything has come from the big bang and eventually it will lead to another big bang, or possibly, in some roundabout way, we will return to the big bang. The universe has been expanding for billions of years to the point in which it cannot anymore. It has been breathing out all this time, now it is time to breathe in, to inhale the elements of the universe that have been created which hold our "energy", the source of life. To absorb all creation at a level that is so incredibly slow, that no living thing is directly affected. And yet, after all this time, it has only been one breathe in the heartbeat of something so big, so old, so unimaginable, that I cannot even begin to describe it in any detail.

Yarkel looks at me, with love and affection, a total look of serenity in his eyes. "You have to leave me here now dear brother, as I will form the link to all your memories, past, present and future. We are in the incredible position of fulfilling our destiny by being an integral cog in the clockwork of time and space. You have to return to your time as Adam and use Kale to ensure our particular future has the chance to exist."

And with that my mind fills with images of the sky falling down, just as it had been predicted in

Stancio's dream, and souls being ripped from their bodies in front of my eyes, as Heirnoymus had dreamt. Even Peter Smith's vision of Sea devils rising from the waves reminded me of man's first ascent from the oceans. All these visions, all these clues, finally revealed as if I can see clearly for the first time in my life. I am no longer blind.

"I don't want to leave you here all alone", I cried, reaching out my hand to reassure him as well as myself, but I could feel nothing. His body began to fade until only his head was left, and then that began to fade too, just leaving behind a translucent face that eventually morphs into a skull before me. A skull. The skull. The skull as in my visions. Has that skull been me all along?

"I won't be alone Adam, I have you, and everyone we have been and will be to keep me company. Your friends and loved ones are my friends and loved ones. Do not be sad for me here, as I am truly blessed". And with that I could just make out twelve other skulls in the background, pulsating gently with the rhythm of life. Is one pulse a breath? Is that breath one breath of the universe, the ying and yang or the circle of life? For me it was a conclusion, as simple as that, the new voices in my head suggesting that now was a good time to return.

And then I was awake. It was good to feel my body again, to be able to touch and hold, to make decisions and take action when needed. I guess those are very important elements of our existence and without them we would just be a shadow. Kale was keen to find out what I had experienced but I doubt that even he could have guessed how far I had travelled.

I told him how I had revisited all my Awakenings, and a few new ones too, but nothing could have prepared him for the news of my future Awakenings.

"You honestly believe you connected with all your future selves?" he asked, looking doubtful.

"I'm not entirely sure, it all happened so fast, but Yarkel followed me through and he seemed prepared for it all. His part in all this has obviously been explained to him and I still feel connected to him. He is now part of my past and future. I can hear whispers in my mind from all my alter egos. I don't like this feeling but I know that I will learn to control it. I will have the benefit of all their knowledge, all I have to do is ask for it."

I was exhausted and thus barely able to speak. Kale let me sleep for the rest of the evening, but was keen to interview me the next day. Unfortunately all I could do was describe my experience as I have here. My new ability to communicate with most of my past and future lives was going to take some time to get used to. I couldn't just answer on demand. Their answer was always... "Be patient."

Chapter 25 – Future

June 21st 2064

Having Kale's personal tuition regarding Awakening was a challenge in itself. His patience was obviously tested by my relatively slow learning curve to his strong sense of purpose. He knew we only had a few more weeks to learn as much as possible before meeting with the skull or skulls in Chichen Itza.

Kale put me through the Awakening process several times, always hunting out my time as Yarkel, but we were never able to lock into the same period I'd had before, as if it was off limits. I saw other parts of Yarkel's life as he grew up, but nothing past the point of me lying there in that dank dark room.

We looked at the Mitchell-Hedges skull when it arrived a few days before our flight to Mexico, trying to fathom how it could be activated for communication but again we didn't want to upset any delicate balance there might be with this strange enigmatic representation of life and death. What secrets did it contain within its crystal edifice?

It has long been known by scientists that you can keep digital data stored within crystal. Photons are key quantum objects that can carry information over large distances and can be entangled in relatively large numbers but are difficult to store. Crystal seems to hold the key though, with evidence that quantum memory can store photonic information in a crystal with efficiencies of up to 88 percent.

With Quantum memory comes Quantum computing. Using a holographic storage system and floating point data processing gives computing power and memory storage on a huge, unparalleled scale. I can only imagine these strange entities within the skulls being able to perfect such a complex task at this point in time, thus giving unimaginable levels of data storage within one skull. Was this its secret, a database of living beings held invisibly inside and able to think and communicate as if still alive?

Kale had decided that it would be good to bring Mike and Millie over as well. He felt that it would reward them for all their hard work with me over the years and give me a portable comfort zone to ensure I was at my best for this meeting. He also knew that they had a better insight to my Awakenings than anyone else and he wasn't leaving anything to chance.

Three days later we landed in Cancun, the hot air hitting us like an oven as we walked out of the Airplane hatch and down the steps to the tarmac below. Late afternoon and the local temperature was still thirty-two degrees Celsius. That, mixed with the high humidity took the air from your lungs and strength from your legs. We had another three days to acclimatise as best we could and spoke to the local Mayans about their folklore and what they knew about the crystal skulls, but there was a lot still to do.

Kale was treated like a president, able to open avenues of dialogue with whoever he needed. Invitations from local dignitaries poured in but we were too busy to attend most of them as we discussed what we felt we needed to say in our meeting with the skull.

Eventually the day arrived. From my hotel room I could see the sun rise over the main pyramid of Chichen Itza, with all its symbolised equations. There are three hundred and sixty-five steps leading up to the top, from which the Mayan king would sit on his ceremonial mat looking over his subjects. Today would have been one of their most important days; the summer equinox, which is shown in the alignment of the pyramid and its surrounding buildings.

The burst of colour from the molten sun was beautiful and scary at the same time, burning over the tip of the pyramid like an omen and sending a shiver down my spine. Was today going to offer hope or despair to our world? Whatever was going to happen, some of its secrets were going to be disclosed and it would never be the same again.

Breakfast was short lived as none of us had any appetite, so we packed a few pieces of meat and cheese to take with us as it could end up being a long day. The morning dragged as we waited for this huge event, time slowing in its predictable manner, so we set off early to the Mayan pyramid, getting a tour from an Awakened guide describing the harsh realities of living within this huge metropolitan complex over a thousand years ago.

It reminded me of the priests I saw as Yarkel, overseeing their subjects, controlling them through their use of knowledge and their submission to fear and superstition. It seems knowledge will always be power, using the brain to overcome the brawn until it finally does its bidding. I suppose ignorance needs direction to avoid chaos, unless the direction given is sullied by lust, greed or power.

As midday approached, we were led up the steep steps that signify every day of the year and offer 360° views around the surrounding jungle; from the top you can only imagine how awe inspiring it must have been when the Maya were at the height of their power.

Kale pulled the crystal skull out of its protective box and laid it on a specially prepared Metate table. The Metate was originally used for grinding corn but became symbolic of the land and how it fed its people. The Metate's three supporting legs were embellished with complex carvings of a wide range of imagery, showing beast and man together. An awkward silence formed as we realised that we could do nothing but wait for something to happen, all the preparation and sleepless nights had been leading to this point. The anti-climax of nothing happening would be too much to bear and I began to sweat from the heat and stress of this realisation.

After what seemed like an eternity, the skull lit up from within, instantly communicating with us all, and with that communication we could read each other's primary thoughts. I couldn't help but "overhear" Millie's pride in me as she watched everything come together, and maybe... something more, a deep seated affection that I couldn't quite fathom, something deep and timeless. Of course, my feelings then became quite obvious too, forcing me to blush, even under these circumstances.

The skull suddenly "spoke".

"Martin Kale, Adam, Mike and Millie, welcome. We have asked you to come here today as it phases easiest with your dimension. Each summer or winter solstice brings our dimensions closer together and we chose this location for many reasons, but mostly its relevance to your past which also relates to your future."

"Your planet, like most, has been hit by several large asteroids in its time, giving and taking life with it. When your Earth was only one hundred million years old it was hit with such force that it scooped up enough debris to form your moon. It also knocked it off its axis by 24.5 degrees, thus giving you your seasons. These changes helped breathe life into the planet."

"Not far from here, sixty-five million years ago, another large asteroid smashed into the Yucatan peninsula, its impact almost undoing the work of the previous one by killing off nearly all life on this fragile planet and left the Chicxulub crater in its place. The power of the blast, along with the dust, created an instant ice age thus killing off your Dinosaurs. The energy of that blast was so great that it still resonates through this area today even though you cannot see it. It is now a fixed point in temporal space from which we can use as an anchoring point for dimensional mapping."

"Now, another asteroid is on its way to your planet and due to hit in 2088. This asteroid is bigger than anything experienced previously, thereby having the potential to destroy all life on Earth. No weapon you have will even come close to destroying it. Nuclear missiles are but pebbles compared to the power of such a large force. We have been planning your salvation for a long time in your terms, but nothing is certain in this regard, everything will depend on your race working together to divert this disaster."

"Two hundred thousand years ago, we intervened, adding to your DNA with the help of the

"Nordics". These beings are from another dimension but are very closely related. Their DNA donation ensured that you would evolve in a much quicker time span, and thus be ready for this period in your history."

"So we have alien DNA?" asked Kale, sounding shocked.

"It depends on what you call alien. We all come from the stars. We are all made of the same atoms which are constantly recycled to make everything around us. Physically, the oldest part of you is only seven to ten years old, as atoms are changing their form all the time, but the elements are as old as the universe itself. Yes, the DNA spliced into yours is from another race of humanoid, but over such a long period of time, when does it stop being foreign and just become native?"

Kale looked down at his feet, not completely comfortable with this revelation. "From the point in which we were being bred to the point we evolved I guess."

"We had good reason Martin. Without it, you would not have been ready at this point in time."

"So who are you?" Kale asked.

"We need to go right back to the beginning of this universe to try and explain who we are, and even then it will have very little reality with your physical world."

"Try me."

"We are thirteen skulls, remnants of a once great race of supernatural beings. We had no form as you would understand it, just pure energy. We existed in a state of harmony with no real needs or wants until the seed of an idea was planted into our consciousness. Just a small idea that seemed harmless at the time, but it grew and grew until it split our race apart."

"And the question was?" I ventured, surprising myself by my sudden boldness in this surreal situation.

"**What if?**"

"What if? What is 'what if?" My mind was racing.

"What if things could be different? What if there was more to our existential existence? What if we were to give ourselves physical bodies? What if our physical bodies were able to use their minds to play with different situations? What if those minds took control? "**What if**" becomes a lot of questions if you let it run amok."

"That sounds very juvenile" Millie interjected.

"It does in the context of our surroundings Millie, but in the right circumstances it becomes all consuming. Juvenile questions can sometimes be the deepest. Do not children easily think outside of the box? Do they not see things that older, wiser, grownups are too clever to see? Clear understanding of perspective is an underrated ability."

“So what happened?” Millie asked.

“It was enough to fracture everything. Our energy exploded, and this is where we enter your scientists’ understanding of your universe. You have heard of the Singularity at the beginning of the Big Bang?”

“Of course” answered Kale, “the theoretical point from which the Big Bang emerged.”

“Yes, the Big Bang, that is when your time and your universe began, and our race effectively died out. We did become mass, but in the form of all the elements of the universe. Out of that Big Bang came the building blocks; matter, anti-matter, dark matter, dark field energy, atoms and all their compressed elements and all the energy that powers your universe. It is a very simplified version of events, but from that beginning in time, dimensional space was also created, and through those dimensions came the power to control our destiny.”

“If your race died out, how come you are still here and how can you still control the universe?” asked Kale

“Our race, as it had been, died out, but our energy went out into the stars that we were creating. We only influence the universe, not control it, the greater we work in harmony, the greater the influence we have. We thirteen skulls are the legacy of our past being, and I died billions of years ago.”

I was getting more confused by the moment, “So

how can you talk to us?" I asked.

"When you see a star shining in the night sky, do you question its existence?"

"No, I guess not, I'd never really thought about it. Surely it exists though if I can see it?"

"It did exist once Adam, and the one you are gazing at may well still exist, but many of them died millions of years ago. What you see is the light they sent all that time ago. In essence, you are looking into the past from the comfort of your own planet."

"Well maybe, but they can't look or talk back like you can."

"That's why we exist multi-dimensionally. Dimensional travel is much easier than time travel and affects the same thing."

We all went quiet at this point, not even knowing how to phrase the next question. The Mitchell-Hedges skull continued.

"Put simply, time in different dimensions can be at different points from your time, and yet hold the same history. In one dimension Adam, you still exist as William Umpleby Kirk. At this very moment you are giving your marriage vows to Ada. Ten minutes later, you are giving the same marriage vows to another Ada in another dimension. Dimensional time doesn't just run forward, it also runs concurrently."

"So everything that ever happened is happening at the same time?" asked Kale.

"Everything that ever happened and could

potentially happen." You have to remember that the universe is infinite. In an infinite universe with infinite dimensions, you end up with an infinite set of times within an infinite set of scenarios. That's the beauty of infinite, it's never-ending and thus makes everything possible even if it seems impossible. As you have already guessed, the real trick is navigating it all. That is why it was easiest to meet up with you during this summer solstice; our particular dimensions are in closer phase."

I looked at the skull wondering how I was now positioned in their phase space.

"You, Adam, are now in almost perfect dimensional alignment with us over many generations. Now that you are linked to your past and future through Yarkel, we can start to build a new age of hope. You will have the wisdom of thousands of lives to draw upon and they will be your counsel, but remember, even though they are all part of you, they are also influenced by their separate nurtured identities. That is their strength and their weakness, but with time your judgement will prevail, you will be the sum of all their parts.

We also needed your help to bring Martin Kale to us, which is why we were trying to contact you throughout your timeline. You both need to stand side by side to bring the whole of mankind together, to join them as one voice.

Mike had been quiet up until this point. "So how

can we help, what can mankind possibly do as a group that science cannot do alone?"

"I was waiting for someone to ask that question Mike. Remember the vocal projection in your fabled Atlantis? The vocal ceremony was a way of focussing our natural energy or Chi. Everyone has varying degrees of this spiritual force."

Mike didn't look so sure.

"A good example is shown every day by your top sportsmen. When you watch a tennis player hit a ball that lands directly on the line, is it a fluke? Maybe once or twice, but they do it many times. A golfer controls a ball using a carefully crafted stick, but his mind is what guides the ball towards the green. A snooker player is able to control the cue ball with levels of precision that you would think impossible if you did not see it with your own eyes."

"Practice makes perfect." Millie quipped.

"Yes, practice does make perfect, but only if your mind is perfectly attuned to your body and its surroundings. If you can get everyone to focus that same level of energy towards a common goal, amazing things can be accomplished. That spiritual energy is our gift to you, the power of the stars built within your bodies. With everyone knowing how to harness that power and focussing it on one point, it becomes amplified from a latent energy to a potent force. Positive thinking is positive energy and positive energy can become positive force."

"So you are saying we can make a difference using this energy?" I asked.

"Yes, just look at home games of football or the Olympics. The last time your country of Great Britain hosted the Olympics in 2012 it broke all records of your wins. It is not only the vocal support that drives your athletes, they were also helped by the huge number of supporters focussing their will and energy for them to win; that is what makes all the difference in home games. Now imagine eight billion focused voices and minds balanced, and us to amplify that power?"

Then a glow emanated towards Kale.

"Martin Kale, you are an evolutionary leap. Very few humans reach your potential, and even fewer use it. Your work in Awakening will save the world from itself and from the asteroid on its way."

Kale looked a little agitated. "I can understand that point, but why are you helping? Why does it matter to a race of beings that died out so long ago?"

"Because Martin, we live on in all of you. Our energy is within your bodies. Your consciousness, your level of self awareness is at a level that no other living creature possesses. It is an integral part of your life force, a part of your soul. We helped you evolve so that we could live on through you. In essence, you truly are children of the stars and we do not want to lose that. Although our future dimensions show your world obliterated by the asteroid, new dimensional space can be created and through that space, your race - our race, can survive. One day, we may all return to being free of our physical selves, back to the original source."

Suddenly it all clicked into place for me. "So our core identity is the personality or consciousness of your race from all those years ago?"

"Yes, in a way Adam, although your independent identities have evolved since their inception. Your understanding shows you will work very well with Martin over the coming years. The more you understand, the better we can communicate through you to Martin and thus through to the whole of the planet. You have almost eight billion souls invested on Earth. We need to save this fragile existence, both in terms of averting the asteroid strike and by you looking after the planet you all exist in. Through Awakening you can all learn that you will be around to claim the benefits of forward thinking or suffer the consequence of wasting this opportunity. We can help, but the biggest part of the challenge is up to all of you."

"So… do you want me to work with Martin as an intermediary between you and him?" I asked.

"Yes, and more Adam. As time passes, your communication of our ideas will become more of your ideas. You justifiably stand by Martin Kale's side, you are a contributor, not just a communicator, and destined for change."

That made me feel a little better about my role, but daunted at the responsibility it would hold.

"So, what's next?" asked Kale, saving me from having to give an answer.

"You have already started with what is next Martin, by continuing to train Adam in every aspect of Awakening that you have so far devised. Your next task is to uncover the other twelve true crystal skulls that are scattered all over the world. Once we are together again, our energy can be amplified and utilised with your energy. I can guide Adam roughly in the direction of these skulls, your job will be to bring us all together and prepare a small team of twelve trusted followers to go into the world setting up communication posts for our task."

Now it was Martin's turn to look a little daunted and slightly put out that he would be assisting me in the search. It was only for a second however, as logic clearly dictated to him that this was by far the most sensible scenario.

"Adam, your first location is the Great Sphinx of Giza in Egypt as shown in your dream. Buried somewhere around her should be another crystal skull, and hopefully still in one piece, we have been scattered a long time. I know little about the location of the other eleven skulls, but with every additional skull will come greater unity and power, thus hopefully leading to our resting places."

"Hopefully?".

"Nothing is guaranteed Adam, otherwise we could all just sit and wait. Fate would take its path and we would have no control, just as it is when you view a past life in Awakening.

The skull then dimmed a little.

"I must go. Do not worry, even though your fate is carried in each other's hands, your unique talents will pull you through this period of history. Remember, if you view God as an entity rather than a deity, then we are all that entity. You are us, we are you, we are all God."

And with that, the skull went back to its usual translucent state, a seemingly empty shell hiding its secrets in clear view. We stared at each other, all wondering what to do next? Everything felt strange, as if the world had shrunk in the wash. Everything felt smaller.

I thought of the dreams of Hieronymus watching the souls ripped out of their human hosts and now understood why our bodies need souls, but souls need bodies just as much; the synergy of positive and negative, light and dark.

Whispers of everyone's thoughts were fading from my mind as the skull's telepathic bridge switched off, but I still had a pretty good idea of what everyone was thinking. How do we tell the world these incredible facts? This life changing information has the potential to cause panic if not handled carefully. You do not proclaim the end of the world without a solid plan.

Night fell in the Mexican jungle, the heat slowly relenting to the cool breeze rustling through the trees. The sound of small creatures fills the air with a jubilant chorus and feels like a comforting blanket being pulled over us on this strangest of days.

It feels like we are about to lose a certain innocence in this new future though. Now everyone will have to play their part and work together in this changing world for the sake of humanity, because if we do not work together, we won't have a future.

And so gramps, you can see how I ended up being at the centre of the universe, metaphorically speaking. Without Awakening we would not have been ready. Now it is time to finally take charge of our destiny for the greater good. Not only for our fellow man, but for the life force that inhabits every point in space, and even every dimension... and that's infinite.

Epilogue

So we come to the end of my journal, my experiences laid bare for all to see. It has truly been the "cathartic" process that every writer claims happens. Going through my notes with Mike, I have been able to re-live my Awakenings again; a third time to live those memories and yet from a third viewpoint. First from living it, second from being in the Awakening and seeing it all happen from inside their / my mind, and thirdly, from being able to see everything from the outside, an observer on myself and my reactions to my adventures.

I was able to re-live all my fears; confronting my death as Cabel, dealing with the apathy and sadness of Methodius and the religious nightmares of Hieronymus. Laying to rest all the small shadow memories of panic, sadness, madness and loss that have so far been unreachable. Seeing the skulls now from the other side, knowing who they are and why they were part of almost every life I can remember. They are a symbol of life, not death, from a race of beings that seem older than time itself. And I am rejoicing in the knowledge that I had not lost my "Adam" personality in the sea of different characters. They were morphed into what I have now, not the other way round. They add to my life experiences, extending my knowledge and understanding to a far wider spectrum than would ever have been possible within one lifetime. Awakening has let me grow, and makes me the man I am now.

The Sphinx of Giza

Only a few weeks after the Chichen Itza experience, Kale had quietly arranged a private archaeological dig around the Great Sphinx of Giza. I doubt anyone else could have organised anything so politically delicate in such a short time or have it backed up with some of the world's leading experts. We were back to the old methods of dig and sift, plan and scan, slowly but surely mapping and examining every inch underneath her ancient feet.

Another three weeks passed in which nothing was found, and we began to think that maybe our first link to another skull had been lost over this huge passage of time and that we might have to wait until the winter solstice before we could even communicate with the Mitchell-Hedges skull again for more information.

Many different methods were employed in trying to locate the skull, but crystal is not an easy substance to find in such a difficult environment; the heat and the secretive conditions only adding to the long list of obstacles in our way. At least a needle in a haystack is made of metal so can be found with detectors or x-rays or a hundred other methods that make this material so easy to find.

Kale turned tack, and went back to finding someone with the oldest memories of the sphinx that he could find. Mujab Hassini is an Iraqi teacher living in Baghdad. Several years ago he experienced an Awakening in which he found he had been an Egyptian priest in Giza over seven thousand years ago. His memories had been scant, but Kale quickly put him through the memories again, unlocking new information about his position within the royal family he had served.

Finally he remembered a small object being wrapped in just a simple cloth and laid within the upper part of the sphinx itself when it was being built. We had gotten it wrong, the skull hadn't been buried beneath her, it had been put into the head of the sphinx as if it were the brain, sitting there patiently all these years just waiting to be discovered. High and proud, above the earth so that it could see the world from its stone eyes, watching it evolve and change into what it is today. How many other places have been left untouched for such a long period? In some ways, it was the safest place in the world, and right under our noses. Strangely enough, when the Sphinx had been rediscovered by Thutmose IV, only the head was visible above the sand, as if she had been waiting to be found.

Mujab seems to think that the sphinx was built for the skull as a resting place after his pharaoh had been approached by strange beings that were tall, strong and fair skinned, with eyes bluer than the sky. They had promised him that this would pave his way to immortality and would one day save the world.

It took another two months to even get close to performing this delicate "lobotomy" on this ancient wonder, a diplomatic challenge that was almost too complex for even Kale to perform. Kale called me back to Egypt when everything was in place so that I could communicate with the skull if need be, even if it was just to reignite some past memory in my mind.

8-8-8-8-8-8-8-8

Light; blinding, warming, comforting light seeped out of the stone structure when the last section was removed from the sphinx. My body seems to absorb this "healing" light, like sunshine on a cold winter's day. It feels good and it feels illuminating. Strength surges through my tired body giving me a feeling of total elation.

This skull is far more powerful...

The End

Thank you for reading.

Please leave a review on Amazon.

Or find me at

www.savantpress.net

Mark William Taylor